THE FRIENDSHIP BREAKUP

THE FRIENDSHIP BREAKUP

A Novel

ANNIE CATHRYN

alcove
press

Published in the United States by Alcove Press, an imprint of The Quick Brown Fox & Company LLC.

Alcove Press and its logo are trademarks of The Quick Brown Fox & Company LLC.

Library of Congress Catalog-in-Publication data available upon request.

ISBN (Paperback): 978-1-63910-238-9
ISBN (ebook): 978-1-63910-239-6

Cover illustration by Sarah Horgan

Printed in the United States.

www.alcovepress.com

Alcove Press
34 West 27th St., 10th Floor
New York, NY 10001

First Edition: February 2023

10 9 8 7 6 5 4 3 2 1

For Mom,

I am because of you.

For Dave and Skylar,

My loves. My everything. All for one, and one for all.

CHAPTER ONE

Right between the milk and the eggs, I go into menopause. Shoving my head into the store's cooler, I pretend to find the expiration date on the eggs as my own unfertilized eggs are expiring.

Please pass quickly.

Oh no.

The water works are starting.

Why am I crying?

There is a feeling of loss, but of what? *Loss of youth. Loss of my eggs. Loss of my best friend, Beatrice. Why is she ghosting me? Did I do something? I must have done something . . .* Before rehashing it for the trillionth time, I swipe at my eyes and chide myself to get it together. *You could be stuck in gridlock traffic with a full bladder.* Pushing this nightmarish thought away, I silently give thanks that I live in the Midwest and not L.A.

As I take my head out of the fridge, a busty blond twenty years younger than me bounces up in a miniskirt, tank top, and lavender Birkenstocks. She's dressed the way I should be right now, with this sudden heat rush creeping up my neck. Then I remember it's only fifty degrees outside. Typical April weather in this small, barely there town. Last week, it dumped four inches of snow on us, and I thought I woke up in Antarctica.

I eye miniskirt girl again. Before Jessica Rabbit can ask me where the whipped cream is, I grab a carton of eggs, lower my head, and see my slippers. Ugh. *How did I forget to change out of them?* I guess I've been too preoccupied with the fact that my "bestie" isn't acting like my friend anymore.

Hurrying down the baking aisle, I park my cart in front of the decadent chocolate and on impulse pull out my phone once again to see if there are any updates from Beatrice. Scrolling through my texts, I stop on the last message I sent her weeks ago, asking how she was doing. She still hasn't answered. Or called me back. I haven't seen Beatrice at our daughters' soccer games either, because I've been using that time to work on my chocolate business. And at school drop-off, it's too rushed to say more than two words to anyone. Just this morning, I thought Beatrice saw me in the school parking lot, but when I waved, she turned and quickly got into her minivan. There's a possibility she didn't see me, I convince myself.

"Excuse me," someone says, startling me out of my delusion. I glance up to see a big, toothy grin with a sprig of greenery stuck in the middle. Cringing, I refrain from swiping a fingernail through my own teeth. *How can I tell the woman about her leftover spinach?* I don't know her—or if she is saving it for later.

"Do you know which chocolate is the best for fondue?"

I'd rather tell her where the toothpicks are, but I swallow down my words and point to my favorite brand. "This works well for dipping," I say with a forced smile.

Then, because I would want someone to tell me I had a sprig in my teeth, I whisper, "You have a little something right here." I point to my own two front teeth.

She throws her hand up to her mouth.

"That happens to me too, so I thought I'd let you know." I suck in a breath, hoping I didn't overstep.

She reaches into her handbag and pulls out a compact mirror. "I appreciate it. Sometimes my smoothies take a detour." She looks in the mirror and picks out the goosefoot. Then she grabs a bag of chocolate and reads the ingredients. The woman's unstained and wrinkle-free white button-down is properly tucked into her designer jeans, and her navy espadrilles are definitely not slippers. I zip up my purple hoodie to hide the red sauce splatter on my yellow T-shirt, then reach up and secure wisps of hair that have broken free from my bun.

"This will do. Thank you so much. I'm having a party tonight. Just a few close friends, and fondue will be a fun treat."

Her little party sounds lovely and reminds me of what I've been missing with my own friends.

"Enjoy," I manage to croak out as she continues down the aisle. "Don't forget the toothpicks."

"Oh yes! The bamboo skewers for the dippers," she calls over her shoulder.

I didn't mean for the dippers.

As soon as she turns the corner, I slap several boxes of baking chocolate and send them tumbling into my cart.

Is this what my social life has been reduced to? Small talk in Aisle 7? Perhaps my rattled appearance these days is one of the reasons Beatrice is disowning me. I cannot believe anyone I know would be so superficial, though. That can't be it. Beatrice has seen me at my worst—with baby spit-up in my hair and black yoga pants I've worn three days in a row. I should make a better effort in the self-care department. It might uplift my mood anyway.

Now in Aisle 8, international foods and packages of chickpeas swimming in red hot chili sauce stare back at me. I flush again, like the scorching sun has bored a hole in the ceiling and found my face.

Is this menopause? My mom told me she'd started experiencing perimenopausal symptoms early. *What did that mean? How early? I'll be forty in three months. This early?* I wish I could call my mom for answers, but she wouldn't be any help on this one. I'm on my own. I sigh and tick off my symptoms in my mind. Hot flashes—check. Weight gain—check. Missed period—um, *maybe?* I need to look at my calendar. Extreme irritability—triple check.

My phone dings and I scramble for it, thinking it could be Beatrice. But it's another mom in our group, Lyla, posting "Lunch" on Facebook. As I examine the photo, I hear my husband Max's words echoing off the walls inside my head. "Fallon, my love, you know social media is the downfall of society." Judging by Lyla's photo of some sort of indistinguishable yellow pureed slop, he's right.

Max doesn't do social media because the last thing he wants is for one of his patients to find him. It's bad enough I see the social media community posts about the "McDreamy gyno" in town. The words conjure up images of my husband's hands between another woman's legs. I've learned to replace those thoughts with ones of cute puppies canoodling by a fireplace. *What choice do I have?* I knew what I was getting myself into when I married him. I tell myself he's not at the strip club or into porn. It's a job. I've learned to roll with it.

As I push my cart into the checkout lane, the cashier eyes the eight different brands of chocolate in my cart. She asks me how I am, and tears spring to my eyes again. Her kindness reminds me of my loneliness. I want to explain the chocolates are for research, and not at all for chocolate therapy. Another delusion. I mumble something. *Who knows what?* I'm not making any sense. I throw on my oversized sunglasses and head for the door.

* * *

Loading my groceries into my Jeep, I repeat to myself, "Turn your pain into power." After reading that mantra in one of my self-help books, I can't stop thinking about it. I have emotional pain these days, with time constraints to get everything done, guilt over trying to do something for me when I feel as if I should be taking care of my family first or hanging out with my friends more . . . and these horrendous hot flashes aren't helping matters. As I toss the last grocery bag in the trunk and reach up to shut the hatchback door, something hard crashes into my backside.

Through gritted teeth, I manage to say, "Turn your pain into power." When I touch the tender spot and feel the bruise forming, I add, "Go stuff your mantra."

"Oh, my gosh! I'm so sorry." A woman pulls back her shopping cart and a box of diapers falls off the bottom. A little boy bounces a toy airplane off her hip. As she steps around the cart, her bulging belly, barely covered by a T-shirt, knocks into the cart, and I grab it before it hits me again.

Judging by the dark circles under her eyes, I realize she may be having a worse day than me. "Here, let me get those for you," I say, bending down to pick up the box of diapers. "It looks like you have your hands full."

"Thank you. I'm so sorry. I hope you're okay." She smooths down her hair, which is standing up in five different directions. Her boy, dressed in *Paw Patrol* pajamas, suddenly runs off, and she's screaming, "Benny, come back here right now!" She waddles after him.

A minute later, she returns with Benny. Tears stain her cheeks.

"Please be careful not to change the settings again," the woman says as she starts to hand him the phone. "Wait, let me open the app for you."

Her words strike me. *The settings!* As she's searching her phone, I pull out my cell and click into my contacts to check if my daughter, Maya, accidentally blocked Beatrice. But the settings appear fine. I wish that was the answer to this ghosting mystery. To be absolutely sure my cell is working, I text my old college roommate, Avery.

"Where is your car?" I ask the woman, who has now managed to smash several bags of groceries in her cart by sitting Benny on top of them.

She points to a silver minivan.

"Let me get this for you," I say and take the cart from her. The woman lifts her boy out and carries him on her hip. I don't blame her. She doesn't know me. As far as she knows, I could steal her child, her phone, and her groceries.

I remember days like this when Maya was a toddler. I never thought I'd fail at anything until I became a mother.

Then I failed daily. The piles of toys and paper in my house grew faster than my lawn grows in spring. Not to mention that I ran behind schedule everywhere I went, sometimes by hours because I couldn't find my keys. One time they were hidden in the freezer next to my emergency cookie stash; another time they were in the trash with the poopy diapers. On most days, I smelled like sour milk and Cheerios. I tried to keep my head up and take deep breaths, but it was hard to breathe under mounds of dirty laundry.

"It's been kind of challenging with my three-year-old and you know . . ." She glances down at her stomach.

"You must be exhausted. When are you due?"

"Two weeks."

"You're in the home stretch," I say and smile, following her to her van. When I was pregnant with Maya, she was late, and that extra week had me going crazy. I ate all the spicy food I could find. I even drove over railroad tracks to induce labor. Nothing worked. She'd arrived when she'd wanted.

While I load the woman's groceries, she straps Benny into his car seat. I want to tell her it won't always be like this—that it gets better—but she doesn't need to hear this from a stranger while she's in the throes of it.

So, when she returns, I say what Beatrice used to say to me, "You're doing a great job, Mama."

She throws her arms around me. Shocked, I slowly raise my arms to hug her back, trying not to squish the unborn baby between us. Then, just like that, she's on her way. Maybe we both needed that hug.

* * *

After returning home, I get busy testing a new chocolate recipe for an upcoming bachelorette party. If all goes well, this could be my big break and lead to more orders.

I whisk the heavy cream and shaved chocolate together, add vanilla, and blend. Inhaling, I'm intoxicated by the rich aroma and think about why it has taken me so long to make my own chocolate.

Once Maya was born, Max and I agreed I would stay home until she went off to school. Now, Maya has been in school full time for two-and-a-half years. It took that much time to organize my closets, sell my maternity clothes, decorate my home, and get a routine down for the million other things mothers do. Of course, I had to account for emergencies, like running to school to drop off stuff Maya had forgotten, like a snack, lunch, and gym shoes, which happens at least twice a week.

I finally got to a place where I could do something I enjoyed. Something so powerful it emanated from the depths of my soul.

Scientific studies say chocolate releases endorphins like sex. For me, making it is cathartic, although why I do it is more than that. If I'm being honest, it's because I'm turning forty and feel as if half my life is over, and I thought I'd have more to show for it. *If I don't do it now, when will I?* I'm starting small, with local orders, but I have big plans to open a chocolate shop one day. For inspiration, I follow a ton of chocolate shops and chocolate-related Facebook pages. Social media is at least good for that.

I lick the spoon and relish in the rush of sweetness on my tastebuds. Immediately, I'm reminded of my childhood with sweet Grandma Rose. Grandma stockpiled her pantry full of

Fannie May so she would always have something delightful to offer for a last-minute gift or to an impromptu guest—or, in my case, a sad child who'd scraped a knee or bumped her head.

With her kind eyes and comforting touch, she'd say, *"Chocolate makes everything better."* And I believed my wise grandma with her nine freckles that speckled her cheeks like kisses left by angels.

I spent a lot of time with Grandma Rose because my parents were workaholics. My mom never had fun parties like my grandma, and didn't make friends easily. I am nothing like my mom, which isn't surprising, now that I think about it.

On any given day, women filled my grandma's home—playing cards or crocheting together. I'd sit at Grandma Rose's feet, with my own box of chocolates, while the women drank tea and talked about the latest buzz in town—the new car the Smiths bought or the renovations on the library or the neighbor's cat who got stuck in the gutter during a rainstorm.

Their stories always started with, *"Did you hear . . .?"* I love those memories. When Grandma Rose got sick, those women were by her side, reading to her, recounting memories, and filling her room with love and laughter right until the day she crossed over. God rest her soul. Now that I'm an adult, those are the friendships I crave too.

Before being ghosted, I would have sworn I'd found this type of friendship with Beatrice. A montage of moments flickers through my mind, like the opening credits of *The Wonder Years*. Seven years' worth of moments, many of them in the mom trenches. Seven years . . . I take out my phone calculator. That's nearly eighteen percent of our lives. I read an article that said if a friendship lasts longer than seven years, it will last a lifetime. I fight back salty tears so they don't drip into my buttery, smooth mixture.

Spooning the chocolate into heart molds, I glance past the oak kitchen table, pausing for a moment on the scattered, million-piece Lego set. Ignoring that mess, I then overlook the fifty-pillows-and-blanket fort covering the living room floor and rest my eyes on the matching framed photographs hanging in tidy rows above the gray sectional—a much more pleasant view. One of the frames holds a picture of me, Beatrice, Elenore, Vivian, Lyla, and Mel standing on the rocks lining a lake at a nearby park in our quaint town.

I remember that day well. Beatrice planned a Sunday Funday family outing for all of us. She reserved a small pavilion with picnic tables that she covered with red-and-white-checkered tablecloths. I made puppy chow mix and brought sliced watermelon. We grazed on finger sandwiches, potato chips, and various side salads. Lyla snuck in flasks of rum, and we spiked our sodas. We reeked of alcohol. When the forest ranger strolled by, we offered him cake, and he turned a blind eye to our shenanigans. Cake always works. As the sun kissed our skin, we played bocce ball, cornhole, and croquet until the kids crashed on a blanket under a tall maple tree.

That day, I ignored some of the women's side conversations about Mel, who was wearing a short skirt and a super tight bright pink tank top that accentuated her slender figure. Mel, a divorced, successful financial advisor, didn't quite fit in with the stay-at-home moms. She was invited because I'd vouched for her. She has since moved away, and I can't help but think she heard the murmurings. I feel bad now for not sticking up for her, but I didn't want to rock the boat with the other women.

Other than my guilt over Mel, I remember the day with fondness, and enlarged the photo of us women and framed it. Never mind that Vivian fell into the cold water right after the photo was taken, and Beatrice jumped in to save her. We fished them both out with a broken tree branch. All in all, it turned out to be a picture-perfect day—a happy day with our perfect friends. We even started most of our stories with, "Did you hear . . .?"

Over the years, these moms, especially Beatrice, had gotten me through days where I would have otherwise curled up into a ball and died from the stress of keeping up with Maya and the housework on very little sleep. The adult conversation stimulated my brain when most of my day consisted of baby babble.

Beatrice listened to me cry over my burnt spaghetti. She told me she had done it too. A white lie, of course, to make me feel better, because even I know it's near impossible to burn spaghetti in boiling water.

I can hear Beatrice's voice ringing in my ears, "You're too hard on yourself, Fallon."

Beatrice was the only friend I let see my daily chaos. She was so easy to open up to without feeling judged. There were a million and one stories of things going south, where Beatrice turned my big, ugly cries into big, snorting guffaws. I know we're worth fighting for.

My phone dings with a text from Avery, confirming my phone is fine. *Great.* Now I know Beatrice is ghosting me. *What did I do? WHY is she ghosting me?*

I shudder to think no woman would be so kind to me as my grandma's friends were to her, now that I'm being ignored. *What is wrong with me?* I sigh and shake my head.

Maybe I'm overreacting.

Or am I?

Am I going to die alone?

Gah! Chocolate is overflowing out of my molds and onto the counter. Ugh, so much waste. I wipe my forehead with the back of my hand, leaving a streak of chocolate dripping onto the bridge of my nose. What a mess.

CHAPTER TWO

I could get a job in logistics after coordinating schedules down to the minute for the last seven years. I fill Maya's water bottle, grab a bag of pretzels, the sunscreen, and the bug spray, and place everything in her backpack.

"Maya, finish your breakfast."

"But it's soggy. I don't like it."

"Well, whose fault is that?"

Had Maya started eating it when I poured it, it wouldn't be soggy.

It's chaos all the time around here, and I only have one child. I don't know how those mothers with multiple children do it, especially the old woman who lived in a shoe. *Didn't she have like one hundred kids?* I get hives thinking about it.

No. I'm not sitting around eating bonbons. Okay, I am, but it's for my business. Totally different. Sometimes they contain alcohol, and I pair them with spiked coffee too.

Speaking of coffee—I need it now. Maya came into bed with us at one AM, and somehow I got sandwiched between her and Max. I had visions of being a slice of cheddar in the middle of a panini. I was hotter than hell. Night sweats—another symptom of menopause.

Last night before bed, I made sure Maya had a small snack. Water on her nightstand. Diffuser pumping out lavender. Salt lamp lit. Night light on. CD player with soothing music. Closet door closed. Bedroom door open. Calming oil on her feet. Digestive oil on her tummy, and monster spray in the air. I cuddled up next to her and fell asleep. *How could I not?* It was like a spa in there, with absolutely no monsters lurking. Somehow, I woke up two hours later and made it to my bed.

Maya's coveted bear sits staring at me from our couch. The one she's slept with every single night since age one. *How could I forget to find her bear?* That's why she climbed into our bed in the middle of the night.

"Maya, can you please put your shoes on? We're leaving in two minutes."

"I need help with my socks," Maya says, standing there with her long, blue soccer socks in her hands. I go to reach for them, then pull my hand back. The pediatrician encouraged me to give her more responsibility to foster confidence. Putting her soccer socks on seems like a good place to start.

"Well, at least start putting them on, then I'll help you." Pulling socks over shin guards is a pain in the butt, even for adults.

Then, I am quick to say, "Bathroom stop before we leave, please." I've been reminding her for three years. If I forget, it never fails that we'll get down the block and she'll announce, "Mommy, I have to pee."

"I don't have to." She shakes her head and her brown ponytail swishes back and forth.

"Try." I shoo her toward the bathroom.

Her blue eyes shoot daggers at me for a moment before she huffs, turns on her heels, and stomps away.

Coffee. I need coffee. I look for the thermos that fits under the spout on the Keurig. Great. It's in the dirty dishes. I pump dish soap into it and quickly wash it.

"Maya, are you going?"

"I'm pooping!" she calls out.

I glance at the clock. Okay, deep breath. We still have time. I can swing by the coffeehouse to pick up five coffees before heading to the field. I debate calling the café ahead of time to place my order, so Maya won't be late, but I think we'll be fine.

I learned early on to give myself at least a half an hour lead time to get out the door. Throughout my life, I've always prided myself on being on time. Having a child makes being on time for anything near impossible. After making a cup of coffee, I resort to washing the pots hardened with spaghetti sauce and piled sky high in the sink.

Staring out the kitchen window as I scrub, I watch as my seventy-year-old neighbor, Mrs. Crandall, crouches over her small vegetable garden. I can't imagine the plants survived the recent one-day winter tundra. Mrs. Crandall has the worst luck. I remember when she decided to keep chickens and got the whole neighborhood up in arms. Apparently, our association bylaws forbid chicken coops because of the high risk of attracting disease-ridden rodents that gnaw through electrical wires, sparking little fires everywhere, which eventually turn into threatening wildfires throughout the entire subdivision. Poof! Everything goes up in smoke. Absolutely no chickens allowed. The whooshing of the toilet flushing and the faucet running interrupts my thoughts.

"Did you go?" I ask.

"Yes."

I resist saying, "See, I told you." I am tired of saying it. I'm sure she is tired of hearing it.

I help her with her socks and redo her lopsided ponytail. She looks so cute in her white soccer uniform with the blue number seven on it. I snap a quick photo of her and kiss her on the forehead.

"Mommy, I want a booster seat like Cecilia," Maya says as she jumps down the four garage stairs. I cringe. She could seriously hurt herself.

"Cecilia is bigger and taller than you," I say, thinking about how tall her mother, Beatrice, is. I always wished for long legs too. "It's safer for you to be in the seat you have."

Dang, I forgot my coffee on the counter. I need my morning coffee before stopping at the coffee shop to get more coffee.

"Buckle in while I grab my thermos."

I remember the days when I had to buckle her in—one less thing to do. Yay for minor victories.

"Yes, Mommy. *Puh-lease*, get your coffee." Maya already understands I'll be a raving lunatic without it.

A wise philosopher once said, "I caffeinate, therefore I am." I fully subscribe to that way of thinking.

Returning from inside, coffee now in hand, I open the garage door. Purse, check. Car keys, check. *Backpack?*

"Maya, where's your backpack? How come you're not buckled in? We'll be late."

"Sorry, Mama."

My heart melts every time she says sorry. She's such a sweet child when she's not taking her sweet time getting out the door.

"That's okay. Just buckle up, buttercup."

Back in the house again, I scan the kitchen counters and chairs and find it in the bathroom. Yes, the bathroom.

Finally, back in the car, I turn the key in the ignition. "Manic Monday" blasts through the speakers. I jump and turn down the volume. Why yes, it is manic, but it's Saturday.

"Why are we going so slow?" Maya calls out.

I tap my fingers on the steering wheel, glaring at the man on the bicycle taking up part of my lane. Cars fly by me in the other direction.

"Oh. We can't get around the *super* slow biker. We'll be late," Maya says, and huffs.

At age seven, she's already showing signs of my attitude.

I don't know why people bike on the busiest street in town. It's just an evil plot to piss off mothers. There are beautiful bike paths a hundred feet away. I should know—we pay taxes for them.

"That's dangerous. He's not even wearing a helmet."

"Yes, Maya. You're right. It's very dangerous."

We get to the coffeehouse with fifteen minutes to spare. I still think I can get Maya to the soccer game on time, with coffees for the other soccer moms. I haven't been to a game in four weeks because I've been renting a commercial kitchen to fill my chocolate orders. Each week, I try a new recipe at home. If I like it, I recreate it at the commercial kitchen. I've come up with half a dozen different chocolate concoctions. I'm growing my business and have given away more truffles than I've sold, but I know that's all part of getting the word out.

Saturday morning is the only time the commercial kitchen is available to me, but today I skipped my time slot to go to the games. Max had been going in my place. It's not that unusual—it's always a mix of moms or dads or both parents. But I know Beatrice, Vivian, Elenore, and Lyla have been there every Saturday without me. I'm hoping the coffee will be a good way to show how much I've missed them.

In line at the café, I tap my foot. The woman in front of me is talking to the barista. "I'll take vanilla. No, wait—hazelnut. And make it coconut milk. No, almond. Let me think . . ."

I check my watch. My window of time to get to the game is slowly dwindling. Finally, I step up to the counter. I know how all my friends take their coffee, and it's not as simple as cream and sugar. Vivian adds a shot of wheatgrass. Beatrice puts a packet of collagen in her Americano. Lyla always asks for two pumps of hazelnut with almond milk. Elenore gets a non-fat caramel macchiato. I take mine with half and half and stevia. I'm thankful this café offers all these unique options.

After placing the order, I catch Maya with her tongue out.

"Maya, do *not* lick the condensation off the glass refrigerator door."

Now there's a sentence I never thought I'd say.

We make it—five minutes late. Before Maya joins her teammates, she turns to me and says, "Mama, I'm so glad you're here."

Her words touch my heart, and I blink back tears. Juggling the coffees, I lean down and kiss her cheek. "Me too. Good luck, buttercup."

This time is too precious to miss. I decide I'm going to change my commercial kitchen hours permanently to be at her games, even if it means finding a new kitchen.

Heading over to the bleachers with the tray of coffees, I'm happy that I haven't spilled any of it all over myself. This coffee run better work as an apology for being MIA. People bond over coffee.

"Maya is being benched. The game has already started." Coach Jack glares at me as I walk by the coaches' bench.

"I'm sorry. It was my fault. I got stuck at the coffeehouse." I hold up the container as proof. "Can you waive the rule just this once?"

"Rules are rules." He turns back to the field. Maya sits on the bench, kicking dirt. Had I known he'd bench her, I would've skipped the coffee.

Crap, I should have brought the coach one. I offer mine up as an apology. "I brought you a coffee."

"Thanks, you can set it there." Coach Jackass waves to an open spot beside him. I consider dumping it on his head. My heart is heavy in my chest. So much for my job in logistics and my perfect timing.

I wish I could take Maya into my arms and apologize, but I don't want to embarrass her in front of her teammates, especially Cecilia, who can be mean sometimes. Like the time she told Maya her pigtail hair ties didn't match and they looked dumb.

I scan the front row of the stands where the soccer moms usually hang out. Something's wrong. I don't see them. Instead, I see their husbands. Vivian's husband, Andrew, half smiles and averts his eyes. I sense something awkward is happening by the way the others barely glance my way.

Lyla's husband, Jim, notices I'm standing there with the coffees. "Those for us?" He laughs.

"Uh, well they were for the moms, but they aren't here."

"We were expecting Max," Jim says. Then he turns back to the field to watch.

"He had to work today . . . I guess you can have the coffees. Otherwise, they'll go to waste."

I hand each husband his wife's coffee. I'm left with Elenore's. Her husband is nowhere around. That's okay. I need it now. I wish I'd brought a bottle of Jameson to mix in.

The husbands say thanks and pretend to focus on the soccer game. Andrew yells, "Go, Grace!" I look, and she doesn't even have the ball.

Andrew takes a sip and chokes it down. "What's in this?"

"Oh, your wife likes wheatgrass. Enjoy."

Not one of them says where their wives are, which is suspicious. I turn to ask them, but they are in serious conversation now about baseball. Making my way up the bleachers to the top row, I take out my phone and click on Beatrice's Facebook profile. I missed the boat on something.

"Psst . . . psst."

A woman skirts close to me. She's wearing an oversize trucker hat, pulled low, and sunglasses that cover most of her face. She's got on black Uggs.

"Fallon, it's me." She clears her throat. "Elenore."

Now I understand the disguise.

"Oh, hi," I say. I haven't seen her in a while. Not since Lyla, the PTO president, and the Springshire Gossip Queen, called to inform me Elenore had gotten caught by the drama club, on stage with her pants down, messing around with the elementary school principal.

I can't imagine how Elenore's daughter, Penelope, feels. I fear the day Maya comes home from school and asks me why Elenore's mommy was kissing Mr. Lox, and I hope to God she hears nothing cruder.

Elenore's husband, Jeff, hasn't filed for divorce. I'm still scratching my head on that one, considering he's a divorce lawyer. Maybe he understands that, affair or no affair, if he divorces Elenore, he'll be the one who's screwed. I heard that some parents of the drama club children are suing the school and Elenore for emotional distress. Lyla recounted how "Poor little Mason, traumatized for days, missed a whole week of classes and won't step foot on the stage." Talk about a showstopper.

Elenore points to my phone. "I see you weren't invited either."

I follow her finger. My heart drops into my stomach. Plastered on Beatrice's page are three moms at the spa, in white robes with green masks, cucumbers on their eyes, clinking together flutes of champagne. I force myself to swallow the lump that's made its way into my throat. Now I understand why the husbands were acting so weird. They figured out I wasn't invited either, and didn't know what to say to me. Blinking back tears, I hover my finger over the "Like" button. *Do I let my "friends" know I know?* Before I spiral down this train of thought, loud clapping erupts, and I look up to see Cecilia limping off the field. Poor Cecilia—I clap for her as the assistant coach ices her ankle. I hope she's okay.

The coach lets Maya into the game, and I jump up and down like a crazy person. "Go, Maya!" After all my hoots and hollers, I settle back down into my seat.

Elenore says, "I've been dropped from the group because of . . . you know." She lowers her head in shame.

I nod and hand her the caramel macchiato. She needs it more than I do. I feel a little sense of relief that I'm not the only one left out, even though I have no idea why I've been dropped.

"Thank you," she says, and takes a sip.

I flash her a smile, then stare at the soccer field.

"You remembered how I like my coffee." Her voice shakes.

Maya scores a goal, and I jump out of my seat and cheer. *Take that, Coach!* I sink back down on the bench, triumphant, before remembering the spa picture, and the pit in my stomach returns.

"Will you meet with me to talk about what happened with the principal?" Elenore whispers.

"Of course," I say, hoping it will help her get things off her chest. Maybe she can also shed some light on why Beatrice is excluding me. "How about Monday after school drop-off? I'll text you later, and we can decide where to meet."

"Thank you," she says.

I open my messages and click on "Beatrice." I'll send her a text to remind her I'm alive and still her friend, which she seems to have forgotten.

Me: *We need to get together soon.*

Then I click on Lyla's name and text her.

Me: *Why aren't you at the soccer game?*

Lyla never misses a game. I need to confirm what I suspect to be true—that Beatrice is the organizer and Lyla is the follower. Lyla wouldn't pass up a good scoop either. She'll lap this one up. I place my phone in my pocket and watch the rest of the game.

* * *

A few hours later, I get a text back.

Lyla: *You decided to go to the soccer game instead of joining us at the spa?*

Exactly what I thought. Lyla is following Beatrice, unaware that Beatrice is leaving me out. I start to text her back, but realize I don't know what to say. She replies first.

Lyla: *I see three dots that you're typing, but nothing comes.*
Me: ⚽

I need to figure out a way to save these friendships. A thought hits me: *I* should plan something. I don't have to wait to be invited by Beatrice. I could be the organizer for once. The thought of planning anything makes me want to hurl, but if I can pull it off and get back into the group, it will be worth the stress.

CHAPTER THREE

Elenore fidgets with her napkin. She's a nervous ball of energy on the other side of the table, clearly already highly caffeinated.

Glancing around the new coffee shop, I take in how cute it is, with its small, turquoise-painted wooden tables and funky artwork. I think the owner's children go to Springshire Elementary with Maya.

"Thanks for meeting me, Fallon," Elenore says, and tugs at her earlobe, a nervous habit I've seen her do many times.

"Oh, no worries." Reading the appreciation in her eyes, it strikes me that I may be the only friend she's talked to in a while.

Blowing the steam from my piping hot coffee, I refrain from asking her how she is. Not because I don't care. I do. It's because I suspect I know how she feels. Overwhelmed, embarrassed, mortified—take your pick.

Instead, she asks me how I am. I say the obligatory, "I'm good."

I can't pour my heart out to Elenore about my hurt feelings over the spa day, like a wounded puppy. I need to stay level headed. Gather intel.

"I've been thinking," Elenore says. "Do you ever get the feeling that life isn't turning out quite like you expected it to?"

I sit up straighter. She's hit the nail on the head. Life is not turning out like I expected it to. *I never expected to be ghosted by my friends.* But I realize she's referring to her life and how it's now been turned upside down.

"I'm here for you," I say, meeting her hazel eyes that are more light brown than green today.

"Thank you." The table trembles with each tap of her foot against it. She continues, "Well, I don't want to beat around the bush."

Those may not be the best choice of words, given her situation. I look past Elenore at the bakery section—or lack thereof: a sad display of picked-over oatmeal raisin cookies and rock-hard fruitcake, proof that no one eats them.

"It's been a rough few weeks dealing with rumors, as you probably can imagine," Elenore says, and leans forward.

I nod. Why yes, I can imagine, but maybe not on the same level.

"I didn't intend for it to happen." Elenore tucks a lock of her brown hair behind her ear.

By "it" I can only assume she means screwing the principal, but she could mean getting caught on stage. I don't ask her to clarify.

"I was feeling unwanted. I thought at first it was because I'm older now. I have wrinkles . . . that maybe I'm undesirable. I never thought I'd feel this way." My gaze is drawn to her crow's feet as water edges to the corners of her eyes.

I, too, have seen the fine lines around my eyes, the extra bulge in my stomach, the creases in my neck, and the chin hairs—gray, nonetheless. I still don't condone her behavior, but I can see where she's coming from.

She goes on. "But the truth is, I found out Jeff was on a dating app. Instead of confronting him, I fell into Mark's arms." She sucks in a deep breath.

It takes me a second to realize she's talking about the principal, who we never call by his first name. It's always been Mr. Lox. This revelation about Jeff being on a dating app surprises me. I would never have pegged him as the type to cheat. He's always been so buttoned up.

A tear escapes onto her cheek, so I hand her my napkin because hers is in shreds.

I want to smack some sense into Jeff for not realizing what he has. Elenore is a classy woman, who at one point had a solid modeling career. Yes, of course, she's older now, but I can still see how beautiful she is—inside and out. None of this is up to me, though.

Elenore sniffles. "I don't expect you to understand. Your marriage is perfect."

I practically spit out my coffee. I wouldn't go that far. If she knew about the three-year period where we were at each other's throats, she'd think otherwise. But that's all behind us now. I don't dredge up the past.

"Everyone has problems," I say.

"What is unnerving is the fallout from the affair. Being shunned by friends, lawyer bills adding up. I don't regret the affair. I regret getting caught."

She lowers her eyes and picks at a chip of loose paint on the table. I shift in my seat, trying to find the words to comfort her.

"Getting caught is unfortunate," I say after a beat. I'd be having nightmares if Maya caught Max and me having sex. I can't imagine getting caught in public. The whole situation is beyond messy and traumatic.

"It's not what you think, though. I didn't get caught by the kids. I don't know who started that rumor. The drama club director found us behind the curtain before any of the kids came on stage. By the time the kids appeared, we had composed ourselves."

My eyes widen. She's being sued and crucified in the neighborhood because everyone thinks the kids caught them. This is a game changer. Talk about drama. "I hope you have a good lawyer."

She nods. Then she chokes out in a whisper, "I love him." She wipes one eye with the back of her hand.

And there it is. The admission. At first, I think she's talking about Jeff, but she means Mr. Lox . . . Mark. Part of me is happy for her, but part of me wishes she would work it out with Jeff. This isn't how it should end. But cheating is tricky. I don't know if I could get over that.

I glance around the coffee shop again, hoping no one is eavesdropping. It's not a conversation you want anyone overhearing. Then I see her—Laura Gibson, Mason's mom. The boy supposedly traumatized by seeing Elenore and Mr. Lox lip-locked and tangled. I swear I have the worst luck. It doesn't look like she sees us. In my rush to hide my face, I accidentally knock my mug, and it goes crashing to the floor, cracking into a million pieces and splattering the rest of my coffee all over my suede boots. Everyone in the coffee shop turns to stare as Elenore jumps up to get napkins. Laura rushes over and gets right up in her face.

"How dare you come in here? Do you even know who owns this place?"

Mama Bear Laura has surfaced. That's the only way I can explain her outrage. You don't mess with someone else's child.

Elenore jerks backward. Her mouth drops open. I remember now who owns the coffee shop—another mom who is suing Elenore.

"And you, Fallon." She points to me. "I thought you had more class than to hang out with her."

I grab our purses and Elenore's arm and head for the door. I want to tell Laura off, but I bite my tongue, not wanting to make this whole situation worse than it is already.

In the parking lot, Elenore throws on her sunglasses and hugs me. "I didn't mean to put you in that position."

It's better than the position the principal put her in, but I don't comment on it.

"It's okay. I'll call you," I say, and get into my car.

As I pull away, my mind drifts back to our conversation. It's heartbreaking that Elenore is being left out because of her affair. Before Laura herded us out of the café like livestock, I never got to ask Elenore why the friend group is excluding me too. I wonder if she knows anything.

I check my phone again. There's still no reply from Beatrice.

CHAPTER FOUR

As I stir chocolate, I'm careful not to drop any on my beloved copy of *How to Win Friends and Influence People*. I'm reading it for the third time. Apparently, I need a refresher.

"Listen. Ask about the person's interests. Make the person feel important."

On top of reading this book, I've been thinking about what type of event I should host for my neighborhood mom friends. Something unique and memorable. Something we haven't done before. Then it hits me—an elegant tea party, just like my grandma used to host. It's a wonderful excuse to use her fine china. I can face my fear of party planning and figure this out. *Maybe.*

I finish my chocolates and head down to the basement to find the china. Switching on the light, a cloud of dust puffs up my nose, and I sneeze. The basement storage area is a dank room with creepy-crawly things I try to avoid. *Be quick.*

Lopsided stacks of unlabeled plastic bins line the walls. I'm hoping I can figure out which one contains the china, but I don't have a clue. My phone vibrates, and I pull it out of my pocket to see a FaceTime call coming in from Avery. I answer, and her wide smile fills the screen. She is just as striking as when I met her in college, with her expressive, brown, doe-like eyes. Sometimes I think I can see straight into her soul, as if hers is a reflection of mine. And we have similar personalities—sassy. Although, my smart mouth has subsided a bit in my Springshire neighborhood.

Avery frowns.

"Where are you? Girl, don't freak out, but there's a gigantic spider web behind you," Avery says.

I lunge forward and screech while Avery laughs. "I'm itchy just looking at you."

"Gee, thanks a lot," I say.

"I was calling to talk about my upcoming visit, but I see you are in the middle of something creepy."

"I'm in the basement looking for my grandma's china."

"Special occasion?"

"I decided to host a tea party."

Avery makes a face at me.

"What?"

"A tea party sounds boring and not like you." She lets out a rather loud, animated yawn.

I agree it doesn't sound like the old me from college. Late-night study sessions included popcorn, Milk Duds, Mountain Dew, and breaks where we blared Whitney Houston's "I'm Every Woman." She knows me better than anyone, and more times than not, she serves as my memory. College is fuzzy at times. After all, it's been more than twenty years since freshman year.

"Is it a party to promote your new business?"

"Not really." I don't tell her I'm trying to save my mom friends. I'm not sure she would understand. "I wanted to try my hand at organizing something fun."

"Fun?" She lifts one eyebrow. "Your life is so different now. I guess that's what having a family and living in suburbia will do."

"Something like that," I say. I can't imagine Avery hosting a tea party for her single friends.

"Stress is written all over your face. Remember, if it doesn't go as planned, who cares?"

She's right. There's a reason why I don't plan parties, but I'm grasping at straws here to save my friendships.

Eyeing her through the phone, I ask, "Did you do something different with your hair? I like it."

"Girl, I just rolled out of bed."

I check my watch. "It's noon, your time." She looks fabulous as usual, even straight out of bed, with her high cheek bones and glowing skin. Avery lives in Atlanta. Sadly, I only get to see her maybe once a year.

"I called off work for a 'me' day."

Sounds about right. Avery has a demanding job in information security, keeping hackers at bay.

"Are you okay?"

"Nothing a little sleep couldn't fix. Speaking of my hair, I wanted to let you know I'm sending hair products ahead of me."

"Okay, I'll watch for them." Avery has always been particular about her hair. Even in college she spent any money she earned working at a bagel shop to buy salon-grade products. She said they controlled her natural "kinks." I loved her tight curls. They were a far cry from my lifeless, dirty-blond tangles that I mostly wore in a bun.

"I'm so excited to see you!" Avery says. "Bringing my mama's famous jambalaya recipe straight out of New Orleans. Your world needs some shaking up."

Little does she know, it's already tilting on its axis. "Sounds lovely."

"By the way, how is Maya Jambalaya?" Maya loves her Auntie Avery for many reasons, one of which is her endearing nature, not to mention her doting.

"She is great and can't wait to see you, of course!" I say with enthusiasm.

"I'll be bringing a family-size bag of gummy bears for her only . . . Anyway, I'll let you get back to it. I'm going to soak in a bubble bath. Watch out for that spider."

After hanging up with Avery, I pull a medium-size bin off the top of the stack and peer inside. My high school yearbooks stare up at me. I don't want to look at my class photos. Braces and stringy hair flash in my mind. They weren't the best four years of my life in terms of my looks or memories. I've tried hard to repress most of my high school experiences, especially the ones involving the mean girls. I pull out my letterman jacket and old textbooks and place them in a pile. I should really get rid of this stuff.

Clearly, the fine china isn't in this bin, but I still rummage through it. Curious about what I might find. *Old love letters?* Unlikely. I had one nerdy boyfriend, sophomore year, and we rarely held hands, let alone wrote steamy letters back and forth.

My hand grazes a torn and tattered notebook. Looks like one I used to take copious notes for chemistry, which I passed by the skin of my teeth. I open it. Nope, not chemistry. It's a journal, and by the date of the first entry it's not even from high school. *How did it get in this box?* I read through it.

May 15, 2002

When I am Mrs. Max Monroe, I will have four well-behaved, beautiful children (two girls and two boys), who always do as I ask. They will be kind, helpful, and intelligent, with IQs in the genius range. My house will always be organized and clean. You'll be able to eat off my floors. There will be no toys out of place. We will have a charming home. Max will dote on me and bring me flowers once a week. I'll be in the best shape of my life because I'll have the time and energy to work out and make healthy meals.

I'll plan all the meals and grocery shop. I'll take time off work to volunteer at my children's school. But I'll still have time for a biweekly get-together with friends for coffee and brunch.

When the kids get home from school, I'll give them a snack, and they'll do one extracurricular activity of their choice. Max will come home from work and play with our kids while I make dinner. We will eat a healthy dinner every night together as a family and go around the table saying what we are grateful for that day. Everyone will help clean up. Homework will be done and lights out by eight p.m. On weekends, we'll take long road trips and have wonderful adventures.

We will be part of a larger community of supportive friends. Our kids will play together. Moms will lean on each other. We'll have the perfect family and perfect life.

It will not be an ordinary life. It will be extraordinary. Mark my words.

I rub my forehead. *Poor baby Fallon. She had no idea.* I'm not sure if I should laugh or cry. There isn't much out of this whole entry that rings true today—twenty years later. *It's been that long?* Somewhere in my subconscious, I still believed my life would be exactly as I had written all those years ago. With a sigh, I shut it and set it on top of the pile.

Okay, the next bin must be it. Peering inside, I see I've struck gold. I remove the bubble wrap from one piece and discover a delicate white teacup with silver trim. A flower with blue petals adorns one side. Simple yet elegant. I always loved this set. *This will work.* I will save my friendships. Closing my eyes, I can feel my grandma and almost smell her citrus scent. A new ingredient for my chocolate surfaces— lemon zest.

Max can help me lug up the heavy bin of china when he gets home from work. I look at the useless high school crap and decide I'll deal with it another day. As I stuff it all back in the box, a paper falls out of my journal.

When I realize what it is, I freeze.

The letter.

I slowly lower and pick it up. I accidentally found it shortly after my eighteenth birthday, right before I went off to college, and I wanted to trash it long ago, but I couldn't bring myself to do it. Seeing this letter made for one of the most shocking days of my life and the start of my questioning everything I ever believed. *Can I deal with this now?*

I can't. I haven't told anyone about this in years, intending for it to remain buried forever.

Taking the letter upstairs to my bedroom closet, I pull my keepsake box off the shelf, where I've saved photos and cards from Max and Maya. I hesitate, wondering if I should put this letter with my beautiful memories. Then I decide this is where it needs to be, with the hope that one day it will lead to something other than dread.

CHAPTER FIVE

I pinch the skin together on my forehead, wishing away my throbbing headache. Glancing at the clock, I realize I've been creating these handmade tea party invitations for six hours. It's just past one AM, and my pillow is calling to me. I flip through the invitations to make sure the calligraphy isn't smeared, and the ivory Chantilly laser-cut lace is tied perfectly with the complementary ivory ribbon. An enthusiastic paper connoisseur at the stationery store today helped me pick out the most elegant decorative paper. Her sales pitch went something like this: "I have paper, yes I do. I have paper just for you!" Then I imagined her on top of a cheerleading pyramid. I have to hand it to her, though—the invitations are stunning. Now I pray I can pull off this party. Maybe I can hire her to be my cheering section.

Scanning my party to-do list, which is seven pages long and broken into five categories, I realize I still need to order matching embroidered napkins, napkin rings, tablecloths, and fancy silverware. It takes me another hour to order everything online. I pay more for one-day delivery. Luckily, I have eight million unused Bed Bath & Beyond coupons that never ever expire.

Reading over the list of finger foods, my eyes glaze over. I have too much to do. *What has gotten into me?* This is why I don't plan events. With all this effort, I can't imagine not getting back into good graces with the Ma Spa Squad, which is my new name for them. I'm even thinking Elenore might benefit from this tea party. She has to come so I can help smooth things over for her and the friend group too. We will all be friends again.

Crawling into bed, I softly pull the down comforter over me.

Max stirs. "Why are you up so late?" he says as he sits up and rubs his eyes.

"I'm sorry. I didn't want to wake you. I was making invitations for a tea party."

"What tea party?" he says groggily.

I haven't told him about the party yet, not wanting to hear the "social media is the downfall of civilization" speech again. But now that he's asking, I should come clean.

It's the middle of the night, but what's a few more minutes now that I'm up four hours past my usual bedtime. I tell him about being ghosted and how I want to do something nice for my friends so we can put all this behind us.

Max scoots closer to me and pulls me toward him. He's half asleep, so it looks like I may be able to avoid the speech. I breathe in his fresh, clean, musky scent with hints of amber and vanilla—the scent of home and comfort. Warmth spreads through my chest.

"You are a much better person than I am for caring so much," he says. "I don't know why you're going through all the trouble, especially since I know how much you despise hosting anything."

Max won't ever understand. He has a few drinking and golfing buddies he sees twice a year, and they talk about sports and nothing at all important. When he returns home, I always ask him, "How are the guys' families?" He shrugs and says, "I don't know." *Really? You're with these guys for eleven hours, and you didn't think to ask how everyone is?*

My friendships are way different. These women are my first mommy friends. We've been through a lot together. I can't give them up. Sure, I have Max, but I crave bonding with my girlfriends. My sanity depends on it, so much so that my bedroom walls would be padded without them.

Max kisses my forehead, turns over, and goes back to sleep while I'm left staring at the ceiling, wondering if he's right. *Can I save my friendship with Beatrice? Is all this planning for nothing?*

* * *

"Why are we stopping now?" Maya asks.

"Good question," I say, and peer around the cars. Orange cones and signs line the road. Seriously, the city plans construction at the worst times. *Hmm, what is the best time to fix this road? I know! When two hundred mothers are going this way to school at nine AM on a weekday.* Just another evil plot against mothers. Seems like they are in cahoots with bicyclists.

No cars coming in the other direction. I make a U-turn and take the first street. I have no idea where I'm going, but I refuse to sit in the long line. Road closed. *Ugh.* Let's try this way. *Ugh.* Another closed road.

"Where are we going?"

"Don't worry. We'll find a way out," I say through clenched teeth.

The road circles right back around into construction. That was a waste of three minutes. I sip my coffee for fear I will lose my shit otherwise.

I'm nervous to hand out my invitations to the Ma Spa Squad.

What if they reject me? The invitations sit in a nice pile on my passenger seat, Beatrice's on top. Once she sees it, everything will be fine again. Plus, now I am prepared to *"Listen. Ask about the person's interests. Make the person feel important . . ."*

"Mommy?"

"What's up, buttercup?"

"Can I have your phone?"

I hand it back to her. *Will the screen hurt her eyes?* I hope not, but I haven't made the time to research it yet. And silence would be best right now.

"Mommy?" I really do love the sweet sound of her voice.

"Yes, Maya."

"Can you turn up the radio? I love this song."

I like this song too, and soon we're both singing along to the chorus, "Watermelon sugar high." It will be a long time until she knows the real meaning of this song, but for now it's simply about watermelons and sugar. Oh, the sweet innocence of childhood—right before the world smacks you upside the head with the thing you never even saw coming, and you're never the same after. I force myself to stuff this thought back down.

I look in the rearview mirror, meet Maya's eyes, and we smile at each other. Still singing together, there's a new feeling in the air that everything is going to be all right. As I turn onto the road for the detour, I hear several dings over our loud singing.

"Maya, Mama needs her phone for a second."

Still stopped in traffic, I see a text from Beatrice. *Whoa!* My eyes widen as my pulse quickens. She's answering me. *Finally!* Relief rushes through me. I smile and click on it.

Beatrice: *Wannabe*

Wannabe? What does that mean? I wrack my brain. I don't understand. *Is she calling me a wannabe?*

Yes, I did *wannabe* at the spa with the Ma Spa Squad.

Before I can respond, my phone rings. It's Beatrice. I stare at it in disbelief. After all this time, she's calling me. Maybe she wants to apologize for excluding me and not texting me back sooner. I pick it up through my car's Bluetooth.

"Hi, Beatrice. You're on speaker," I inform her to preempt any swearing about construction, because I know that's what I would do. Maya is too young to hear us cuss.

"Oh, hi, Fallon. Sorry, Cecilia must have dialed by accident." *Ugh. Seriously?* Beatrice had no intention of calling me. My heart hammers in my chest.

"Hi, Cecilia," Maya calls from the back seat. Cecilia greets her back.

"Gotcha. I got your text," I say in a singsong tone, trying to sound chipper.

"Oh, sorry again. That was Cecilia asking Siri if we were on Wallaby Road. She must have clicked on your name."

Wallaby not *Wannabe.* I frown. Beatrice had no intention of making up with me. *How foolish am I?*

Traffic starts up again. "We just started moving on Durand, so definitely take that. It's fastest," I spit out and clutch the steering wheel tightly to let out the rage that's building inside me. I can't believe she's acting like this exchange is normal after not acknowledging my texts and calls, and leaving me out of spa day.

"Okay, see you at school," she says coolly, and hangs up.

"Okay, see you at school." I shake my head and mimic her.

"What are you doing, Mommy?"

I glance in the rearview mirror at Maya. "Oh, nothing," I say. I turn my focus to the road again. That's when I notice the street sign. Wallaby. We're on Wallaby.

Oh no. Did I tell Beatrice to take Durand? In my flustered state, I gave her the wrong road. I click her name to call her back, and it goes straight to voicemail. I try again. Same thing.

There's no fixing it now. I hand the phone back to Maya. "Crud!"

"What, Mommy?"

"Train."

Getting to school is like one of those word problems. If train A leaves the station going thirty miles per hour and train B leaves the station going twenty miles per hour, how fast do you have to drive to beat both trains at the crossing so your kid gets to school on time? Like a bat out of hell. That's actually how I got my first speeding ticket. I'm clearly not good at word problems.

After ten minutes, we make it. Maya jumps through to the front of the car and comes out the driver's door. I'm used to this routine, especially after the first time she did it, and I accidentally slammed the door in her face. That was a fun day.

Vivian rushes up beside me, with her three kids in tow. "Hi there!"

"Good—you're just as late as us."

"We're fashionably late."

Fashionably? Well maybe you, Vivian, with your short dress, accentuating your porcelain skin and your shiny, straight black hair, grazing your bare, toned arms. Not to mention your sparkly sandals showing off your pretty manicured toes, which you probably had done at the spa day.

I mean, how do you do it with three kids? I glance down at my T-shirt and notice the spattering of coffee from my quick rush to get out the door. My hair is in a messy bun as usual. And I just now realize, I forgot to brush my teeth and apply deodorant. *Fashionably?* No, as far as I'm concerned, there is absolutely no fashion involved in this whole affair. Now I remember my pledge for self-care. Guess that's not working out for me.

"Chaotic?" she asks, raising one sculpted eyebrow.

"Bingo," I answer.

We've learned over the years to talk in short sentences. Saying what we mean the quickest and easiest way possible. What made us friends—well, *used-to-be* friends—was the common bond we shared: mothers of small children.

"Maya, where's your backpack?" I ask. Maya looks up at me, gritting her teeth.

"Sorry, Mama. It's in the car." I remembered I left the tea party invitations there too.

"I'll take her to the door," Vivian says with a look of understanding. Vivian, with three kids, is helping me with my one kid. Somehow it makes complete sense.

"What's one more?" Vivian shrugs, taking it all in stride.

"Maya, you listen to Ms. Vivian."

As I rush to get Maya's backpack, Beatrice swerves into the parking lot like a mad woman. She slams her brakes inches from the curb next to me and rolls down her window. Her hair is matted in weird places, like she got out of bed five minutes ago. Good. At least we have something in common today, and I can cross off "the way I look" as a possible reason Beatrice is ghosting me.

Ask her something that interests her, I remind myself. I smile, ready to ask her when she's planning on opening her pool for the summer, when she starts screaming. I mean, full out like a banshee. I don't think I've ever heard something so primal come out of someone's mouth. *Who is she screeching at?* My mind races with ideas of what I can grab to shove into her mouth.

Moms and teachers are staring. I can't make any sense of what she's saying until I hear clear as day, *"Fallon, what is your problem lately?"* In fact, I think they heard her in Bosnia Herzegovina.

A flush of warmth creeps up my cheeks.

"Excuse me?" I holler back. "My . . . my . . . problem?" I stutter. My ears burn and my heart beats rapidly.

She hisses at me, "Yes, your problem. You sent me down the wrong road on purpose!" While she's shrieking, her kids jump out of the minivan and scurry toward the school. They can't get away fast enough. Cecilia sprints like her life depends on it.

Shit. I clear my throat and put on my best cheery voice. "It was an accident, but look, you made it!" I don't want this to escalate further. It's already measuring ten on the Richter scale.

"I swear you can be a real bitch!"

Rubbing the back of my neck, lightheadedness moves in. I'm speechless. I certainly didn't expect this response from Beatrice, or anyone in Springshire, for that matter. Even rabid monkeys have better manners.

Not wanting to make a bigger scene, I flee to my car. Beatrice squeals her tires and speeds out of the parking lot. My blood boils. *How am I the bitch?* I'm not the one excluding her.

After getting Maya's backpack to her, I sink into the driver's seat and inhale deeply. I can't believe Beatrice. I take three more deep breaths. I consider calling Avery, but she will just ask me why I didn't call Beatrice a bigger bitch right back. *Why didn't I?* First, I was shocked at the words coming out of Beatrice's mouth. Second, I wasn't thinking straight. Third, that part of me that used to go off at a moment's notice got left behind the day we moved into Springshire.

Where did all of this go wrong? There must be more to the story than a few missed soccer games. Beatrice's reaction bordered on hysteria. I need to get to the bottom of this. *Text her? No. Better let her cool off first.* I need to literally cool off too, I realize. Sweat is pooling under my armpits, and I'm burning up like a marshmallow over a campfire.

The tea party invitations still sit on my passenger seat. After that completely insane blowup with Beatrice, I'm not sure I'm in the mood to host anything. I pick up Beatrice's invitation and look at it. Then I wave it to fan my flaming face. At least, it's good for something.

CHAPTER SIX

At home, I crawl under a throw blanket with a box of chocolates. I think of the Forrest Gump quote, "Life is like a box of chocolates. You never know what you're gonna get." *Isn't that the truth?*

Tears slide down my cheeks as the vanilla buttercream melts in my mouth. So much for my tea party. I can't remember the last time I felt so excluded. Maybe it was high school when I was left out of the biggest party of the year. Crying for weeks, my seventeen-year-old self was left heartbroken and shattered. I'm not sure I ever pieced myself back together from that exclusion. Now I find myself practically in the same situation, but for different reasons. I've grown older and wiser, yet I feel like I'm still in high school in a lot of ways.

When I was seventeen, it had been an accident. Not wanting my date to see me stuffing my face with a hot dog at junior prom, I snuck into the hallway. They were about to announce prom king and queen, and I needed to get back quickly—not that I was in the running.

I could hear Whitney coming toward me. Not expecting her to be peering into the glass trophy case at her reflection, I turned to say something and ran straight into her with my hot dog. Mustard splattered everywhere, and yellow streams of liquid dripped down her dark blue dress just as the principal's voice came over the loudspeaker. "Your prom queen is Whitney Ross." I reached out with a napkin to clean it, smearing the mustard into a big circle that looked like the sun, and thus transforming her prom dress into something she would have worn in kindergarten. But unlike the cheery sun, she became a fierce storm, thundering obscenities at me. Whitney made me switch dresses with her right there. Ironically, in her dress, I looked like a plump foot-long hot dog stuffed into a regular-size bun. She hated my pink taffeta dress that draped over her thin body two sizes too big.

And just like that, in a matter of ten seconds, I had managed to get ousted from the popular crowd and excluded from the annual end-of-school party hosted by Jason Martin—the richest kid in town. Whitney started nasty rumors about me and hot dogs, which I will not repeat. I haven't eaten a hot dog since.

But where did my friendship with Beatrice go wrong? I can't recall a traumatic event anywhere close to the Great Hot Dog Disaster.

The day I met Beatrice, I was taking Maya for an early morning walk in her stroller around the neighborhood on a warm summer day. She was facing me, and I was describing the trees and the birds. I kept chattering about the chalk drawings and basketball hoops in the driveways and the bikes left out on lawns overnight. I told her one day she'd enjoy these activities.

I didn't even notice the pile of shit in the middle of the sidewalk. I rolled over it and proceeded to step in it in my new shoes. Everyone who knows me knows not to mess with my shoes. I have about a hundred pairs of them, and they are my most coveted possessions. I proceeded to screech a few choice words, startling Maya enough to make her cry.

A woman in a pink bathrobe and multicolored foam rollers in her hair called out from her front porch, "Oh no! I meant to clean it up."

I must have looked at her accusingly, because she held up her hands to indicate she wasn't the one who had taken a huge dump in the middle of the sidewalk.

"It wasn't my dog," she said with a horrified expression.

I thought we lived in a nice neighborhood where people cleaned up after their dogs. I was wrong. There was clearly at least one inconsiderate jerk who lived here. The association rules stated in bold print: **"Pick up after your dog."**

The woman rushed toward me in her slippers. "Let me help you. I have a hose around the side of the house."

I followed her, and she sprayed the stroller tires and my shoes, managing to also soak my leggings and top. I looked like I had entered a wet T-shirt contest.

"I'm Beatrice." She held out her hand to me.

After that day, Beatrice and I began power-walking through the neighborhood with our girls in strollers—always watching out for dog poop.

Then, as our girls got older, we had endless playdates at the park to get us out of the house and keep us sane. Beatrice had Benjamin and got busier with two kids. School happened, and we went to lunch on occasion, when she could get a babysitter for Benjamin and the girls were gone all day.

Shortly after meeting Beatrice, we met the other moms at the neighborhood playground. We became close—Beatrice, Lyla, Vivian, Elenore, and me. Our kids are the same ages and in the same grade. But it's more than being bound together by our children. Our husbands golf together too. It works for all of us. This is the dream group of friends I've always wished for. We've become so close these last few years: brunches, ladies' nights out, family gatherings—even weekends away skiing or at a water park.

We've been through a lot together too. When I got a concussion from falling out of the bed and banging my head on the nightstand—I still don't know how I managed that—and during recovery I couldn't do anything but stare at the wall, Beatrice bought a whole slew of tabloid magazines and read them to me. That was the only period in my life I was caught up on Hollywood gossip. It kept my spirits up, and I'm convinced it's what cut my recovery time in half.

And I jumped into Beatrice's pool fully clothed to rescue her one-year-old son while Beatrice yapped away with the pool boy.

The last time I was with the whole gang had been in early March for a park playdate. *Did I say something to offend any of them?* I talked about my chocolates and some new recipes. Nothing out of the ordinary there. Lyla caught us up on teacher talks with the union about negotiating for more money. Lyla said a strike might be imminent if the school board didn't meet their demands. Still, this had nothing to do with me. I remember Cecilia and Maya fighting over the last swing. I don't know who started it, but Beatrice and I ended it and gave them each a time-out. By the end of the day, they were playing with each other nicely again.

There was one remark from Beatrice that struck me. I'd thought it was funny at the time, but maybe there was more meaning behind her words.

"I hate how the garbage collectors leave the top of my trash can open when it's raining, and when I dump it out, it splashes everywhere and always on my shoes," I said.

In response, Beatrice said, "Oh, Fallon, it must be so difficult having your problems." She had never judged me like that before. "Besides, they're just shoes and you have, like, a hundred of them."

Then the fight broke out between Maya and Cecilia, so I hadn't responded.

Feeling sappy, I search the internet for friendship quotes, as if that will make me feel better.

"Good friends are like stars. You don't always see them, but you know they're always there."

I miss Beatrice. She used to text me daily, relaying some new tidbit about the stupid stuff people do. These things are usually absurd and make me feel like a better parent. Like the time she texted, *Did you hear about the guy who strapped an inflatable pool to the hood of his car and had his two children sit in it while he drove them home?* Luckily, the kids hadn't gotten hurt.

She is often my only comic relief throughout a mundane day. But now, I can't remember the last time she texted me something funny. I haven't seen her in four weeks, and she'd planned a spa getaway without me. I move on to the next quote.

"People come into your life for a reason, a season, or a lifetime."

Struck by the profoundness of these words, I continue to read the page's long passage. Whoever this unknown author is, they're deep and quite smart. I begin to contemplate the meaning and where my mom friends fit in. *These are lifetime friends, aren't they?*

I go on to read more quotes.

"If a friendship lasts longer than seven years, psychologists say it will last a lifetime."

"If a friendship lasts longer than seven years, you are no longer just friends, you are family."

Seven years. This is the make-or-break year for my mom friends. I take a deep breath.

Craving a connection with them again, I click over to my text messages and open a group thread I couldn't bear to delete.

Beatrice: *If u ever think u had a shitty day . . . just think of this. I put the steaming hot coffee pot in the pantry.*

Lyla: *I've done that before. U know it's really bad when ur looking for ur phone and ur talking on it. That was me yesterday.*

Vivian: *I can top all of that. I accidentally sent an email to Grace's gym teacher meant for Andrew and addressed it "Sexy."*

Lyla: *Lol. Did he respond? He is kind of sexy in a boyish way.*

Vivian: *Ewww if u like lizard faces. I sent an apology right away.*

Elenore: *I just spit my coffee across the room, and now I have to clean brown spots off my white walls.*

Me: 😂 😂 😂 *I told a telemarketer I loved him before I hung up.*

Elenore: *Now I have two walls to wash.*

Beatrice: *Did he get you a good deal on car insurance?*
Lyla: *I've done that before too, except it was to our accountant. Technically, he found a loophole on our taxes, so we got more money back, so I wasn't totally off base.* 😏
Me: 😂 😂 😂

I can't help but laugh again. I want more of these exchanges. Need them. I haul myself off the couch to make some tea to comfort me, and my eye catches my trusty "Joyful Jar" sitting on the bookshelf next to my self-help books. I only open the mason jar when I'm feeling particularly down. I take it in my hand and blow the dust off the top of it. It's my most treasured gift from Mel from when she hosted a Day of the Dead celebration. We all attended because of the mystery and excitement it promised. I was dying (pun intended) for intrigue. Parties like this were not held in Springshire—birthday parties, book clubs, and backyard barbecues, yes. Day of the Dead—totally out of the ordinary. The subdivision, with cookie-cutter houses, three-car garages, 2.5 children, white picket fences, and camera doorbells to track the whereabouts of coyotes, lacked excitement.

So I jumped at the chance to do something new. We dressed in black and painted our faces white, black, and red. Mel created a beautiful altar decorated with photographs of her ancestors, candles, marigolds, skulls, a cross made of salt, and perforated colorful paper. I can still conjure up the image of it in all its glorious detail.

After way too much mezcal, Mel handed us mason jars, scraps of paper, and red pens. The assignment—for each person in attendance to write what you would post on your friends' social media if they died. Then stick the paper in their jars. You could choose to sign your name or remain anonymous. I crossed my fingers before writing my notes in hopes that would ward off death. *Did I even want to read what my friends would write?*

In the end, the only one to sign her name was Mel, and we were instructed to open hers last. She wrote hers on yellow paper, so it would be easily recognizable. We took the jars home and during a warm bath, I read them. I sobbed. Alcohol may have played a factor in their sappiness and my response.

I unscrew the jar now. I reach in and pull out a tattered piece of paper. Chocolate thumb prints mark the crease from the last time I was sad, which had to do with a fight with Max. I read the note.

Fallon didn't deserve to die from the pigeon poop that fell in her eye and infected her whole body. If she had seen it had gotten on her shoes too, she'd turn over in her grave. Okay, I wouldn't write that first part but thought you'd appreciate it.

Fallon Monroe was a beautiful soul gone way too soon. It's rare that someone like Fallon comes into your life. She was like a beacon of light in a storm, helping you navigate your way. She was the type of person who wouldn't think twice about ruining her coveted new shoes to save your child from drowning. She jumped right into any situation if it meant saving someone she loved. I owe a lot to her and now she's gone. I'll never be able to repay her for all the last-minute babysitting or child pickups from school. Godspeed.

This note, written by Beatrice, is proof she loved me. That's why this whole situation with the Ma Spa Squad is confusing. I want to snap a picture of this note and text it to her.

I pull the yellow note from the jar.

Okay, chica, I'm not going to write anything sentimental. I'm surprised you took me seriously. Who wants to think about their death or their friends' deaths? Well, anyway, you have some nice notes that say you're wonderful. So, you're welcome. Enjoy your Joyful Jar. Remember, though, you still live in Shitshire, so be careful.

That was Mel for you. Always with the surprises. *Did she write the same thing on everyone's note?* I've never asked her.

I replace the jar on the shelf and move to the kitchen to make my tea. Here I am still having a tea party. By myself. As I steep the tea bag, the doorbell startles me. Setting my teacup down, I head to answer it. A big box from Bed, Bath & Beyond sits on my porch. *Great.* Now I have everything I need for my tea "pity" party of one. I pick up the heavy box and bring it to my dining room table. Scorching overtakes my neck and cheeks like I just finished an Olympic marathon and face-planted into the torch.

This is not normal. I'm too young to be experiencing menopause symptoms, *right?* I freeze. I'm too old to be pregnant, *right?*

I retrieve my phone from where I left it on the couch and open my calendar.

I've missed two cycles.

CHAPTER SEVEN

I rummage through my bathroom cabinet and drawers. I know I have one in here. It's been a while, though. After sifting through what feels like a hundred half-empty hair and makeup products—I really should go through them and trash what I don't use—I find the pink box. I search for the expiration date, but I don't see one. I'm sure it's fine. I inhale deeply. In a few short minutes, I'll know if I'm pregnant.

As I wait for the results, I think about the many downs I've had with these tests. Lots of tears and frustration for months from negative results. I turned to Ben & Jerry. They lifted me up time and time again with a pint of half baked. I'd play hide-and-seek with Maya and hide in the back of one of our six closets and stuff my face. By the time she found me, I had one large spoonful left for her. She loved this part of hide-and-seek best.

After the fifth negative test, I'd gained ten pounds from my Ben & Jerry therapy. It was like baby weight without the baby. We finally went to see specialists when we hit one year of trying. My eggs were fine. Max's low sperm turned out to be the problem.

With Max's medical background, he understood the medical terminology, which I have now forgotten, and his condition more than I did. From that appointment, we learned it would be near impossible for us to have any more children. No treatments would work, and adoption would be our best option, which was not right for me.

This revelation threw me into a state of despair that I hid from Max and just about everybody who knew me. My mindset added to the stress of our marriage and to the difficult years raising Maya through the terrible twos and trying threes.

Thinking back, I recall the time Maya got a hold of a permanent marker at age two and decorated her face as well as the walls. I had gone to the bathroom for literally two minutes and couldn't believe how much damage she'd done in that amount of time. It took me a week to get it off her face, and the wall needed repainting.

When she was three, I accidentally left a pair of scissors in her room after using them to open a box of pull-ups. She was supposed to be napping, but somehow thought it would be a good idea to cut her hair and her American Girl doll's hair to match. She had patches of baldness all over her head, looking as if she had mange. I cried for two days and had nightmares it would never grow back.

I barely survived her tantrums, and it took years to recover from Max's infertility. Now, here I am again in limbo. I don't like this feeling. *What if the test is positive?* I have resigned myself to the fact that one child is enough. I've convinced myself that I couldn't do it again. As much as I want another child, in all honesty, I'm finally at a place of mental stability—well, I have a much better handle on things now at least—and another child at the age of forty might just push me into a mental breakdown.

On the other hand, the pitter patter of little feet again, along with giggles and coos, counting fingers and toes, and snuggles might brighten my mood. I could push through the exhaustion. I did it before. I survived. Like they say, "What doesn't kill you makes you stronger." Maya would have a playmate. She would be a good big sister and help me.

I swipe my clammy palms on my sweatpants, take a deep breath, and I'm about to check the results when my phone dings with a text from Mel.

Mel: *Hi, Chica, como estas?*
ME: *I'm good. How are you?*
Mel: *Same. How's Shitshire?*
Me: *Not the same without u. I was going to host a tea party for the group.*

Mel moved into Springshire like a strong wind no one was prepared for, and she left the same way. She viewed life a bit differently because her experiences were jagged around the edges. Mel moved out of our neighborhood six months ago to take a job in New York City.

We met commiserating over the stupid neighborhood association rules after one of their meetings where they explained how the grass should never be more than four inches tall, and they would be measuring. Mel whispered to me that she had something they could measure and flashed her middle finger. We became fast friends.

She moved shortly after she received a photo of her dying bushes from the association police. She was told to remove them or pay a hefty fine. She didn't dig them up, nor did she pay up. The new owners of the house have no idea how deep those roots run. Mel said, "It's not my problem anymore." I agreed.

Mel: *What? A tea party? Nah. Snoozer. Forget about your fake friends. Visit me in New York.*

That would be amazing, but I don't know if I can take time away from Maya or my chocolate business. I tell her I'll think about it.

* * *

I scoot closer to Max's side of the bed. He's busy reading a medical journal, most likely about whatever gynecologists read about—STDs, pap smears, advances in those cold metal objects they shove up a woman's vagina.

"I took a pregnancy test today." I pull the pillow over my stomach.

Max sets his medical journal down on the nightstand and raises his eyebrows. "What?"

"I skipped two periods."

"Oh?" His deep brown eyes widen.

"Negative," I whisper.

Max draws me into his arms, and I breathe in the blackcurrant scent of his cologne. "I'm so sorry. Are you okay?"

"I'm okay. I mean, we were told no." I place my head on his chest, listening to the thumping of his heart. He strokes my hair as we lie in silence for a few minutes. A part of me has still hoped we could have another child. Then my life would be closer to the way I envisioned it.

Annie Cathryn

"I don't mean to be the bearer of bad news, but you may be experiencing perimenopausal symptoms." Max switches into Dr. Monroe mode.

My heart sinks. *So, it really could be menopause?* I'm not ready for everything that comes with that—hormones out of whack, weight gain, moodiness, vaginal dryness—although Dr. Monroe would have a cure for that. "I know," I say. "I was afraid of that."

"Or it could be stress," he adds to soften the blow. He brushes a strand of hair off my face.

"You think?"

"Absolutely. You're still on the young side to be experiencing symptoms associated with menopause," he says, and tucks a tendril of hair behind my ear. "Stress causes all sorts of havoc on your body. Fallon, you have a lot on your plate with starting your business."

"But chocolate makes me happy," I say.

"Things that make you happy can still be stressful. Think of our wedding."

He's right. Planning our wedding was one of the happiest times of my life, but also one of the most stressful. I hired a wedding planner because even I know my limits. A lot of the stress had to do with his parents wanting to invite all one thousand people in their small town, and third cousins twice removed that they hadn't seen in thirty years. Plus, his mom insisted on having the local baker make our cake with miniature pigs on it to represent their farming community. In the end, I put my foot down on the pigs and invitations to people we didn't know, with Max backing me up.

I skipped two periods during that time as well. *How could I have forgotten?* I had been absolutely joyful at the prospect of being pregnant then. When I found out I wasn't, I hadn't been too upset—we had time, I remember thinking.

So now again, not getting my period could be stress related, and I have a sneaky suspicion it's because of my friend situation.

Max inhales a deep breath, as if he is readying himself to say something important. Then he purses his lips and kisses my forehead.

CHAPTER EIGHT

It's Saturday, and I beg Max to go to the soccer game with me. I don't want to face the Ma Spa Squad alone for fear Beatrice has brainwashed them into believing I'm Cruella de Vil incarnate. Being around ninety-nine yapping dogs *is* my idea of personal hell, but I would never steal their fur. It's just the type of comparison she'd make now that she had called me a bitch in front of all the stay-at-home moms at school.

Max says he can't go because he has to be at work today. I can tell by the way he's slamming kitchen cabinets he's annoyed at the state of the house. I've never let it get this bad. Well, not since Maya was one and I couldn't get ahead of the cleaning in between breastfeeding, drinking wine, pumping and dumping, and changing diapers. Rolling the vacuum around, I make an effort to clean up now for my lack of it then.

* * *

We are fifteen minutes early to the soccer field. It's better than being late, but Maya complains. I tell her to kick the ball around. It will do her good to warm up. The grass squishes under her shoes, soggy from last night's rain. Puddles of water and mud dot the field. I stare at my rain boots, satisfied with my choice of footwear this morning.

I take my normal seat in the front row of the bleachers before all the other moms show up, hoping they'll sit with me, and I can take this opportunity to use the principles from *How to Win Friends and Influence People*. Maybe this time will be better than the encounter with Beatrice in the school parking lot, which proved that it's one thing to read a book full of advice, but it's another to put it into practice. My hands sweat at the thought.

Lyla approaches me with a thermos. "Fallon, you made it!" The warmth of her breath hits my face, and I detect the scent of vanilla, cinnamon, and rum. As they say, it's five o'clock somewhere.

We are the only two on the bench. "It's good to see you," I say. Then I realize maybe she can tell me what's going on with Beatrice. "You know, I haven't heard from Beatrice lately." Lyla "loose lips" loves to offer up information any chance she gets.

"I don't know why everyone is being so secretive. Beatrice needs to tell you, but she won't, and being her oldest friend in the neighborhood, you of all people deserve to know what's going on," Lyla says, and waves one hand in the air.

So, there *is* something going on.

Lyla's daughter tugs on her pants. "Mommy, my cleat won't go on."

Lyla bends over to help with Jenna's shoe. Vivian greets us and sits next to Lyla. I sigh loudly. *Am I ever going to hear the scoop?*

"Good to see you, Fallon!" Vivian says. They're acting like I've been out of the country for a year. She dabs her lips with gloss. Then rubs them together as the sweet scent of watermelon wafts toward me.

"Hi, Vivian. I was here last week too." I want her to know that I'm not skirting my mom responsibilities going to a spa. I say it to convince myself that I'm a good mom. Then I cringe. Will she pick up on my snarky tone? *How to Win Friends and Influence People* advises against criticizing. I did say her name, though, which the book says to do.

I should be keeping score on this conversation like the soccer game. That would be three points for me. Two for using her name and one for smiling.

Vivian doesn't mention the spa. I'm tired of pretending I don't know, so I address the elephant on the bench. "How was the spa?" There, I recovered by asking about something that is important to her. Another point for encouraging others to talk about themselves. I'm up to four points.

Lyla, finished with Jenna's cleat, greets Vivian. I wait for the pleasantries to pass and ask again, "How was the spa, Vivian?" Another point for using her name (five points). She's digging through her purse, so I am not sure she's heard me.

As people fill in the surrounding seats, the whistle blows, indicating the start of the game. Maya takes the field, and I breathe a sigh of relief that she's starting today.

I don't see Beatrice anywhere, but her daughter, Cecilia, is also on the field.

"Good. Why didn't you join us?" Vivian finally answers me.

"Yeah," Lyla says. "I was sad to hear that you were too busy to come with us, but then you chose to go to soccer anyway." She turns to me. Her long red curls fall in front of her face, and the aroma of her floral-scented perfume fills the air between us.

"What do you mean, Lyla?" Another point for using a person's name (six points).

"What do *you* mean, what do I mean?" Lyla raises her eyebrows, and her green eyes widen.

"I didn't know about the spa," I say.

Vivian gasps. "Oh, Beatrice said she invited you but that you said you were playing with chocolate."

Playing with chocolate? You play *with Play-Doh. You don't* play *with chocolate. Is this a joke?*

"I took the day off to watch the soccer game and see you ladies. It wasn't until I got to the game that I noticed you weren't here." Another point for showing them they are important to me (seven points).

"Must have been a miscommunication," Vivian says, brushing fuzz off her casual black jumpsuit with her travel lint roller.

I don't understand how not being invited in the first place is a miscommunication. Cecilia scores a goal, and everyone cheers.

"Well, maybe you can make it to the paint-and-sip night," Vivian says.

Paint-and-sip night? I don't know what that entails, but I hope they choke while sipping their paint. Another outing I clearly wasn't invited to. This friend situation keeps getting worse.

"Well, you know Beatrice isn't herself lately. It may have slipped her mind," Vivian says.

Whoops and hollers erupt again. Maya jumps up and down. The score reflects a new goal. I cheer.

"Speaking of Beatrice, where is she?" I ask. There are more cheers, and my question gets lost in all the hoopla. It's too hard to hold a conversation during the game.

Just then, Beatrice walks up and sits next to Vivian and waves in my direction. I turn to see if someone is behind me, but I think the wave was meant for me. When I turn back around, she's watching the game. Maybe she was waving a fly out of her face. *Shit does attract flies,* I think, but now I'm being petty.

I must admit Beatrice looks vibrant and healthy. Her brown hair is glossy, her lips plump and painted, and her cheeks are tinted with rouge. The only thing amiss is the glob of mascara in the corner of her eye. She's a bit overdone for a soccer game, though. It's as if she came directly from the salon and is going to a swanky night club. *Does she have a sequined dress under her raincoat?* I must stare at her a little longer than is comfortable, because Lyla nudges me.

"Your daughter has the ball," Lyla says.

I hoot and scream Maya's name. As I watch her kick the ball caked with dirt, my mind wanders back to Beatrice. My first assumption is that she might be sick with something dreadful that no one wants to talk about. But after seeing her today, she can't be sick. In fact, I don't think I've ever seen her glow so brightly.

Maya kicks the ball to Grace, along with a splash of muddy rainwater. Their white uniforms are now sopping wet and dirty. Andrew screams from behind me. The husbands sit two rows behind their wives so the women can catch up, and the siblings of the players sit directly between us. I look past the kids behind me to see which husbands are here. *Where's Craig?* Beatrice leans back and says something to Elenore's husband, Jeff, and they both laugh. I look past them to the top row. Craig is sitting with Elenore. My eyes widen. *Am I in a husband swap reality show?* I search for the cameras. I'm being ridiculous, but something's off.

Why isn't Beatrice sitting with Craig? He's her lobster. That's what she told me once, anyway. Lobsters mate for life. We used to have long conversations over coffee about how in love they were. He'd often bring her flowers just because, and the jewelry she flashed must have cost a fortune. This happened to be during the time Max and I had hit a rough patch. I remember feeling envious of their relationship. It doesn't make sense to me that they're sitting so far away from each other today.

Maya has the ball again. I press "Record" on my cell phone. Max will want to see it, especially if she scores a goal. Maya is slipping and sliding all over the place, but she keeps control of the ball.

"Come on, Maya. Come on," I say under my breath.

She is good at maneuvering and anticipating the moves of her opponents. I watch in awe as she fakes her moves, left and right. She's running the ball all the way to the goalie. She's fast. Her opponents have lost steam. She kicks the ball hard over the goalie's head and straight into the net. The crowd goes wild. I'm screaming and jumping.

Someone brushes my arm as I settle down. It's Max.

"My appointment got canceled," he says, and sits on my left.

I couldn't be more relieved, for my sanity, that he's here. I pat his leg and lean my head on his shoulder.

"You just missed the best play of the game, but don't worry—I got it on video."

"Thank you," he says, and kisses my forehead. "Looks like they're winning. There wasn't a doubt in my mind."

Maya's coach calls a time-out, and I replay the video for Max. I can hear people talking on the recording. It sounds like Beatrice's voice, but I can't decipher her words while Max is watching it. Max finishes the video and hands my phone back to me.

"That's one of her best scores," he says proudly. "Great job getting that on video. She's going to love seeing it."

I excuse myself to go to the bathroom. Locking myself in a stall, I play the video again, but this time I hold the phone up to my ear. I turn the volume all the way up, catching a few words here and there.

"Not a good friend . . . thinks she's better . . . surprised she's here . . . daughter's a bully . . . husband is snobby . . . busy playing with chocolate . . . friends with Mel, if that tells you anything."

What? It's one thing to call me names, but another to bring my family into this. I know Beatrice is calling Maya a bully because of the fight over the swing at our last playdate. *Get over it! Kids fight.* As far as my husband being a snob, he's successful and good-looking, and people will assume he thinks he's all that, but I never thought I'd hear those words from a friend. I fight back tears.

When I return, the scoreboard indicates the game is a close one. Each team keeps scoring, and it's super loud. Jeff gets kicked out of the stands for calling the ref a rat bastard. I wouldn't have used those exact words, but he was right about the ref making bad calls.

With thirty seconds left in the game, the score is tied, seven to seven. Everyone is on their feet now. Maya has the ball. She fake kicks with her right foot, then immediately kicks it the other way with her left, surprising the goalie. Score! I scream my head off, and Max whistles.

Overtaken with a sense of triumph, I'm high-fiving people I don't even know. Parents are storming the field to congratulate and retrieve their daughters.

"I see you've made up with them." Elenore walks beside me.

Appearances can be deceiving. Sitting with the Ma Spa Squad didn't improve matters. I think it made them worse after overhearing Beatrice's rant.

"Not exactly," I say gruffly in a strained voice. If only it were that easy.

CHAPTER NINE

As I sit on my couch, I play the soccer video again, holding it up to my ear. Yes, Beatrice has said some very mean things about me, but I know Beatrice, and she doesn't really mean any of it. There's something else going on with her, and I'm going to get to the bottom of it.

I make up a story in my head that she's pregnant and Craig doesn't want another child. I cringe at this thought. The idea of an unwanted child hits too close to home for me. *But what if it is true? What if he's threatened to leave her and move to Bora Bora or some place to provide chiropractic services to travelers after long flights?* Geez, no wonder Beatrice is distraught. I have faith, though, they'll work it out before the baby arrives. Whatever it is, their problems have nothing to do with me. Like Lyla said, I slipped her mind. Then I think maybe I am a horrible friend if Beatrice can forget me and feels uncomfortable turning to me.

After contemplating whether to host something yet again, I decide a party will fix everything. The tea party wasn't enough. It would have been too small, just like the coffee run. I will throw an epic party. It will prove I'm not only a good friend, but a *great* friend.

I text Mel since she has experience in spicing everything up. She'll know exactly the type of party I should host. As I begin typing, I remember that Beatrice hasn't been the nicest to her either.

> **Me:** *Can I pick ur brain about hosting something fun?*
> **Mel:** *If ur inviting ur neighbors, ur already at a disadvantage.*

Mel thinks the women in Springshire are jerks. A single mom in Springshire is the equivalent of a witch in Sunday school. Mel got the memo right away and had a T-shirt made with a scarlet *A* on it. Although she said she never cheated on her ex-husband, she enjoyed mocking the neighbors.

Mel was continually left out for not having a husband to take to the neighborhood parties. I wasn't hosting the shindigs, so I felt I couldn't invite her. Somehow, she found out about the parties, probably from social media, and she went anyway, wearing low-cut tops. She couldn't care less. These women would never show off their boobs. They smacked their husbands every time they were caught ogling over Mel's size B that looked like size D, with the help of a padded push-up bra. I didn't worry about my own husband. When you see boobs all day long, what's another pair? Before I can respond, another text comes through.

> **Mel:** *Have a dildo party*

I choke down my coffee.

> **Me:** *Now that would really get a rise out of people!*

Mel: *Ha! Okay, I get u have to live there and be somewhat normal. How about a Mexican Fiesta?*

I contemplate this. Suddenly I recall last summer when Beatrice and I sipped margaritas poolside. I'd said, "We should have a Mexican Fiesta," and she'd replied, "Oh yeah." A buzz of energy courses through me. This is a phenomenal idea.

Mel: *Then fill the piñata with penis suckers and have your camera ready standing by to catch those bitches' faces!*

I am literally dying at her texts. I wish she still lived here. Before I can respond, she texts again.

Mel: *Ditch the party. My offer still stands to visit me in NYC.*

It didn't help Mel's reputation that she made more money than any of the men in a five-block radius. The rumor mill claimed she was an exotic dancer. I mean, they said she'd have to be with that killer bod. They glossed over her Yale finance degree and the fact that you could do a simple internet search and find her as one of the top financial advisors in the nation. You would think they would be knocking down her door for investment advice.

If you ask me, they were all jealous. *How dare a woman make more money than my husband?* Come off it. This isn't 1950. Although, the way the households are set up here, you would think we'd reverted to the 1950s white-picket-fence-stay-at-home-mom philosophy. I didn't know the women back in the '50s mostly kept it together by drinking alcohol mixed with crushed pills. I mean, I do know now because I've considered it.

When Mel moved, she didn't get a proper sendoff—not even a measly goodbye wave. But I'm not Mel. I still have to live here and play nice. A Mexican Fiesta with a piñata filled with liquor bottles. Hanging chili lights. Salsa dancing.

I can do this. We'll all be friends again. Swaying with our arms around each other and singing "Livin' la Vida Loca."

CHAPTER TEN

As I drive to make my chocolate delivery, I'm lost in thought about my budding business. I know I need a website, from the many self-help business books I've read, but orders keep rolling in by word of mouth and from the fliers I've distributed. The fewer expenses I have to undertake, the better. This delivery is for a relative of one of Max's patients. They ordered one hundred pieces of liqueur-filled chocolates.

With all my tinkering, this is my best recipe. I can feel it, and not because I've been buzzed all week taste testing. It takes the edge off my crappy mood since hearing Beatrice's conversation with Jeff at the soccer game.

This is my first official order for someone I don't know. This could be my big break into a ton more business. By the size of the order, I imagine fifty women trying my chocolates and thinking of me for their next party. This batch of chocolates is proof that I'm not playing around.

I pull up to the address on the order slip. It's a small, older apartment complex with cracked siding and overgrown shrubs. Parked cars line the street, and I sigh, realizing I'm going to have to parallel park, which I haven't done in a hundred years. Thank God for bumpers. After ten minutes of maneuvering and bouncing off the front and back bumper of the other cars, I squeeze my Jeep in and leave it at a sharp angle. It will have to do. I'm only running in for a quick minute anyway.

I carefully take the chocolates out of the hatchback. I packed them securely, so they arrived safely. This was one of my largest orders to date and the farthest I had to drive to deliver them.

There's a sign on the elevator that reads, "Out of order." Inconvenient for me and for the residents. As I climb the stairs to the third floor, I think that in the future I should ask for more details on the layout, like stairs and parking. Next time, I'll charge for exertion. I make a mental note.

It becomes evident which unit I'm delivering to by the loud music, cheers, and thumping echoing down the hallway. I'm used to high-society brunches, upscale restaurants, and kids' birthday parties, which sound like a cakewalk compared to the raucous sounds coming from behind the door. I knock. I wait. No one answers. I knock louder. Still nothing. I pound. My hand hurts. I try the door handle. It's unlocked, so I push the door open.

I can only guess it's the guest of honor on a chair in the middle of the room, wearing a tiara. Women surround her with their arms around each other, dancing and singing. I bite my lip at the scene before me. Everyone looks so messed up, but that's not what my mind processes. They are having fun. Letting loose. I squeeze my eyes shut for a moment. Opening them again, my gaze falls on a sweaty, hairy, muscular man gyrating near the tiara woman's face. He's got a lot of back hair for a stripper. *Isn't he supposed to wax that?* Heat rushes up my neck as a young woman moves toward me, and I turn my attention away from Dirty Harry.

"Can I help you?" she screams over the screeching women.

"Chocolates."

She raises her hand to her ear.

I point to the box and hold up the invoice. The woman motions for me to follow her through the small apartment. Presumably to the kitchen. There must be thirty women in here. Someone needs to crack a window. The stench of the wafting cigarette smoke is stifling.

"Fallon!" I think I hear my name over the music. I glance back. It takes me a second, but I recognize the woman with a ridiculous penis balloon on her head. It's my sister-in-law, Maeve, Max's sister.

"Hi!" Maeve is so close to me I can smell her beer breath. I try not to breathe through my nose. There's no way to talk to her without her being up in my face. I wish someone would turn the music down. "Do you know Misty?"

I assume she means the woman with the tiara. "Oh no. I'm delivering chocolates." I show her the box.

"Yum," she says, and licks her lips. She's drunk like the rest of them.

Maeve lives one town over, where she and Max grew up on a farm. Their parents, Melvin and Milly—yes, their names all start with M, and Max insisted on the name Maya to continue the Monroe tradition—still live in the area but sold the farm when it became too much for them to handle. Their mom, Milly, is a farm girl through and through. I'm sure it just about killed her when she had to give up hers. I know she blames me for Max not wanting to be a farmer. I had nothing to do with it. Max wanted to live close to them, but not in the same town. He said it was way too small and everyone's always in your business. He called it Nowhereville.

Maeve looks cute tonight in a sparkly silver top and capri jeans. The last time I saw her, she was dressed in an adult-size zip-up pajama onesie covered in printed yellow duckies. She welcomed Maya into her home for a cool aunt sleepover while Max and I went out for our anniversary.

"Is Sarah here?"

She's been dating the same woman for years. We gave up asking her if they were ever going to make it official.

"No, she's not feeling well. She said I should come without her."

"Oh, I hope she feels better. Tell her I said hi. It was good seeing you," I say. "I should drop these off in the kitchen." The other woman stands waiting in the doorway.

"Okay. Good to see you. Come over for dinner soon."

As I walk away, a hand grabs my right shoulder and pulls me back. I lose my balance and stumble. I whip my head around to tell Maeve to let me go.

It's not her.

Dirty Harry is humping my leg like a dog.

What? Is that what I think it is sliding up and down my right calf? Ew! Are those spiky pubes poking through his speedo and scratching me? Oh, the horror of it. I jerk away so fast that I knee him in his nuts. *Oh crap!* I didn't mean it. But it's too late, as his flailing arms smack the box of chocolates. I struggle to hold on to the box, but it slips from my hands. The lid separates from the box and the chocolate splatters all over the floor, squirting the grenadine and gin filling everywhere. It looks like a crime scene. The stripper backs away with his hands up and slips on the red goo. He grasps at the air for his balance and knocks two women flat on their asses. Yelps ring through the room. A mess of contorted arms and legs remind me of a game of Twister gone terribly wrong. I freeze with my mouth wide open.

The woman with the tiara and a banner that reads "Bride" grabs my elbow.

"Get out of here," she shouts like a lunatic.

She pulls me across the apartment and pushes me out the door, slamming it in my face. I stare at the door for at least three minutes in stunned silence. My heart races. *What the hell just happened?*

The music stops.

I knock.

The bride swings open the door. The stripper is sitting on the couch with an ice pack on his head.

"What?"

"You owe me three hundred dollars," I say.

"I don't think so. You ruined the chocolates."

I furrow my brow. I can feel my heart beating in my ears. "Not my fault."

"We're not paying for something that we didn't enjoy."

She slams the door in my face again.

"BRIDEZILLA!" I scream.

The door opens again.

"Fallon, I'm so sorry," Maeve says. "I'll talk to her when she calms down."

My face is on fire. I need water.

"Thank you," I say, and storm away.

I hadn't thought through what I would do in a situation like this. *Why would I? Who could even anticipate this scenario?* This is not how it was supposed to play out. They were going to love my chocolates and recommend me. Orders were going to roll in.

I get into my car and a paper flapping on my windshield catches my eye. I open my window and grab it. You have to be kidding me—a ticket for parking in a no-parking zone. *Ugh!* I avert my eyes to the curb. Sure enough, a "No Parking" sign stares back at me. I swear someone just erected that. This night is just full of expensive surprises. Then I see another paper stuck under the windshield wiper on the passenger side. I get out of my car to retrieve it. In big block letters, it reads:

NICE PARK JOB JERK

I blow out a breath. With shaking hands, I pull out my cell phone. This is when I would normally text Beatrice, asking for her advice. She would text me back some tidbit about strippers, like how often they get waxed, to which I would reply that this stripper must have missed his last several appointments. I call Avery instead.

She answers on the first ring.

"What's wrong? You never call me on a Friday night."

"I got stroked by a stripper, and he destroyed my chocolate."

Avery snorts loudly. "Um . . . Congrats?"

I laugh, realizing how salacious it sounds. "Then I got a parking ticket for parking like an a-hole."

"OMG! You just made my night," she says to me.

"I'm glad I can be your amusement."

She snorts again. "I'm sorry. I'm having the worst first date. Tell me more, so I don't have to go back to the catfish."

"You're being catfished? Ugh. Rough night for both of us."

I recount my story to her. By the end, we are in stitches. Neither of us can catch our breaths we are laughing so hard.

"Thank you," I manage to choke out. "I needed this."

"Anytime."

"What happened to your date?"

"If he can catfish then I can phantom . . . besides, you needed me."

Warmth spreads throughout my chest.

Avery says I should take Bridezilla to small claims court. Too much of a headache.

"I don't know if I'm cut out for this chocolate business."

"You're going to let one party sabotage your dreams?"

It's not just that. I missed a bunch of Maya's soccer games. My friends in Springshire are excluding me, and I spent all week on these chocolates, only for them to be ruined in a matter of seconds. No one got to enjoy all my hard work. It was all for nothing.

I don't tell Avery any of this for fear I won't be able to drive home through all my blubbering. Instead, I whisper, "I thought this would be my big break into getting more orders."

"I'm sorry, hon. Maybe it will help to remember why you're doing it. Tell me again."

I take a deep breath. "Chocolate brings me joy, and I want to bring joy to others just like my Grandma Rose used to."

"Then don't give up. I love your chocolates, and I believe in you."

A tear slides down my cheek, and I choke out a thank-you. She asks me how my tea party went.

"I was thinking about throwing a Mexican Fiesta instead."

"Now you're talking. Suburbia could use a little spicing up, and just in time for my trip! I'll help you host."

CHAPTER ELEVEN

Instead of making fancy invitations like I created for the tea party, I design an Evite with chili peppers strung across it. I spend an hour getting the words right:

"Taco 'bout a Moms' Night Out Fiesta!"

"Nacho Average Celebration!"

"Catered by Sergio's, the *newest* and *best* Mexican restaurant in town!"

"Mariachi band!"

"Door prizes!"

"Piñata filled with mini tequila bottles!"

"Margaritas!"

Pressing "Send," I fist pump the air. I love it so much. Never mind I paid extra to have the party catered by Sergio's on such short notice, as the woman on the phone told me they were already booked up. Beatrice is dying to try the restaurant, so I know this will seal the deal in all the women coming to my party.

After the blowup with Beatrice in the parking lot and the fact that she was talking about me to Jeff, I wasn't sure if I should plan anything. She did wave to me at soccer, so that showed promise. Maybe she'll see this party as me extending an olive branch.

I hid the guest list on the Evite because I invited Elenore. I don't want the fact that I asked the person who slept with the principal to be the reason for anyone declining. Besides, they should let that go. Elenore didn't hurt any of them or their children.

Max didn't flinch when I told him I wanted to host a Mexican Fiesta. He knows I've been feeling down lately. He says some liveliness will do me good. I'm getting ahead of myself now. I don't even know if anyone will come. I bite my lip and check the invitation one more time after sending to make sure I spelled everything correctly. I notice Beatrice has already viewed it. I refresh several times, eager to see how she responds, but she doesn't.

* * *

Within a few hours, the "yes" responses start rolling in. Relieved that I can officially start planning, I pull the chili spice from the cupboard. No Mexican Fiesta would be complete without some spicy truffles.

In the middle of mixing all the ingredients together, my phone rings. I wipe my hands on a towel and place the phone on speaker. As soon as I hear Avery's voice, I know something's wrong.

"Are you okay?"

"Not really. I was waiting to cross the street, and a car jumped the curb. My leg is broken."

"Oh my God! That's terrible. Where are you now?"

"I'm home. My mama is taking care of me."

"I'm so sorry, but I'm glad to hear you're in good hands."

"Anyway, I have to postpone my trip to see you. I'll make it up to you, I swear."

"Don't even worry about that. Just get better, okay?"

"I will. I have to take my meds now and rest."

"I'll call you soon," I say.

I feel so sad for Avery. I hop on the internet and buy the largest flower arrangement I can find that doesn't look like it's being ordered for a funeral.

Turning back to my chocolate mixture, I lift the spoon to my mouth to savor the taste. A sharp stinging immediately overtakes my taste buds. My tongue is on fire. Tears surge from my eyes. I cough and choke. Gasping for air, I grab the milk from the fridge. I don't bother with a glass and drink straight from the carton. When the pain subsides, I pick up the bowl and scrape the chocolate into the garbage disposal. This better not be a bad omen for my Mexican Fiesta.

CHAPTER TWELVE

I'm so excited about my party that at school drop-off and pickup, I'm in a better mood and briefly talk to the Ma Spa Squad minus Beatrice, who hasn't been walking her kids up to the door. She's the only one who still hasn't responded to my invitation. It feels good not to avoid the rest of them, though. I won't see them at soccer for the next few weeks. The park district needs to figure out where and when the championship game will be played.

Apparently, the ground maintenance crew treated the fields with the wrong chemical. Within days, the grass died, and they still have to haul it away. On top of that, it's been raining almost every day—so the fields are a muddy mess. I'm waiting for the announcement that they're going to put in AstroTurf and our taxes will go up yet again.

I scroll through social media, like I do a hundred times a day. I dare not check my data usage, which usually says I've been on it for six hours. That's preposterous. An app must be running behind the scenes on my phone, driving up my usage.

I remind myself that I'm searching for chocolate inspiration too. It's not all fun and games. My eye stops on a photo of the Ma Spa Squad holding up the same painting—well, various versions of the same scene. I can't quite tell. Some of them look like they painted with their toes.

Then I remember Vivian mentioning paint-and-sip night. I take a deep breath. This excluding me is going to end. My party will be epic. It will be the talk of Springshire, and it will save my friendships.

* * *

"How much, Mommy?"

"A teaspoon."

Maya sniffs the vanilla before pouring it into the bowl.

"Can I lick the spoon?" Maya points to the one I'm about to shove into my mouth.

I hand it over to her as her eyes light up. She makes sure to lick every last bit of chocolate off it. It really is the best part of making chocolate. I tell her to put the spoon in the sink. No double-dipping even though this batch is for us. Better to teach her young.

"Skylar told me at recess that her parents don't let her eat candy," she says.

"Really?"

"Yeah, and sometimes she sneaks it. I would sneak it too because life without candy is no life at all," she says, shaking her head.

That we can agree on. I laugh, wondering if she's channeling Grandma Rose. "You're so funny."

"You have the best job, Mommy. I want one like this when I get older," she says with a ring of chocolate around her mouth.

"I think Daddy's job is cool too," I say, to let her know she can be whatever she wants.

Maya crinkles her nose like I just told her to eat ants. She doesn't entirely understand what Max does for a living. She knows he's a doctor, and that's all she needs to know right now.

"Nothing is as fun as making chocolate."

"Well, you have many years to decide."

I like this me with Maya. It's the relaxed I-don't-have-to-rush-out-the-door-like-a-crazy-person me. I'm sure Maya appreciates it too. That's probably why she wants to be a chocolatier. She sees the good mood I'm in.

"Mommy?"

"What's up, buttercup?"

"Will you volunteer for the music concert?"

I frown. "Maya, I don't have a musical bone in my body."

"Puh-lease?" She tilts her head down and looks at me with puppy-dog eyes. She should be an actress, or maybe a saleswoman.

I pull her toward me into a hug.

"Okay."

She squeezes me hard and buries her chocolate face into my apron. I have no idea how the school can use me for the concert. Failing to play the kazoo as a child is a good indicator I am not musically inclined.

"Mommy?"

"Yes, Maya."

"Cecilia is having a sleepover for her birthday." She stops talking, and a flood of tears pour out of her little eyes. She's sucking in air fast now. "And I wasn't invited."

I'm too shocked to speak. *WTF. Now Beatrice is turning her daughter against Maya?*

"Is it because we fought over that swing at the park?" she asks.

If I were a dragon, smoke would be billowing out of my nose.

"Oh, honey. Maybe the invitation got lost," I say, hoping it wasn't lost in the same place as my invitations from the Ma Spa Squad—in an abyss of ignorance.

"You think?"

"Yes, honey. I do."

My hope is that she'll forget about the invitation. In the meantime, I'll find the date of the party, and that night I'll take Maya somewhere that will be so fun that she won't care that she wasn't invited to Cecilia's stupid party. I knew Maya would one day be subjected to mean girls. I just hadn't expected it to be in second grade.

"Okay. I'll look for the invitation at school," Maya says.

I smile with a clenched jaw. I want to shove my foot so far up Beatrice's ass she'll taste the rubber of my shoe. I pull out the chocolate molds from the cabinet. We need to finish fast so I can march over to Beatrice's and give her a piece of my mind.

As we're filling the heart molds, my phone dings. Beatrice RSVP'd yes to my party. I take a long, calming breath. Change of plans. I'll talk to her there.

CHAPTER THIRTEEN

I snap a photo of my backyard. The small, rented white tent looks amazing with red chili peppers dangling from the awning.

After I started planning, I realized I had overdone the arrangements for five, so I asked Lyla to invite the PTO moms. I couldn't let the food and drinks go to waste. I catered for twenty people and hired a bartender to keep the margaritas flowing.

On one end of the wooden pallet dance floor, four men dressed in charro suits and sombreros set the mood with "La Negra," and I can't help but wiggle my hips.

Scanning the food table, I make sure the restaurant didn't forget anything—guacamole, four different kinds of salsas, corn and flour tortillas, ground beef, chicken, carne asada, grilled veggies, shredded cheese, lettuce, rice, onion, cilantro, and sour cream. That will do it.

On the dessert table, my appropriately spiced chili chocolates, sopapillas, and Mexican wedding cookies look and smell delightful. I saunter over to the five tables arranged next to the dance floor and smooth out the pink, purple, red, yellow, and green striped serape blankets doubling as table-cloths, and adjust the cacti centerpieces. The blankets and cacti plants will be fabulous door prizes. I'm ready for this party to get started. My stomach tingles.

Balloons and a sign direct guests to the backyard. I lucked out on the clear blue-sky weather. One never knows, not even the meteorologists, if May will be cold and rainy, but today is sunny and seventy degrees.

Impressed with myself, I snap some more photos. With the vibrant colors and lighting, they're good enough to send to *Good Housekeeping*. These pictures would make the publisher weep with joy.

"Hi, this looks amazing!" Vivian kisses my cheek. She's wearing a form-fitting, off-the-shoulder, flower-print red dress. She has a keen eye for fashion. I thought my simple yellow sundress with a layer of ruffles at the bottom was stunning. Now, I'm not so sure. I look past her to see if Beatrice has arrived too. Not yet.

"You've gone all out." Vivian takes two maracas from the basket. I like her enthusiasm. She hasn't even had a margarita yet.

The bartender reads my mind and approaches with margaritas. He can't be more than twenty-five. He's thin, with a thick head of black hair. "For you, señora," he says in an accent, and lowers his head in a bow. Vivian smiles.

"Thank you, Rodrigo," I say.

"This looks fab. I didn't know you had it in you to host such a party," Vivian says.

I'm not sure if I should be offended. I sip my margarita. It's already my second one.

"Oh my gosh! Look at those lights!" Lyla enters in a pretty white capri jumpsuit and gorgeous, hot pink stilettos that make her legs look extra long. Her curls fall over her shoulders in ringlets. Three women follow her in. I exhale when I realize Beatrice is not one of them. Lyla introduces them as her fellow PTO moms. I greet them, and Rodrigo motions them over to the bar to his premade margaritas. He hands each of them a glass. The women gush over him, the spread of food, and the band.

We fall into easy conversation—could be with the help of tequila. An hour and two margaritas later, more PTO moms show up, and a few of us are attempting the cha-cha on the dance floor. I'm spilling my latest margarita, and Rodrigo is, thankfully, wiping it up. Not one of his responsibilities, but I don't stop him. He'll get a good tip.

The other women are working through their plates of tacos. I glance at the gate every so often. *Where is Beatrice?* Then I see her. She hesitates at the gate. I wave her in and rush toward her.

"Glad you made it." I force a smile.

Rodrigo hands her a margarita. "For you, señorita."

Beatrice reaches past me and snatches the drink out of his hand. I catch Rodrigo's greeting of "señorita" and glance at her left hand. There's no ring. My mouth drops open. I quickly close it before she sees me.

"Come in. Are you hungry?" I recover from my surprise.

Her denim dress hangs loosely over her frame. She's lost weight.

"No, this is fine," she says, holding up her glass.

The coloring in her face is off. Deep circles pool under her eyes. Now I'm back to thinking maybe she's sick or extremely stressed. I want to hug her, but she's giving off a don't-come-closer vibe.

I hold up my margarita to hers. "Salud."

She doesn't respond. I sip my drink while she heads over to Vivian. *Are Beatrice and Craig Splitsville?* She's always worn her dazzling three-carat ring. Even to the gym for Pilates. If this is the case, all the recent moms' nights out make sense now—a way to deal with the pain without wallowing at home. But that still doesn't explain why she excluded me.

I grab the piñata stick and the blindfold. The band is taking a break, so I use their microphone.

"It's time for the piñata!" My words are met with cheers, and the women rush to form a line. I laugh. The margaritas must be kicking in. That or these women, like me, are starved for excitement.

Lyla is first up. I tie the blindfold around her and spin her three times. I step out of her way as she swings like a mad woman from side to side. After the third swing, she strikes it hard enough to leave a hole the size of a golf ball in its body. Vivian's up next. Her strategy is to swing up and down, and she manages to whack off the donkey's ear.

"Hi, lady. Sorry, I'm late." Elenore hands me a bouquet of purple and pink flowers. "They're sweet peas," she says.

"Thank you. They're lovely. So thoughtful of you."

Elenore scans the tent.

"Looks like a lively party."

Rodrigo hands Elenore a margarita. "For you, señorita." I glance at Elenore's bare left ring finger.

"Jeff filed for divorce," she says.

"I'm sorry," I say and place my hand on her shoulder.

"Thank you. Let's not talk about it now," she says and takes a sip of her margarita. "Today is supposed to be fun."

"Okay, we'll talk later," I say, shifting my gaze to the flowers in my arms. "I'll put these in a vase. Join the others and I'll be right back."

My eyes mist over as I think about Elenore's impending divorce and now possibly Beatrice's. Divorce is not something I wish upon anyone. A terrible thought strikes me. *What if my marriage failed?* I'd be devastated. I take a deep breath, brush a single tear away, and glance back at the party. I must make my relationship with Max a priority so it doesn't happen to us. Beatrice is up next for the piñata. I watch Vivian blindfold her as I walk toward the house.

In the kitchen, filling a vase with warm water, I peer out the window into the backyard. Beatrice is swinging at the piñata and missing. After what is sure to be her tenth attempt, she hits it with a sharp blow and the piñata plummets. Mini plastic tequila bottles scatter. Vivian rubs her head where one hit her. Most of the women are on their hands and knees, grabbing for bottles. Geez, I didn't know these ladies would be so enthusiastic about tequila. This is better than I'd imagined. This party will go down in Springshire history. Maybe I'll make it an annual party.

Beatrice holds several bottles in the crook of her arm and thrusts her index finger close to Elenore's nose. *Wait, what's going on?* She may hit her. Rodrigo stands near them and leans forward like he's about to lunge. He's readying himself to break them up if a fight ensues. I fling open the window. Beatrice's voice carries throughout the yard.

"You aren't welcome here. I can't believe you have the gall to show your face . . . and you're already flirting with the bartender." She snatches a tequila bottle from Elenore's hand.

This confrontation is eerily like the one in the coffee shop. I can't let this happen . . . again. I drop the vase, and it crashes into the sink. As I swing open the back door, a man enters the yard. All eyes turn to stare.

"Hello, lovely ladies. Your entertainment has arrived," he says. A few women gasp.

His hair is feathered, and his yellow-armpit-stained white shirt is unbuttoned to his navel, exposing his hairy chest.

What? That's not . . .?

Dirty Harry.

What is he doing here?

He sets down his 1980s boom box, switches it on, and gyrates toward the women as "I Want Your Sex" blares from the speakers. Most of my guests shrink in horror away from him. The Mariachi band members are frozen in place and stare dumbfounded.

As the stripper shimmies out of his pants like a newborn baby giraffe finding his footing for the first time, a PTO mom I don't really know, and who clearly has had too much to drink, dances up behind him, shaking her booty directly into him. He trips over his pants and slams into Vivian, causing her to drop her margarita glass. *Holy smokes!* Not again. Dirty Harry leaves a trail of destruction wherever he goes.

Vivian bends over, picking up shards of glass from the dance floor. It's all happening so fast. My head swivels to see Lyla running to help Vivian, and she slips, landing in the pile of glass. She lets out a blood-curdling scream. It's as if I'm watching a horror movie unfold in front of me, and each scene is more frightening than the last. Vivian lifts Lyla up, and blood spurts from a gash on Vivian's hand all over Lyla's white jumpsuit. My eyes focus on the blood dripping down the back of Lyla's lower calves. Blood. Everywhere.

Beatrice whips a blanket off one of the tables, and more glasses tumble to the floor. The cacti centerpiece catapults and hits Elenore's thigh. The needles prick her skin, and she releases a high-pitched screech, snapping me out of my shock. *This is terrible.* Beatrice spreads the serape on the lawn. Then she hurries back, taking Lyla's arm and leading her away from the glass to the safety of the blanket.

I reach the dance floor and grab the white rag that is tucked into the back of Rodrigo's pants and hurriedly tie it around Vivian's hand to stop the bleeding. It soaks through with blood in seconds.

"Are you okay?" I say, taking a deep breath. She stares blankly at me. "Here, sit." I pull out a chair and help lower her into it.

The stripper stands off to the side now. He's wearing the same blue speedo from the bridezilla party. He must be the only stripper in this town.

"You ruined my party and my chocolate, and you owe me three hundred dollars!" I scream.

He looks at me as if I'm crazy. Then recognition registers on his face.

Beatrice turns toward me. Lyla leans against her. "Why did you invite her?" She points to Elenore who is being attended to by Rodrigo.

"Now's not the time, Beatrice." I motion toward Lyla's injury. When Beatrice and Lyla exchange a glance, I say, "She's our friend."

"Not anymore," Beatrice says. "She ruined our friendship when she cheated on Jeff."

What! How ludicrous. "One doesn't have anything to do with the other," I say. "Besides, this is my party, and I can invite who I want."

Beatrice huffs.

What I thought I could gloss over and move on from, I bring up. "Why did you call me a bitch in the school parking lot? And I overheard you telling Jeff at the soccer game how I'm not a good friend. What have I ever done to you?"

"Oh, you and your arrogance," she slurs. Ah, tequila is truth serum.

"What are you talking about?"

"Never mind."

"I will not 'never mind.' And not inviting Maya to Cecilia's birthday party? What is that all about?"

Mama Bear inside of me is getting ready to release the biggest roar of her life.

"Cecilia didn't want to invite Maya, so I said she didn't have to."

"They've been friends since they could walk," I practically growl at her.

"So? I can't help who Cecilia chooses to be friends with."

"Unbelievable. Like you had nothing to do with it. I call bullshit." I clench my free hand into a fist at my side as I apply pressure to Vivian's cut with my other hand. It takes all my strength not to unleash the beast on Beatrice.

I think about Maya being left out of the party and how sad she'll be. I try to sweep the thought away to attend to Vivian. Pulling back the rag from her hand, the cut is proving to be deep and still gushing blood.

"Call bullshit all you want. I'm calling an ambulance for Vivian and Lyla," Beatrice says.

My head feels heavy. I glance toward the dance floor. Huge amounts of glass covered in blood is strewn all around. Tingling runs down my left arm. At the same time, heat rises fast to my face like I'm being cooked alive. I swallow hard. My throat constricts. I take ragged breaths. Sweat drips from my armpits, but I'm chilled to the bone. My mind is racing with thoughts of a heart attack and dying. I shake and clutch at my heart. My head spins. The scene before me melds together in blurred colors.

Darkness.

* * *

I awake to Max standing over me. Blinking, I try to figure out if he's a figment of my imagination.

"Fallon, are you okay?"

"Where am I?"

"You're in the hospital. Mrs. Crandall our neighbor called me at work. She got concerned when she saw the ambulance."

"Where's Maya?"

"She's at my parents'. Remember, they were watching her so you could have your party."

Everything is fuzzy. "What . . . hap-happened?" My mouth feels like the Sahara. "Water." I manage to say. Max opens a bottled water and places it to my lips. I take small sips.

"You fainted. They ran some tests. Now we wait."

That tequila must have done a number on me, because I don't remember going through any tests. Max sweeps my hair out of my face and tells me everything is going to be okay. I hope he's right.

I sit up in the hospital bed, and Max adjusts the ice pack on my ankle. I don't remember twisting it. He asks me how it all went down. I say I don't know. It just did—downhill and fast, like an avalanche.

"The stripper gave me this to give you." Max holds up three crisp one hundred dollar bills. "Do I want to know what this is for?"

I assure him I didn't order the stripper. I explain to Max how the stripper ruined my chocolates at the bachelorette party and how I confronted him.

"Are Vivian, Lyla, and Elenore okay?" I close my eyes. I wish I could disappear.

"They'll be fine. Vivian and Lyla need stitches. They will be treated and released. Elenore didn't need medical attention," he says. "It's okay. One day you will look back at this and laugh."

He's not helping.

Snippets of the day flash through my mind. I remember the bartender calling Beatrice "Señorita" and that she wasn't wearing her ring. Signs are pointing to what I hope isn't true.

Someone knocks on the door and enters the room. "Hello, I'm Dr. Pain."

Dr. Pain? Seriously? I hold in my breath to suppress my laughter and steal a glance at his name badge. Sure enough, his name is in fact, Dr. Pain.

"Judging by your expression, I see there is nothing wrong with your cognitive processing," Dr. Pain says, and laughs. "And I assure you, I am not here to cause you . . . you know . . . more pain." He winks.

I release my breath and laugh as Max says, "Well, that's comforting."

"How are you feeling?' Dr. Pain asks.

"I'm fine. My ego is bruised, though."

He laughs again. I can already tell he has a good bedside manner—kind and friendly.

"Well, I have good news for you. Your EKG came back normal. You didn't experience a heart attack."

I sigh. "That's good news."

"You've had a panic attack." He looks at the paperwork on his clipboard. "Based on your symptoms—hot flashes, I see—and what your husband has told me about your life lately, I believe you are under some stress."

Max and now Dr. Pain have both confirmed my hot flashes are due to stress, but I need to know if it's not really perimenopause. Turning forty is doing a number on me. "So, it's not the start of menopause?"

"No. It looks like stress, which wreaks havoc on the body. Now you've suffered from a panic attack."

I swallow hard. "Is a panic attack serious?"

"They can be frightening to the person, but they aren't dangerous. Normally, you won't faint from a panic attack. It's a possibility you fainted at the sight of your friends' blood."

I take a deep breath. Seeing the blood shooting down Lyla's leg, spurting out of Vivian's hand, and all the blood-covered glass had freaked me out. I push the gory image from my mind.

"Will I have another attack?"

"It's hard to say. Many people just have one or two throughout their lifetime, and they go away. If you start having recurrent panic attacks, you could be diagnosed with a panic disorder. For now, it's my recommendation you see a therapist to work through your stress."

How did I get here? Failed chocolates, failed parties, failed friendships. A Great Big Failure. This isn't how I imagined my life.

CHAPTER FOURTEEN

I stand in tree pose, willing my foot not to slip down my leg. Yoga is my only saving grace on Wednesday mornings. Without its calming benefits, I might have spiraled out of control. It's probably what saved Beatrice from getting kicked in the shins. The only drawback is that Lyla is in this class too. I'm certain Lyla got on the phone and called everyone she knew about the glass in her ass. This is the price I pay for living in a small town. Everyone knows everything about everyone.

The instructor is contorted, with his legs behind his head, his feet wrapped around each other above his neck, and holding himself up by his arms. I don't even attempt to try it. They would have to call an ambulance. I need another trip to the hospital like I need another stripper encounter.

My mind drifts to thoughts of all the errands I need to run, even though the yoga teacher encourages us to stay present and focus on our breathing. I can focus for only five seconds at a time before reverting to my list of to-do items.

As class ends, I see Lyla, out of the corner of my eye, returning her exercise ball to the storage room. I purposely picked a spot on the other side of the studio, to avoid her.

My cell dings with a Facebook alert from one of the chocolate pages I follow.

Clicking on the chocolate post, I see it's for a chocolate expo in New York. My mouth salivates over all the pretty chocolate photos. Drizzled, dusted, and decadent. The event is soon. I think about Mel's invitation to visit her in New York. *Could I go?* It could be a combined trip to do some research, see Mel, and get out of Springshire.

Glancing up, I see Lyla walking toward me. The last thing I want to do right now is rehash the events of the Great Mexican Fiesta Fiasco. I'm happy she is recovered enough to return to yoga, but she never responded to my text after the party.

I avert my gaze at the same time my phone rings. *Saved by the bell.* I don't even look to see who is calling me. I would talk to a random person telling me a distant relative named Aunt Bertha died and left me twenty-eight billion dollars, and all I have to do to claim it is give my bank account number. Thankfully, it's Avery. Although, twenty-eight billion dollars is nothing to snub my nose at, and oh gosh, poor Aunt Bertha.

"So, spill the beans. Was your party fabulous or what?" Avery asks. I hold the phone between my ear and my shoulder as I roll up my yoga mat.

"Or what," I say.

"What? The stripper showed, didn't he?"

I gasp. "It was you?"

"Of course it was me. I said I would make it up to you for not being there . . . you know, with my bum leg and all. So, tell me he livened up the party and gave those women a show they will never forget," Avery says.

"Oh, they'll never forget. That's for sure."

I recount the events leading up to my hospital visit.

"Wait, did the stripper cause all that?" Avery stifles a laugh. It's quiet now. I'm fairly certain she's put me on mute, so she can bust a gut.

"No, it was the tequila."

She clicks back on. "I would apologize, but it's just too damn funny."

"I'm glad you find it amusing, because not one of those women is talking to me. Plus, I've now made even more enemies." I think about the PTO moms.

I texted all of them the day after my party, even Beatrice, asking how they were. The only one who responded was Elenore. Max told me to give it some time. I had a feeling they wouldn't answer.

"Look on the bright side. I got you your three hundred dollars back," Avery says.

I explain to her how I've been left out for weeks, and I planned the party to win back my friends. It wasn't her fault it turned out to be a colossal failure and I'd made everything worse.

"Listen, it will blow over. I promise. Everything is going to be okay. Tell them it was my fault for ordering the stripper."

"Don't be silly."

Lyla has gotten closer to me, and I shift my body away.

"Did you see last night's episode?" Avery asks excitedly, switching the subject. She calls me every Wednesday at the same time, right when I'm leaving yoga, to talk about *Dude and Dudettes*, the hottest reality show, about a group of promiscuous twenty-somethings living together and hooking up. It's one of my guilty pleasures. I settle in with a glass of red wine and a bowl of popcorn every Tuesday night to watch.

"Yes. I did. I can't believe what Craig did this time!"

This douchebag has called the women fat and unattractive more than once. He needs his eyes examined because all the women look like models.

"Craig's the worst in the house—next to Jamie, that is," Avery says.

Lyla is staring at me with an odd expression. It could be that her bun is so tight and pulling her skin taut. I wave to her and leave. She shouldn't be surprised. I'm always on the phone after yoga. Talking to Avery about *Dude and Dudettes* is a priority. Besides, Lyla can call or text me any time if she has something to say.

CHAPTER FIFTEEN

"How is Max?" Dr. Josie asks.

"Fine," I say, and sip from my glass of water. "Things are better. Have been for a while now."

Dr. Josie smiles. "That is wonderful news." She draws out her words in a slow and deliberate manner, enunciating every syllable like she's teaching me the English language.

I glance around the office. It's brighter than I remember. Fresh yellow paint. New beach-scene paintings hang on the walls. I unbutton the top button of my shirt and roll up my sleeves. Along with the beach ambiance, it's like one hundred degrees in here. She's gone to the extreme with her tropical theme and is clearly not going into menopause herself. She's wearing a cardigan too. I melt back into the microfiber couch and think about turning into a popsicle—anything to cool me off.

Behind her on the desk is a vase of pink calla lilies. They must be from her husband. I've always admired her wedding band, inlaid with emerald stones. I look to her left hand to get another glimpse of that beauty. I suck in a breath. Her left ring finger is bare. *Where is it?* I swallow hard, forcing down a gasp. *Not her too? What is in the water these days?* I set my water glass on the coffee table. I can't ask her—she's my therapist. We're supposed to talk about me. But . . . *How could she save my marriage, but not her own?*

She raises her eyebrows expectantly and clicks her pen. I realize she's silently questioning why I am here. It's been two years since Max and I stopped seeing her. The last time we were here, we held hands on this very couch.

I clear my throat. "It's stress. I ended up in the hospital after a party, and they ran some tests. All my bloodwork came back fine, so I'm not physically ill or going into menopause, like I thought. I've been experiencing hot flashes, and I had a panic attack."

"I see. Panic attacks can be scary. I will walk you through some breathing exercises and other coping mechanisms that will help you." Dr. Josie pauses. "But first, tell me what you think might be causing this stress?" Dr. Josie crosses her legs and folds her hands together in her lap. She always comes across as composed. Whereas I'm tapping my foot and fidgeting with my cuticles. I didn't want to make this appointment, but I need ways to sidestep another awful panic attack.

"Friends," I say, and raise my glass of ice water to my lips, then change my mind and set it back down. I'm being silly—there's nothing in the water causing divorces—but part of me is superstitious. There must be another reason she's not wearing her wedding ring. In my head, I explain it away that it's at the jeweler being resized. Now I feel better.

"Friends?" Dr. Josie prompts me to keep talking.

I tell her about the Ma Spa Squad leaving me out, the Great Mexican Fiesta Fiasco, the video of Beatrice talking smack about me at the soccer game, and the pending divorces. Not to mention my thoughts about turning forty. It takes me about ten minutes to walk her through it all. She remains quiet and makes chicken scratches on a pad of paper.

"It sounds like you have been through quite a bit recently," she begins. "I think most people would feel stressed with all of that going on. I'm sorry you have been feeling that way. Friendships can be hard and complicated. Why do you think all of this is happening?"

I clench my fists to keep myself from crying. I can be strong. I answer her with a shrug. Dr. Josie must know how bad this situation is for me to be sitting across from her.

"What do you tell yourself when you discover you've been left out?" Dr. Josie asks.

I consider her question. "I make snarky comments in my head about my friends that I don't really mean."

"I see. How does that make you feel?"

"Well, it's not like I'm saying them out loud, so I'm not hurting anyone's feelings," I say, and rub the back of my neck. "But I don't like thinking this way."

"You're hurt, Fallon. It's a natural response. Your comments are a defense mechanism." She pauses. "If your thoughts are adding to your stress, it might be helpful to realize they are not a reflection of who you are."

I let her words sink in. On top of being left out, I'm beating myself up for how I'm reacting to being left out. Now I'm starting to understand my stress.

"Are you thinking about letting go of your neighborhood friends?"

I thrust my head back like I'd just been smacked. *No.* For me, that's not an option. I need these friends. "I want to save my friendships," I say with measured words.

I think about all the fun times we've had, and it's so hard to think that letting them go would mean we'll never be close again. No more pool and park playdates, scavenger and egg hunts, dance parties, lunches, brunches, arts and crafts, cookie and cupcake decorating—if it was on Pinterest, we did it. We may not have done it exactly like the pictures, but we had managed.

We'll never drink together on the first day of school or rotate houses for mom's movie night—gorging ourselves on candy and popcorn and watching *Magic Mike* for the hundredth time.

We'll never compete again for the worst rendition of the floss dance, or vote for who had the worst mom fail, which I won once when Maya was three and ran out the front door and down the block while I washed the dishes. A neighbor walked her back. I jumped at every knock on our front door, worrying it was Child Protective Services and the police, ready to haul me away in handcuffs for being an unfit mother.

"Tell me why these neighborhood friendships are important to you."

I don't tell her the friendships are based on our love for booze and Channing Tatum's abs, which is partly true. Springshire has a reputation to uphold, and I'm not about to share our dirty little secrets. Truth be told, failing together at motherhood made failing tolerable.

"They're my first mommy friends. We've been through a lot together," I blurt out, then pause to compose myself. "I've invested so much time into them. It's been seven years."

"Ah. I see. You've heard that if a friendship lasts more than seven years, it will last a lifetime?"

"Yes," I say. "This is the year that will either make or break our friendship."

"I understand where you're coming from and the importance of this year to you, but I don't know that it's that set in stone. Do you think you have a time limit on making new friends?"

I stare up at the ceiling. "Well, I'm not getting any younger." After all, I'm turning forty soon. Then I look her in the eye. "Do you think I can save these friendships?"

Dr. Josie pinches her chin in thought. "That's for you to decide, Fallon. What would you have to do to save them?"

"I'm not sure. I already threw a disastrous party," I say in frustration.

"What if you let go of these friendships? What is the worst that will happen to you?"

"I'll be . . ."—the words catch in my throat, and I force them free—"left out and lonely."

Dr. Josie pauses for a beat. "Fallon, have you been hurt before in friendships?"

I think back to high school. "When I was younger."

All of this may be my fault for wanting to move to a small town. I thought it would be good for me. A chance to get to know my neighbors and forge friendships that would last a lifetime. The kind my grandma had. Living in Chicago, in a big city, I'd always felt lost. Friends I went to high school with lived twenty to thirty minutes from me. None of us had cars. Buses took too long. When I'd finally made friends who lived close to me, the Great Hot Dog Hot Mess with Whitney had ruined those friendships. I went away to college and never returned. Then friends from college were from all over the country. I couldn't win. I had high hopes for a small town for me and Maya. The last seven years had been amazing for friendships. Now I was once again the outcast.

"You have grown, have you not? Have you had a hard time recently making friends?"

I shake my head. I had met the moms' group easily.

"Fallon, I know very little about your family life growing up. I'm trying to connect some dots here."

I shift in my seat and cross my arms over my chest. I wait for her to ask a question.

"You're an only child. What was it like growing up without siblings?"

"Fine. I played on my own a lot."

"Did you feel lonely?"

"At times, yes. I wonder what it would have been like to have a sister."

"Did your parents ever explain to you why they didn't have more children?"

I bite the side of my lip. I knew at some point I'd have to address this. I'm surprised it hasn't come up with Dr. Josie before now. It's a rather important aspect of my life.

"They couldn't," I say, and take a deep breath. "I was adopted."

It's been a long time since I told anyone this. I didn't even tell the Ma Spa Squad. When I moved to Springshire, I wanted my new life to be perfect, and tried hard to pretend everything was, and that meant not talking about my adoption. I only allowed Beatrice to see my daily mommy chaos because she was going through it too. Only a handful of people from my past know about my adoption.

Dr. Josie leans forward. Her eyes widen. She looks as if I told her she's won the lottery. I wish that were my big news because I don't like talking about being adopted.

"When did you find out you were adopted?"

"I accidentally found out when I was eighteen."

"How did that make you feel?"

Like an elephant hit by a tranquilizer gun. Everything blurred. I confronted my parents, and they said they were going to tell me when they thought I could emotionally handle it. I didn't stop spontaneously crying about the news for probably four years—all through college. I wish they had told me years before. It would have explained a lot of my questions, like how come I didn't look like them or seem to have any of their mannerisms or personality traits.

"Like my whole life was a lie."

"Do you have a good relationship with your parents?"

"It's good now. For a period of time, it was volatile." Like mixing Mentos with soda. They never knew which words would set me off.

"Over the years, I worked through my hurt feelings. My parents gave me a good life and were only trying to protect me. That's why they didn't tell me right away."

"Did they tell you they were trying to protect you, or did you surmise this?"

"They told me they didn't want me to feel different. But the funny thing is, growing up I *did* feel different. I just couldn't explain why. They were trying to protect me from heartache."

"Do you know who your birth parents are?"

"No." I stare at the clock, willing the hands to fast-forward. I rub my eyes. I don't want to talk about this anymore. I'd rather talk about being old and having no friends.

Dr. Josie must sense my discomfort, because she doesn't press me to talk about my biological parents.

"Fallon, you mentioned feeling hurt and misunderstood by the friends who were leaving you out. Do you think this deep-seated hurt about finding out you were adopted could be the reason you're attached to saving your adult friendships? Is there a possibility you fear abandonment?"

Sherlock Holmes just cracked the case wide open.

CHAPTER SIXTEEN

Standing in my closet, I handle the letter in my hand like it's a bomb about to detonate. My mouth is cotton. I'm still debating if I should make contact. Whatever I find out could blow everything I've ever believed into smithereens, which might not be an issue anyway, because I've already imagined the worst. My mind transports me back to the day I found it, and my shell-shocked response.

"Can you explain this?" I hold out the letter with "A Caring Place Adoption Agency" printed across the top. I found it tucked away in one of my mom's classic books in her vintage trunk. My search for a good classic read turned into a horror story.

My mom and dad sit across from me with blank expressions. All personality is removed from their faces like a vacuum suctioned them off.

My dad wipes his forehead with his handkerchief while my mom pats his leg. Goosebumps rise on my arms in response to their deafening silence. This situation is eerily similar to the time they told me Grandma Rose passed away.

My mind spirals. The silence is heavy between us.

"What is this?" I ask as my pulse quickens. I read off the information listed in the letter. "Baby Girl was born July 2, 1982, at Holy Cross Hospital, Chicago, Illinois, weighing six pounds two ounces and twenty inches long. Birth mother is Irish, French, and German." I stop to catch my breath.

"You know how much we love you, right?" My mom's eyes meet mine.

A shiver runs down my spine.

Mom leans forward. "There's no easy way to say this." She sucks in a deep breath. "Fallon, we adopted you as a baby."

There's a moment of stunned silence followed by my breath, leaving my lungs like a blown tire. I figured as much, but hearing the words come out of her mouth still blindsided me. She may as well have said they dropped me as a baby. That would explain the pounding and ringing in my head right now.

The words "we adopted you" repeat over and over in my mind like an alarm blaring.

When I don't respond because I'm paralyzed, she continues. "We've always loved you like we created you. You have to understand this."

"No." I shake my head. "This is not true." It's not true. The same way Elvis is not really dead.

"It is true, Fallon," Dad finally says, and reaches for me. I pull away. This is not happening.

"Don't touch me right now," I raise my voice. Steam is practically blowing out of my ears.

Dad sinks back into the couch.

"Why didn't you tell me before? Why did I have to find this before you told me?" I wave the paper in the air and drop it in mom's lap. I'm hurt beyond measure.

I try to remember their exact words, but they've sunk into the deepest recesses of my mind, lost and comingling somewhere with chemistry formulas.

"This is the adoption agency." Mom pushes the paper toward me. "Now that you're eighteen, you have the option to contact the adoption agency for more information."

I recoil from the paper like it's laced with poison. I blink back tears. After a moment, I take the paper from her. One teardrop escapes from the corner of my eye, landing on it and causing the black ink to smear.

Now, as I look at the paper, the memory of that day slips away. I chose not to contact the adoption agency, but I carried the paper with me to college in case I got up the nerve. I told only Avery and Max about it. They both said I would know when I was ready, and it was okay if I never felt ready. Then I thought I'd lost the letter, but here it is.

After my session with Dr. Josie and the discovery of my abandonment issues, I think it may be time. My hand trembles at the thought. I need to talk to someone. I call Avery.

"Avery." Her name catches in my throat.

"Fallon, what's wrong?"

"I found the letter," I choke out.

"What letter?"

I realize Avery can't read my mind. "The one with the adoption agency information. I don't know what to do. It's been so long."

"What are you afraid of?"

"The truth about why they gave me up."

"Have you ever thought that knowing might give you a sense of peace?"

"You sound like my therapist."

"I'm here for you whatever you decide to do. You know that, right?"

"Yes."

We are silent for a while. I feel as if I'm clinging to a wood plank in the middle of an ocean, surrounded by circling sharks, waiting to be rescued.

"Fallon, are you still there?"

"I'm here."

"I'll stay on the phone as long as you need me to."

"Thank you. That means a lot."

I know what I need to do first.

CHAPTER SEVENTEEN

I pour the three-ounce bottle of rum into my soda. The slightly plump woman in her sixties, with tight curls, sitting next to me sighs loudly. *Listen, lady, I could be a screaming child kicking the back of your seat, but I'm not, so count your blessings.* I need something to take the edge off. Flying unnerves me. I rub my temples because my head is throbbing. I pop two ibuprofens and down them with my mixed drink. The lady next to me sighs again. *Really? You're going to keep sighing at me?* She bends down to wipe a nonexistent scuff mark off her immaculate Gucci flats.

I take another swig, close my eyes, insert my earbuds, and lean my head against the seat. After hanging up with Avery, I'd called my mom to ask her if it was okay to contact the adoption agency. It felt good to get her blessing. But the call to the adoption agency wasn't as seamless. The counselor requested I fill out their online forms and submit them so they could retrieve my files. Her words still ring in my ears, "These things don't always turn out like we hope." My mind hasn't turned off since. That's why I need this break.

I wasn't sure if this weekend away would materialize, especially after Maya clung to my leg, refusing to go into school today. Apparently, Jonas professed his love for her in front of all her classmates on the playground yesterday. The entire class proceeded to sing the K-I-S-S-I-N-G song, "First comes love, then comes marriage . . ." I didn't even know kids still sang it. Mortified, Maya spent at least an hour in the school bathroom, hiding in the stall, until the assistant principal dragged her out and called me. I don't blame Maya—I remember being embarrassed about boys at her age. But hiding in the bathroom is the stuff teenagers do. I'm afraid for me and Maya in six years.

Of course, it had to be the craziest morning ever. It couldn't be smooth sailing—that would be too easy. I blame it on Jonas. If he hadn't proposed to Maya, I'm convinced things would have been a little less chaotic. From the time Maya got up, she was even slower than usual. Throwing a tantrum because her favorite shirt had paint on it. She cried because she couldn't find the matching sock to the pair she *had* to wear today. In a rage, she threw her shoes down the stairs, knocking over a plant. That was fun to clean up. Plus, the whole grabbing onto my leg and sobbing for five minutes before the teacher peeled her off me at drop-off was quite the spectacle. I could feel the glare of the Ma Spa Squad through the back of my head, especially Beatrice, who has been shooting me daggers all week. *Whatever.* It's Max's problem now.

I chuckle at the thought of Max dealing with Maya as I sip my third cocktail. All the stress of getting out the door this morning fades away. I relax my shoulders and open my newest self-help book—*Stretch Marks: A Self-Development Tool for Mothers Who are Being Stretched in Every Direction.*

*   *   *

The flight ends up being uneventful, exactly how I like it. The cab ride from the airport is a whole other story. It must be a requirement in New York to drive like a maniac. That's why I doubled up on the drinks. I hop out of the cab in front of Mel's office just as she exits the building.

"Well, don't you look relaxed." She hugs me, and I breathe in the coconut scent of her hair.

"I knocked back a few at the airport and on the plane." And I may or may not have taken a muscle relaxer. I really can't remember. She steps back to look at me.

"It shows. The wrinkle in your brow has disappeared." She looks chic in her black pencil skirt and fuchsia blouse. Her thick black hair cascades over her shoulders in beautiful waves.

I did my homework and dressed in all black, which I read is the go-to color for native New Yorkers. I feel oddly like I'm going to a funeral, and maybe I am—the death of the Ma Spa Squad friendships.

I swing my arm around her. "I do appreciate that you invited me."

"Of course—we'll have fun. What's the book?" Mel points to my self-help book peeking out of my purse.

"I need tips for overwhelmed moms."

"I didn't know you were into self-help books."

"I'm one book away from having it all figured out. I have about a hundred of them." Sun reflects off the windows of the building, shining in my eyes. I fish my sunglasses out of my tote and put them on.

Mel whistles. "Kind of like your shoe collection."

"Ha. Yes, both make me feel better about myself." I glance down at my black traveling boots and hope I don't look like a tourist.

"Let's head to my apartment, get you unpacked, and freshen up." She waves her arm for me to follow. "It's not far. We can walk."

"Sounds like a plan." I look up at the skyline and marvel at the architecture.

"So, what's the big gossip in Shitshire these days?" She squeezes my arm.

"That didn't take long."

"Well, I've been dying to know since your last cryptic text about hashtag friend fail."

"I'll need a few more drinks to talk about it," I say.

"That bad?"

I nod.

"Okay, I know just the place. My co-workers and I like to frequent it. It's a rooftop bar. You can drop their names over the edge. You'll feel much better." Mel clenches her fist and releases it mimicking a dropping motion with her hand, then raises it and waves. "Hashtag ByeByeBeatrice."

* * *

Stirring my drink with the two cocktail straws, I glance around the outdoor bar. It's swanky, with modular, blue fabric sectionals and a spectacular view of the city. I can see why it's one of Mel's favorites. It's packed but we got lucky and grabbed the last two spots at the bar.

"So, yeah, on social media all these photos keep popping up of the women getting together and toasting with champagne like it's going out of style," I say.

"They've reached a new low." Mel swivels in her stool.

I rehash the whole embarrassing Great Beatrice Blowup with her screaming like a banshee in the school parking lot.

"I can't believe it. I would have punched her." She pumps the air with her fist, and a ringlet of hair falls over her eye.

"I know you would have."

"Do you think they've been excluding you because of me?"

There's no reason to bring her into my misery. She's been lucky enough to escape it.

"No, no."

I tell her about my party and how Elenore is going through a divorce, and I suspect Beatrice is having issues with Craig.

Her eyes are bugging out of her head. "Chica, sounds like Shitshire is up shit's creek."

She laughs hysterically and struggles to catch her breath. She's enjoying this way too much. I don't blame her. She finally recovers and says that the party is the funniest turn of events she's ever heard. Now that I am distanced from it and the Ma Spa Squad, I manage a chuckle. Well, what do you know, Max was right about me laughing about it one day. I didn't expect it to be so soon.

"It's good to be away for a while," I say.

"How's your new side gig going, boss lady?"

"Good. Outside of the neighborhood, not so much inside."

"Sounds like you got a great support system," Mel says, and rolls her eyes. "Well, you know my motto, right?"

I scrunch my nose. "I can't remember."

"If nobody hates you, you're doing something wrong."

She makes a good point. I should be flattered my friends now hate me, because it may mean I'm on the verge of success, but I feel deflated. I wanted my friends to be as excited as I am about my new venture, but I've never received any orders from them, and they all get my products free when I attend the kids' birthday party circuit.

"That reminds me. I meant to give these to you at your apartment. I brought you some." I reach into my bag and hand Mel the box tied with yellow ribbon. "Lemon zest. My new flavor."

Mel takes the box from me, unties the ribbon, and opens it, exposing eight dark truffles striped with white chocolate and topped with candied lemon zest. "These look to die for!"

Mel pops one into her mouth. "Seriously, you need to open your own chocolate shop."

"That's the plan eventually, but I need to drum up more business to see if I can make it work."

"Aw, come on! You'll make it work."

I shrug. *Will I?*

"It's about time you use your business degree for something worthwhile."

I have a bachelor's degree only because my parents sent me kicking and screaming. It was either a college degree or the nunnery. In hindsight, it turned out my parents did a good thing, because I met Max when he rolled over my foot with his skateboard on his way to biology. He broke my toe and left wheel marks on my new pink Converse. Not a great start, but he got my attention. My heart fluttered in his presence, and it didn't take me long to be head over feet for him.

It was even fitting that I lost my virginity to him at the school library on a copy machine somewhere between the sexual education and pregnancy books.

People are mostly shocked when I tell them I married a male gynecologist. Like I should be upset that he gets to see naked women all day. Last time I checked, there are many options to see women naked. I say at least he's getting paid and not shelling out money for cheap thrills.

"You do know what I do for a living, right? I can help you get angel investors—that way you don't have to bear the brunt of the start-up costs."

"Really? That's a generous offer. To tell you the truth, I haven't thought that far ahead."

"Aw, honey, you have a business plan?"

I point to my head. "It's all up here right now."

"Write it down. That's your first step. Once you have it on paper, contact me. I'm serious."

I sip my martini. I need Mel to move back to Springshire or I need to move to New York. She is the realest friend I've ever had, next to Avery.

"You will be very successful with these." Mel crams another chocolate into her mouth. "And seriously, you need new friends. I mean, these are amazing. Who wouldn't order these at least once a week?" She waves her hand to get the bartender's attention. "Let's do a tequila shot."

"No, I can't do tequila after the Great Mexican Fiesta Fiasco. It'll leave a bad taste in my mouth, literally."

"Okay, whiskey it is. Whiskey is strong like you, my friend."

I roll my shoulders back. "Strong" is not how I would describe myself.

Mel orders and tells the bartender to keep them flowing. Before I know it, there are three shots lined up in front of me.

I pick up a shot and take it in one gulp. The whiskey burns a path from my throat to my stomach. I scrunch my face.

We settle into easy conversation. I ask her how she's enjoying New York and if she misses her children away at college. She married young and had her children young too. While we're drinking and chatting, some random guy taps Mel on the shoulder.

"Are you Alejandra?" he asks, and looks down at his phone. "You kind of look like the woman in this photo."

Mel catches my eye and winks.

"What took you so long? I friended this nice woman at the bar while I waited for you." Mel bats her eyelashes as I snicker.

"Oh, I thought we agreed on eight thirty."

"No, I'm sure it was eight fifteen."

The guy pulls at his collar and shifts his weight from one leg to the other.

I extend a hand to him. "I'm Kara."

"Smith," he says, taking it.

"That's your first name?"

"Yes, I promise you my last name is not Smith too." He pulls his hand back.

"Smith Smith, clever," Mel says.

I give him a once-over. He's tall, fit, and around our age, with gray speckles in his hair. I glance at his shoes.

"So, Smith, where in the Midwest are you from?"

He looks at me with wide eyes. "Wisconsin. How d'ya know? It's the accent, isn't it?"

"Lucky guess," I say. "What brought you to New York?"

"Work."

"You're an accountant."

"Oh, I get it. Alejandra, you must've told your new friend all about me."

"Guilty." Mel laughs and throws me a look that says, "How the hell did you do that?"

I shrug like it's no big deal. *How is Mel going to get us out of this one?* Then a woman who looks like Mel taps Smith on the shoulder.

"Hi, are you Smith?" He turns to her startled.

"Yeah," he says hesitantly.

"I'm Alejandra."

Smith shoots us a confused look. Then the realization of our practical joke registers in his eyes.

Mel laughs and turns her back to them. I take another shot, trying to hold it together until they walk away. When they are out of earshot, we both burst out laughing.

"Oh, how I miss you, Mel."

We clink our drinks.

"Chica, how'd you size him up so quickly?"

"He's wearing Allen Edmonds. You can tell a lot about people from their shoes."

"Oh yeah, I forgot about that shoe sixth sense you have. What do my shoes say about me?"

Mel kicks up her feet.

"Your wedge heel reveals you are sensible, and the peep toe says there's more to you than meets the eye. You are a high-class, self-made woman who knows what she wants and is not afraid to go after it."

Mel flips back her hair like only Monica Geller would do on an episode of *Friends* if someone complimented her on her organizing skills.

"Wow, you got all that from my shoes? I'm not sure that's fair. You know me." Mel scans the bar. "Okay, read her." She points to a woman in knee-high snakeskin stiletto boots with a white side zipper.

"She's a confident young woman who isn't afraid to march to her own drumbeat." I pause, studying the woman more closely. "She is so cutthroat she could have skinned the snake for her boots."

Mel lifts up a shot. "You never fail to amaze me. She's an attorney at my company and you pegged her perfectly."

"Ah."

"I heard she's on a dating app too and is quite specific about what she wants. I've never tried the dating apps, but now that I had a little taste of it with the Smith boy, it's just the spice I may need in my life."

"I'm glad I never had to use one. They should have one to meet new friends, though."

"Totally. You can write a description of a perfect friend and meet them for a drink."

That's not a bad idea. In fact, it's genius. I reach into my purse for my phone to google friendship apps, but then realize the drinks are catching up to my bladder.

"Be right back. I have to use the bathroom," I say.

I rise from the barstool and sway a little.

"Are you okay?" Mel asks, grabbing my arm to steady me.

"Oh, I'm fine. Just a little head rush." Truth is, I think I've had just a bit too much to drink.

As I weave my way to the bathroom, I see Smith sitting at a corner table with Alejandra. That gives me an idea. I rudely interrupt their conversation. "What dating app are you using?"

He must be mad because he averts his eyes to Alejandra. She answers me, "It's called Fireworks."

"Is there a way to meet friends on it?" I slur.

Alejandra sighs, like I'm stupid. "Yes, there's a version called Fireworks Friends."

"Thank you . . . hope your night ends with a grand finale," I say, and stumble to the bathroom.

* * *

Back at the bar with Mel, I take out my phone. "You inspired me to find new friends. I'm joining a friendship app." I fling my arm around Mel.

"Whoa, easy there, chica. You better sit before you fall over."

I pull out the stool and lower down onto it, careful not to tip over, then fumble my way through downloading the Fireworks Friends app. My eyes aren't focusing.

Mel grabs the phone from me. "Here, let me help you," she says.

"Be my guest," I say, and tell her to create a profile.

I squint as I look through the floor-to-ceiling windows and into the inside bar. Everything is a bit fuzzy. My eyes land on a group of guys playing pool. The woman in the snakeskin boots sits on the edge of the pool table, with her legs and arms crossed, clearly hindering the game. One of the guys lifts her off and sets her down. As she waves her arms around, I lean forward to get a closer look at what's going on, and someone whacks into me. *Oh no.* I fling out my right hand to grab onto something, anything, but my arm flails, and I can't catch myself. I slide off the chair. *Wham.* Now I'm on the floor with something heavy on top of me, and my breath has left my lungs. It happened so fast.

Someone is lifting me up.

"Thank you, Smith," Mel says. "I've got her." Mel takes my arm, leading me out of the bar. "Are you okay?" Mel says to me.

"I thinks so," I say, and rub my head. I turn to Mel and see double. "Thanks, Mels. You're such good friends to me."

CHAPTER EIGHTEEN

We trip out of the taxi and into her building at three AM. I've heard that the city never sleeps, but damn if I'm going to stay up with it. I've been reminding myself all night I'm almost forty. NYC doesn't care how old I am—it's thrown drinks and food at me all night. The doorman holds open the door for us and smiles.

"Hi, Ralph," Mel belts out in a singsong tone to the older gentleman. She must still think we're singing at that show tunes bar we ended up at. "You're still working?"

He checks his watch. "My shift is ending now."

I try not to puke and shift my eyes to the doorman's shoes. I'm taken aback by their beauty. I purposely drop my lipstick to get a closer look. I brush my fingertips against the raised bumps lining their exterior. Mel pulls me up.

"Come on, Fallon." Then she whispers in my ear, "You can't fondle my doorman's feet."

As we fall into the elevator, I point out, "But he's wearing eight-hundred-dollar dress shoes!"

I don't know why this surprises me. It's New York. Even doormen are affluent. My head spins. I hope I can make it to her apartment before passing out.

* * *

It takes me a minute to acclimate. As I sit up, my head pounds. I swallow hard. My mouth is sandpaper, and my hair is stuck in a sweaty mess to my forehead. On the nightstand is a glass of water and two little round brown pills that I assume are ibuprofen. The clock reads five AM in big red numbers. I have to remember to thank Mel for being a great hostess. I take the pills and let my head fall back into the down pillow.

My phone dings, and I shove my head under the pillow to ignore it. *Who is texting me this early?*

It's Max, and as I look at my phone, I notice a risqué photo of me with my cleavage on full display. I sent it to him last night, and his response was, "Me likey." I must have been more drunk than I thought.

I read his texts from this morning.

Max: *Where are Maya's pink, sparkly Converse sneakers?*
Max: *She refuses to leave the house without them.*
Max: *Are you there?*

Welcome to my world. I type back that I don't know. And I don't because Maya throws her things everywhere. Last week I found one Converse shoe in the laundry room and the matching one under her bed. I go back to sleep.

* * *

A knock jolts me.

"Wakey-wakey, we have a big day of chocolate and shopping ahead of us."

I mumble, "Be right there."

The clock indicates its ten AM. I don't think I've slept this late since college. My phone lights up, and I see fifteen missed texts from Max. I bite my lip. I hope everything is okay. I read through them. They are asking where things are and where he needs to take her. *Didn't he read the three-page detailed itinerary under a magnet on the fridge?* The second-to-last text he wrote said he managed to figure everything out. I scroll to the last text.

Max: *Are you okay? Call me.*

When I call, it goes straight to voicemail. I leave a short message saying I'm alive, but barely.

I stare at Mel's floor-to-ceiling bookshelves. My eyes stop on Mel's Joyful Jar and the folded notes inside. I'm curious about what they say. I tiptoe over to it and remove it from the shelf. She did leave them here in the guest room, in plain sight. It wasn't like I was rummaging through her underwear drawer. Besides, it was a big joke to her anyway. She's not going to care. I debate some more whether I'm invading her privacy. She won't know I looked. I remember vaguely what I wrote on my note to her. Mostly about livening up Springshire.

I unscrew the cap and pull out a piece of paper. I hear her footsteps in the hall, and I shove the paper back in the jar, screw the cap back on, and carefully place the jar back on the shelf.

Pulling on my robe, I head to the bathroom to brush my teeth and smooth down my hair. Mel is sipping coffee on her small balcony. A to-go cup of coffee sits on the kitchen counter, with my name scrawled on it. I pick it up and head outside to join her. As soon as I open the door, sirens from the street scream at me.

I rub my temples. "Geez, it's loud."

The coolness of the metal chair feels good against my legs as I sit.

"You get used to the sounds. You slept right through them last night, didn't you?"

I notice how close her neighbors' balconies are. I could jump from one to another.

"That's because I passed out drunk." Turns out I packed way too much. I didn't need my ear plugs or my lavender balm to fall asleep in a new place. I just needed whiskey.

"That's how most visitors deal with the noise. So, you fit right in," she says. "Bagels are on the counter. They're soft and still warm. I ran out and got them this morning."

"You're an overachiever."

She shrugs. "I wanted you to try them. If I waited until you got up, the line for them would be around the block and they may have run out . . . they're that popular."

"I appreciate it." I push myself up out of the chair.

"Stay. I'll get them." Mel signals for me to sit.

She goes inside and grabs the bag as I breathe in the aroma of my coffee and admire the small arrangement of yellow flowers in a wooden box secured to her railing.

Mel returns and holds out the bagels to me. I take one and hope I can keep it down. I rip off a piece and pop it in my mouth. It practically melts.

"Good?" she asks.

I nod with my mouth full and hum "mm-hmm."

"It's the best hangover food around."

When there's a lull in conversation, I ask her about her Joyful Jar.

"Ah, yes. I like to keep it as a reminder that bitches can be nice when faced with their own mortality and that of others."

I snort. "I recently reread my note from Beatrice. It was nice to go back to a time when we were on good terms."

"For me, that was the *only* time my friendships with those women were good. That's why I did it. To find the good in people. I know I didn't fit in with that group, but for one moment in time I did, and I wanted to bottle it."

Wow! Her words cut straight to my heart. I had fit into the group once too. "That's deep."

"I can be sentimental, but only for a minute. Don't get used to it."

"Did you write the same thing on my note as the others?"

"No, I wrote, 'Thanks, bitch, for the wonderful note. Have a nice life or death.'"

"Oh my God! You didn't?"

"I sure did."

"I wondered why they never talked to you after that."

Mel shrugs. "It was totally worth it."

CHAPTER NINETEEN

On our way to Fifth Avenue, I marvel at the beautiful brown-stones with their tall windows and million stairs leading up to their gorgeous, intricate doors. People shuffle past us, most with earbuds in, coffee in one hand, and a leash for their dog in the other.

This morning, I applied a heavier layer of makeup, covering up the dark circles from our late-night drink fest, so my selfies will still be fabulous. My stomach cramps as we walk. I don't know how Mel is so chipper. She claims vitamin B is the miracle vitamin. I hope I can taste-test chocolate without puking.

The scent of chocolate filters through the air, and the corners of my mouth reflexively turn up in response.

"This is going to be heavenly," I say as we enter the fancy hotel. A sign catches my eye, "Chocolate Contest. Win $5,000." *There's a contest?* Before I can read the details, Mel pulls me toward the center of the lobby, where a fountain of melted chocolate flows like a river into a large metal basin.

People dip various sides into the creamy fondue. I can't wait to grab a skewer and dip too. The queasiness in my stomach has subsided. The fresh air from our walk put me in a better mood and the vitamin B that Mel insisted I take has kicked in.

We stop at the registration table to sign in and get our tote bags and a map of vendors. I scan the list to see where we should start. The woman hands us a separate paper with specific locations to visit. She explains to us if we get a stamp at each of the twenty places listed, we will be entered into a raffle for a Bahamas cruise for two.

"I'm in," Mel says. "I could use a free vacation. I'll take you if you agree to take me."

"Of course," I say. I know the chances of winning are slim. There are like five hundred people here.

Mel says we should work our way through the exhibition from the back to the front. That way we can avoid the crowds. But first we hit the fondue fountain.

"You've picked a delightful business to be in," Mel says, and pops a truffle into her mouth from a nearby vendor. The woman behind the table hands her a card. "Think of us for your next event." Mel smiles, takes the card, and drops it into her tote.

She turns to me. "Of course, *you're* the only one I'll be calling for chocolates." She swings an arm around my shoulder. I am grateful for her support.

"Sample a chocolate-covered pretzel?" A woman holds out a tray to us.

I take one. The combination of sweet and salty makes my taste buds jump. "Thank you," I say. "Delicious."

"I'm going to gain five pounds this trip."

"Most New Yorkers walk off everything they eat. You don't have that luxury."

I make a note to take extra walks when I get home. We push our way through the throngs of people, toward the fountain. Soon, I'm holding a skewer with pineapple and strawberries with marshmallows squished between them and dipping it in chocolate. The fruity aroma mixed with the notes of vanilla in rich cocoa heightens all my senses, and a tingling sensation runs up my arms. I've died and gone to heaven. This is truly a chocolate lover's dream come true.

Mel moves on to the beautiful display of macarons in every flavor under the moon. I join her, take a small box of assorted cookies, and place them in my bag. I have to pick and choose what I'm going to stuff my face with; otherwise, they'll have to wheel me out of here.

On the way to the last row of vendors, we hit every booth on the end of an aisle. My bag is overflowing already with everything I haven't eaten—chocolate-covered bacon, chocolate-covered raisins, brownies, cupcakes . . . I'm getting my three hundred dollars' worth for sure. We selected the VIP ticket, so we didn't have to pay as we go. That meant most of the desserts were included in our entrance fee. There is no way we can eat all of this during my trip. Mel is going to have a freezer full of delights.

Two hours later, I've hit a wall and am crashing hard. We've found fifteen of the twenty vendors, and I've lost count of how much chocolate I've consumed. If I had to guess, ten pounds because that's how much heavier I feel.

"I need to sit."

Mel looks at her watch. "Okay, in about ten minutes they're announcing the winner of the chocolate contest."

I recall the sign in the lobby. "You knew about it?"

"I read about it on their website. They called for entries for chocolatiers who are just starting out."

"Like me?"

"Yes, like you."

I feel like kicking myself for not knowing about it. It would have been the perfect competition to enter. I could do a lot with five thousand dollars. It could help jump-start my marketing. Maybe I'll enter next year.

We find a seat in the front row, and I slip off my shoes. I wore my comfiest boots, and yet my feet feel like they've been crammed into Maya's shoes all day. I reach down to rub them. A large blister has already formed on the back of my heel. People are filling in the seats all around us. Five judges are seated on stage, eating various chocolates and recording their scores. Not a bad gig.

A man dressed in a tuxedo speaks into the microphone and gives an introduction of the contest, the prizes, and the judges. He makes a joke that there were more than fifty entries, and all the judges are on a super sugar high. So, he wants to give them a moment to compose themselves. There are three winners with monetary prizes.

I scroll through my phone and check social media to see who has liked my latest posts from the convention. The last photo is of me and Mel biting into a chocolate chip cookie bigger than our heads. I read through the comments.

Whoa! That's real?

Did you bake that?

Where can I buy one?

I answer each one and notice the Ma Spa Squad don't account for any of the ninety likes on it. Of course, instead of focusing on who liked it, I'm preoccupied with who didn't. Their silence speaks volumes.

They've already announced the third- and second-prize winners of the chocolates. I glance up to see them standing on stage with their oversize checks. Third prize went to a woman who combined chocolate, sea salt, caramel, and coconut in a flavorful, mouth-watering recipe. It didn't sound incredibly inventive to me, but I'd have to try it, to give my honest opinion. The second-place winner's recipe contained cherries and pistachios. To me, that's an acquired taste. I don't like cherries in my chocolate.

I'm ready for them to announce the first-place winner, so Mel and I can finish getting the five stamps we need to complete our cruise entry.

"Our first-place winner created a unique flavor that caused our judges' taste buds to zing right out of their mouths. The twist of lemon puckered their lips and now they're asking for more."

My ears perk up. I would agree with this assessment. I had used lemon in my new recipe.

"Our winner is Fallon Monroe!"

My mouth drops open. I lean forward. *Did he just call my name?* Mel is shaking me.

"Fallon Monroe? Are you here?" The man at the podium says, and tents his hand over his eyes, looking into the crowd.

"She's right here." Mel pulls me up. I don't have my boots on. I sit back down. "What are you doing?" she whispers to me.

I slip my boots on. "There's some mistake."

"There's no mistake. I entered you into the contest this morning."

I stare at her with wide eyes. "So, I won?"

"Yes, you won!" she screams. The audience around us claps as I move in a fog through the row and ascend the stairs to the stage.

"Congratulations, Fallon!" the announcer says, and hands me a huge check. I read the numbers: five thousand dollars. I can't believe it. I won. My heart swells as I try to wrap my head around this. I grip the check tightly to my chest, as though someone will rip it away from me, claiming there has been a big mistake and I'm not the winner. I push the thought away and smile so wide my cheeks hurt. A professional photographer takes my picture while Mel snaps photos of me with her phone. *Is this really happening?*

* * *

I blow on a spoonful of soup. I tell Mel I'm still not that hungry after all the chocolate we consumed, but she insists. Since it's my last night here, I must try the clam chowder. No trip to New York is complete without it.

"What do you think? Amazing, right?"

"It's delicious. You sure know where all the best food is."

I ask her if it's okay that we are at this fine dining restaurant with white glove service and all I am eating is soup. She makes it up to the server by ordering the surf and turf.

"I still can't believe you entered me into the contest, and I won."

She cuts into her steak and dips a piece into a side of blue cheese.

"I knew when I tasted your new chocolates that I had to."

I stare into my soup, entranced by this amazing thing Mel did for me. I look up and meet her eyes as I fight back tears.

"You were snoring away when I called to ask if it was too late to enter. They said if I got them there by eight AM you would make the deadline. So I grabbed a cab, and the rest is history."

"I don't know what to say. Thank you doesn't seem to be enough."

"Chica, a thank-you is enough. Just leave it at that—and maybe a lifetime supply of chocolate?"

"Done."

"I'm kidding."

"I'm not."

"What will you do with the money?"

Turning my gaze toward the dark cherrywood bar where luxurious, glittery glass mirror balls hang, I think about how this is a big win for me. It's not only about the money but also the acknowledgment from the judges that my chocolates are worthy. Maybe I can do this after all.

"Well, it makes sense in the short term to use it for leasing the commercial kitchen, buying supplies, and marketing."

"Good idea, and now you can add 'award-winning' to your promotional materials. I already posted it on Facebook." Mel raises her glass. "Cheers, my friend. To your success."

"Cheers," I say with a smile as we clink our flutes filled with bubbly.

I sip my champagne and stare past Mel at the abstract painting. The colorful strokes are mesmerizing "This is an elegant restaurant."

"My ex-husband and I used to frequent this place."

I raise my eyebrows. "I didn't know you lived here before."

"Yes, before moving to Shitshire. After the divorce, I wanted to get as far away from here as possible. It was hard for me to be in the city where we had our best memories. I needed a break." She sips her drink.

"What made you move to the Midwest?"

"I wanted to go where none of my New York friends would find me. I was too embarrassed to face them after what Roberto did, so I opened a map and pointed." She drills her index finger into the table. "It was nice to be on my own in a different town and to heal from the trauma I felt from the betrayal. Turns out, though, I was fine without Roberto." She takes a sip of her champagne as if she is swallowing down her sadness.

This is all news to me. I could tell that under her tough exterior is a woman who has haphazardly pieced her life back together after a lot of heartbreak. I've caught glimpses of it in her eyes when she thinks I'm not paying attention.

"What betrayal, if you don't mind me prying?"

She fingers one of her diamond earrings. "He embezzled roughly a million dollars from his employer."

I set down my spoon and stare at her with wide eyes. "Whoa! Seriously?"

"I had no idea. I had to prove my innocence." She raises her flute and takes another sip. After a conversation like this, it wouldn't surprise me if she finishes off the half-full champagne bottle.

"That's messed up." I sip my drink in solidarity.

"Yes, you think you know someone, and then bam!" Water edges to the corner of her eyes. "He's still serving his sentence."

Before the moment passes, I place my hand over hers. If I could wring out her tears like a sponge, I would.

"I'm so sorry you went through that."

"What doesn't kill you makes you stronger," she says.

I can't help but think of my own trauma. I stare at the flickering flame of the votive candle set between us.

"I'm adopted," I blurt out, and meet her eyes.

She lifts an eyebrow.

"You say that as if you just found out."

"No, but after all these years I finally contacted the adoption agency."

It's her turn to comfort me.

"Why did it take you so long?" Mel asks.

"It came out in therapy, and I decided it was time to deal with my past."

"Ah, therapy can bring the buried to the surface," she says, and squeezes my hand. "I hope it works out for you."

"Me too."

CHAPTER TWENTY

With renewed vigor after my trip and winning the chocolate award, I dive right into my business plan. I use the template Mel sent me. The questions are hard. What's the competitive landscape? There is no shortage of popular chocolate shops in the area, but not one of them is a local chocolatier. I have that going for me. I've already written the section explaining my product and vision. I need to offer something different. Something unique that no other chocolate shop is doing.

I think about Maya and our coveted chocolate-making time. I love watching her face light up as she follows the recipe with me. It's truly a Hallmark moment. Maya is my inspiration for adding "Mommy and Me" chocolate-making classes. I don't stop there. I include romantic partner classes, girls' night out, and Chocolate 101. My little chocolate shop will be more than a storefront. It will be an experience.

Next, I need to include the financials—guesstimating what I should price my chocolate at. I'm not even sure I'm turning a profit with my current orders. With all the time

I spend perfecting my recipes, it's probably working out to be no more than two dollars an hour. I tell myself it won't always be like this. I remember reading that most businesses lose money in their first three years.

I review my plan one more time and shoot it off to Mel.

I'm about to close out my email when a message pops in with the subject line "Chocolate order." I immediately open it and see it's for a kid's birthday party—a referral from Vivian. That's surprising. I haven't talked to Vivian since the Great Mexican Fiesta Fiasco a couple of weeks ago. Perhaps she's not mad at me after all. I begin typing a message back, when my phone dings.

I check the alert and scrunch my nose at the message notification from Fireworks Friends. I never set up a profile.

When I click the alert, it takes me to a message, "Brava! Love your profile! You said everything most of us are thinking but are too afraid to say!"

There are several exclamation points in that message, and I'm adding more in my head along with a series of question marks. *What is she talking about?*

In the app, I click on the "Profile" tab. Staring back at me is me in a skintight black top, revealing my cleavage. It's the photo I vaguely remember taking in the bathroom at the bar in New York and sexting to Max with lots of heart emojis. It was for his eyes only. *Did I send it to someone else by accident?* My heartbeat quickens, like I'm having another panic attack.

I scan the bio. "I'm looking for new friends because my friends in Shitshire are jerks." *Shitshire.* Those are Mel's words. Bits and pieces of that night at the bar come back to me. *Crap!* Mel set up my profile. I set my Fireworks Friends account to private as I dial Mel.

Pick up. Pick up.

"Wait, slow down," Mel says into the phone after I've frantically spilled out five questions.

I take a deep breath. "Did you set up my Fireworks Friends profile?"

"Yes, you let me at the bar. Wasn't it funny?"

"*No!* It's not funny. Some random woman messaged me. That's how I found out."

"What do you mean? I saved it, but never published it." She sucks in a breath. "Didn't I?"

"Apparently you hit the wrong button."

"Now that I think back, you fell off the stool and . . . oh no! I must have accidentally published it. I'm so sorry."

"I hope no one in Springshire saw it," I say as I pace the kitchen.

"The chances are slim that anyone from Shitshire saw it. They wouldn't be on the app. They are too busy being cliquey."

"I hope you're right."

I don't need any more ammunition against me. The Great Mexican Fiesta Fiasco from hell is more than enough. If anyone saw my profile, I may as well plan a Day of the Dead celebration and create an altar for my friendships because they are as good as gone.

After hanging up with Mel, I hop back on the app to rework my Fireworks Friends profile as I can already tell I'm going to need new friends. It's the only good solution, because I'm starting to worry there is no fixing my old friendships. I get busy striking through Mel's lovely write up:

Username: ~~FedUpWithFriends~~ ChocolateLover411

Title: Woman Seeking ~~Kick Ass~~ Platonic Women Friends

~~I'm looking for new friends because my friends in Shitshire are jerks.~~ I am a married, middle-aged ~~very attractive~~ woman who is looking to meet new badass female friends. I am not on this app for sex or romance ~~or any kinky shit.~~ I am looking for platonic, real relationships with other like-minded, supportive women. ~~I find myself pissed off with my current toxic friendships.~~ I am looking for women who ~~are also fed up with their stupid friends~~ have the time to invest in a long-term friendship ~~and who don't plan secret getaways.~~ Someone who sends ~~hilarious~~ texts and has time to meet at least ~~thrice~~ once a week for coffee or drinks ~~and can get shitfaced on demand. Also, must be able to go on one vacation per year~~ ~~to take duck-face photos and make others jealous on social.~~

Interests:

I make chocolate for a living ~~and will have an awesome shop opening soon.~~ I enjoy drinking alcohol ~~(but not tequila because my jerk friends ruined it for me)~~ and ~~spiked~~ coffee. I like to travel. I enjoy running, yoga, and shopping. ~~I'm a self-help book junkie. I have a shoe fetish and enjoy gossip, plotting revenge, and social stalking.~~

~~Hit me back~~ If you'd like to meet ~~for a drink,~~ please respond.

There, that sounds better. I leave out the fact that I am a mother. I don't want to divulge too much information about my personal life. I skip the boxes asking what I'm looking for physically. Nothing is a deal breaker for friendships. I check the box for those located within twenty-five miles. Anything farther and we might as well be pen pals. I check the box for nonsmoker. I gag at the smell of cigarettes.

Taking the perfect selfie proves to be challenging at such a close-up angle. I want my photo to come across as fun and friendly, not sultry and sexy like the one I sent Max.

I load my photo and my description onto the app. I hover my mouse over the "Submit" button. My palms sweat. My heart races. Weirdly, I feel like I am seeking a boyfriend. Or maybe I'm just having another hot flash. I click "Submit" and take a long sip of my ice water.

CHAPTER TWENTY-ONE

I'm in line for my second coffee of the day at Brewed, my favorite local café, when I feel a tap on my shoulder. My shoulders tense at the touch, and I hope it's not someone I don't want to see right now, like Beatrice. But when I turn, it's Vivian. *Phew.*

"Hi," Vivian says, holding a coffee and a muffin. We had the same idea to come here after school drop-off, which isn't surprising since she and I used to frequent this place with the other Ma Spa Squad members when our kids were toddlers. The kids would run in the caged play area as we drank our coffees while they were still warm, and tried to maintain some sense of normalcy in our chaos.

"Hi," I say back. I'm next in line, so I hold up my finger to signal her to wait a moment as I place my order.

After I pay the barista, she says, "I've been meaning to reach out to you. You know, since the party," Vivian says. "I didn't want to bring it up in the school parking lot. We're so rushed there."

"Oh," I say. Now I understand her curtness this morning. Although, instead of pointing out it's me who is frazzled in the morning, she blames it on the situation. If I had to guess, Vivian secretly has a nanny, a chef, and a hair salon and full-service spa in her basement. She's always so put together. From the outside looking in, her life looks like a fairy tale. I imagine a tiara on her head.

"I'm really sorry about your party."

I nod and move to pick up my coffee order.

"Do you have a minute?" she asks.

I check the time on my watch. "I have a few."

"I was wondering if we can chat." She points to a table near the window, and we both walk toward it.

We settle in. She picks off a piece of her muffin and pops it into her mouth.

"I'm sorry about the party too," I say. "How's your hand?"

"It's fine. Just had a few stitches." She holds up her palm, revealing medical tape across the wound.

"Oh gosh. That doesn't seem fine."

She waves her hand to brush away my concern. "Nothing to worry about. How are you?"

"I'm okay. I passed out from the sight of blood." I skip the part about the fake heart attack and being ordered to therapy. I don't want her sympathy.

"Terrible." She takes a sip of her coffee. Then she asks, "Did you order the stripper?"

"No, it was my college roommate. She thought it was a good idea."

"Well, it wasn't necessarily a bad idea. I was hoping he'd look and dance more like Magic Mike," she whispers. "He just caused a chain of unfortunate events."

"Wouldn't be the first time and probably not the last," I say, then sip my coffee. Vivian raises her eyebrows but doesn't ask me to clarify.

If he had looked like Magic Mike instead of Dirty Harry, maybe he would have been hailed a hero, not some random guy with an above-average body who barreled into my backyard like a runaway truck.

I take another sip. "Have you spoken to Beatrice?"

"Yes," she says, and picks at her muffin.

"So, are Beatrice and Craig divorcing?" I'm afraid what the answer might be.

Vivian looks at me like I asked her to clip my toenails, but then her features soften. "Yes, they've been having problems. I'm surprised you didn't know," she says.

I squeeze my eyes shut for a moment. I had suspected this, but hearing Vivian confirm it saddens me deeply.

"Beatrice has distanced herself from me." Like I hadn't washed my hair in days and wore the same black, sweaty leggings every day for a week. No, that's not right. Beatrice hung out with me on days like those years ago, when our girls were babies. This was more serious. She avoided me like I had the plague.

"I know that now. I thought you were invited to all the get-togethers, but you didn't come because you were too busy."

"No. I would have joined you and supported Beatrice through this."

"I'm sorry. I don't think Beatrice wants to see you, though. I think the party . . ." Vivian clears her throat and takes a sip of her coffee as I wait for what she's going to say next. "You know, with Elenore being there. Elenore's husband is

Beatrice's divorce lawyer, and she's taking Jeff's side. Personally, I wouldn't have gotten involved in that whole situation."

I raise an eyebrow. So, Jeff is Beatrice's lawyer. It's all clicking, and I understand why they were friendly at the soccer game.

Vivian is a voice of reason in all this craziness. So, she thinks it's because of Elenore that Beatrice is distancing herself from me.

"I know it's none of my business, but did she tell you what their issues were?"

Vivian crumples her napkin. "Oh, the normal stuff. I don't think it's a big secret. You know. Craig doesn't help with the kids, and Beatrice is exhausted. Plus, Craig is like a big kid who needs attention and stuff done for him too. She's had enough. She thinks if they split, she'd have one less person to cater to. Those are her words, not mine."

Interesting. "Did they try marriage counseling?"

"Craig doesn't believe in it—oh, look at the time," she abruptly says as she glances at her watch and gets up. "I'm sorry—I have to go. Heading to Zumba class."

"Before you go, I want to thank you for referring your neighbor to me. She placed a big order for her son's birthday party."

"Of course! Your chocolates are delicious."

We say our goodbyes, and I stay seated, sipping my coffee. *Did I hear her right? Did she just say she liked my chocolates?* Mel's voice takes over my mind: *"Chica, believe it already. Your chocolates are amazeballs."*

I chuckle to myself. But then I think about Beatrice and her divorce. Poor Beatrice. Craig doesn't even want to try counseling. At least Max was willing to meet me halfway.

Max let me choose the therapist. Little did he know, I wanted to go to a counselor who was a married woman with children. Someone who would take my side. Enter Dr. Josie. Well, Dr. Jadalavalich, but no one can pronounce it, so she goes by her first name. She turned out to be professionally impartial, but at least I had tried. I liked her despite her non-taking sides approach. In another lifetime, we could have been friends.

Max and I faced some hard truths with Dr. Josie. For example, if I had been more communicative and asked Max for help, he would have been more involved. But I'd thought I shouldn't have to ask, that he should automatically be present and take initiative. But that's the difference between mothers and fathers. Mothers know instinctively what a child needs and when. Fathers aren't as intuitive and thus need direction. That's what Max admitted to, anyway. He thought I had it all under control.

I said it was physically and mentally impossible to have child care under control. Just when I got the knack for something like naps—Maya started teething and threw everything out of whack—or she got a rash or constipation or diarrhea or a cold—or a million and one other things. I'd put out one fire, and another one would start.

I began resenting Max for not knowing what to do, not acknowledging what I was doing was difficult, and not raising a finger to even try to help. I often wondered if we were living in the same house, because our perceptions were completely opposite. It wasn't until we started opening up about our feelings, with the therapist, that we got to a better place.

At that point in our marriage, the only time Max and I made time for each other was to see the therapist. Max's sister watched Maya so we could go. Ironically, we hadn't even thought to ask Maeve to watch Maya so we could go on a real date.

The two-hundred-dollar therapy sessions were worth it. We started understanding each other. I probably could have saved us a lot of money and reread *Men Are from Mars, Women Are from Venus* and gotten the same understanding, but somehow reading anything sounded daunting to me at the time. I could barely keep my eyes open. There was no way I could focus on a page. That's how exhausted I was.

In the end, I learned to tell Max what was needed, both for Maya and for me. I started doing small things for myself, like taking a break to walk around the block. Then I made it a priority to fit yoga into my schedule. Small changes that allowed me to focus on my own well-being made a huge difference.

In Beatrice's case, even though Cecilia was in school, Beatrice still had Benjamin at home. So, the patterns repeated themselves with a second child. She must have thought Craig would be more involved with the second child. After all, they had already been through it once and probably thought the second child would be easier. I'm making this all up in my head. I think I know how she feels.

I never told Beatrice that Max and I went to see a therapist, for the same reasons I didn't tell anyone. I was embarrassed to admit that things weren't perfect. *Aren't we supposed to put on a smile and act like everything is okay?* Maybe if I had told Beatrice, she would have come to me first.

The fact that Beatrice chose not to reach out to me weighs heavily on my heart.

My phone rings, jolting me out of my thoughts. I don't recognize the number, so I let it go to voicemail. *What if it's a chocolate order? Ugh.* I should have answered it. After a few seconds, my phone indicates I have a new message. I click to listen.

"Fallon, this is Pam, from the adoption agency. We've located your records and letters. We will be mailing your documents with additional nonidentifying information. You should receive them in two weeks at the latest."

I place my head in my hands. *"Nonidentifying" information?* That doesn't sound promising. Those words conjure up an image of Maya with a disgusted look on her face, holding up mystery meat at a buffet and asking, "What is this made of?"

That's me—a sad lump of mystery meat.

CHAPTER TWENTY-TWO

It's been two days since redoing my Fireworks Friends profile, and I still haven't gotten any responses. I now know what it feels like to be Avery and dating—annoyed. I check my photo to see if it's okay and not cropped in a weird way. *Is it my photo?* Sure, it's close up, but I look presentable. I put on makeup for the occasion—bronzer and a bit of shimmery eye shadow. At least I look better than I usually do in the school carpool line.

Turning back to my chocolate, I mix in vanilla. It takes all my might not to lick the chocolate from the spatula. I review the recipe I wrote down for Vivian's neighbor. She ordered one hundred chocolate vanilla truffles. The orders have been steadily coming in from word of mouth. The stripper situation hadn't hurt my business, like I originally thought. One of these days, I'll create an official website.

My phone buzzes and an alert comes through from the friendship app. *Finally.* My heart drops into my stomach. This could be my first real local friend! Licking the chocolate off my fingers, I scan the message.

"Hi there. I moved to the area recently and I'm looking to meet new people, whether for dates or friendship. I just graduated college and I'm . . ."

I had selected an age group, hadn't I? I click the link to my profile. Nope, I missed it. Now I enter an age range from thirty-five to forty-five. I'm not sure I can hang with twenty-somethings. We wouldn't have anything in common, especially now that I've started growing chin hairs. Seriously, I think they grow overnight. Or at least I hope they do, because if I've been walking around with them for a few days without noticing, just kill me now. *What if most of the women on this app are between eighteen and twenty-five?* That would be just my luck.

I consider hiring her as a babysitter. I'll carve out time later to answer her and to look through other profiles of women I find interesting. I don't know why I've been waiting for women to ping me first. I guess I'm afraid of rejection. *Ugh.* Now Beatrice is infiltrating my search for new friendships. I have to nip my negative thoughts in the bud.

Another message comes through. I'm starting to feel like the cool kid. *Only took nearly forty years.*

"Interested. I need new friends. I'll explain why over drinks. Tomorrow seven PM? Carrie."

This Carrie woman sounds more like me. Short and to the point. I click on the woman's photo. It's sexy and sultry. She's probably on the dating side of this app too and used the same photo. She's a lawyer, or so she says in her bio. I can't be too sure. I don't know how many women inflate their profiles to attract friends or mates. She likes to travel and has been to more than thirty countries. She's a runner. She's never been married and doesn't have children.

I wash my hands and finish up my recipe before I respond. I don't want to seem too eager. I'm sure there is a rule on how fast to answer, even for friendships. *What is an acceptable response time so you don't look like a loser—twenty-four hours?* She's obviously expecting a response sooner because she asked to meet tomorrow.

After an hour, I message Carrie back, suggesting a new local pub I've been dying to try. I know it will be crowded, and that's fine, because I'm not taking any chances. There are a lot of crazy people out there.

She messages back instantly. She's winning at friendship already.

* * *

I get to the bar early so I can watch the door and choose to chicken out if needed, and to order nachos and truffle fries.

"I'll have a vodka and club soda," I say to the bartender.

Scanning my social accounts, I look up every time I hear the door swing open. A photo on my feed catches my eye. It's Beatrice, Vivian, and Lyla clinking champagne flutes hashtag TBT. Oh, great. It isn't bad enough they aren't talking to me—well, Vivian kind of is—now they are throwing it back in my face for throwback Thursday. I gulp my drink. I sure hope this Carrie chick is someone I can hang out with.

Someone taps me on the shoulder.

"Are you Fallon?" says a tall woman with long, curly, brown hair and a beautiful complexion. Carrie looks just like her photo. She obviously didn't use one from ten years ago. I missed her entrance, and there's no chance of running for the hills now. Thank God she looks like someone I want to talk to, anyway.

"Yes, hi."

She wears a black suit and carries a black leather brief-case. The suit looks expensive. Could be Armani, but I don't know much about professional clothing. When I worked in an office in another lifetime as a project manager, it was business casual.

We make small talk about the weather, parking, and the bar. It's quiet tonight. As she orders a glass of red wine, I survey her shoes—Christian Louboutin's. I can tell by the shiny, red-lacquered soles. I gasp. They are even prettier in person. I take a closer look at her briefcase—Louis Vuitton.

I order us mind-eraser shots made of vodka, coffee liqueur, and soda water—a delightful indulgence. I used to drink them in college, and I can't remember a thing, so it's a good choice for us, to forget our friendship woes. Carrie doesn't decline the shot. Good sign.

I push the plate of nachos in front of her. It's not a test, but I'll like her more if she isn't a health nut. I mean—everything in moderation, *right?* She takes one of the chips loaded with chicken and cheese. I smile, but then I realize we might have a different problem—fighting for the most coveted covered nachos on the plate.

"I'm curious. What made you message me?" I ask.

"I resonated with the fact that you're unhappy with your friends. Then when I saw that you run too, that sealed it for me. Maybe we can run sometime together."

Crap! I forgot to delete that from my profile. Mel, being the funny girl she is, knows I abhor running. So much so that I'd rather eat liver. I gloss over Carrie's statement. "So, we'll drink the shots after you tell me why you need new friends," I say.

As the bartender delivers our shots and the wine, Carrie goes right into her explanation, sounding like a lawyer delivering closing arguments. She captivates me with her eloquence. "Picture this: It's a balmy day in June. The sun hides behind the clouds, but you can feel its warmth on your skin. It's perfect beach weather. You invite all your girls to a getaway at your lake house. You have your own private beach front. The water is cool and calm. No water sports or boats to interrupt your swim."

She takes a sip of her wine. I can imagine her lake house is secluded and breathtaking. From the way she describes it, I want to escape to it now.

"You provide ample alcohol. It's flowing. You think you should hide some bottles because things start getting out of hand and some of your friends are skinny dipping. But you're too drunk to care. One woman is already passed out on the cool tiles of the bathroom floor. Another woman is so drunk, she can't even make it to the toilet and pees in the bushes."

She's setting the scene nicely, intriguing me. It sounds like a party I attended in college.

"You continue to drink and play loud music. The sun sets, and you start a bonfire. You and your friends play 'I never' and 'truth or dare.' It's one of those nights you can feel you'll always remember, bonding with your girls."

I nod, thinking about my party. It should have brought us all together, not torn us apart.

"Then secrets start unraveling, and women are sharing comments said behind the others' backs, such as how so-and-so thinks so-and-so has gained weight, and another has crooked eyebrows, and someone else wants to sleep with someone's husband. It goes on and on. Before you know it, women are tackling each other. You're dousing the bonfire with water so no one gets thrown into it."

I stifle a laugh. I almost wish I was there, watching with a bowl of popcorn. Then I snap out of it. This is serious to Carrie.

"So, after that, no one is speaking to anyone. Not even me, and I wasn't the one divulging information. I'm used to keeping secrets. I have to be secretive for my profession." She takes a sip of water.

"That's some story. What a shame. I was rooting for you," I say.

"Yep, total cluster. Anyway, that's why I'm looking for new friends. Friends I can have a fresh start with." She points to the shot glass. "Now?"

We grab the mind erasers and throw them back. Our friendship is sealed. After a while, I share my story with her. We take a selfie, and I post it, #BFFs.

Take that Ma Spa Squad.

CHAPTER TWENTY-THREE

Carrie and I had a great time chatting and getting to know each other. She didn't even bat an eye when I told her how many shoes I have, and I accepted her love for expensive designer fashion. Now I'm feeling good about meeting new friends.

I open my friendship app and see I have two new messages. One is from a woman who wants to know if I sew and asks me if we can sew over tea. I'd rather stick my eye with a needle. The other message is from a man who asks me on a date. *Has he even read my profile?* No. The fact that he started with "Hi, Sexy" turns me off. Not that I should have been turned on, anyway. *What a creep.* It's called Fireworks FRIENDS for a reason. Some people just don't get it.

I close the messages and swipe through profiles. My eyes stop on a friendly face of a woman who looks to be around my age. I click on her profile. Her name is Stacy. I read her profile more closely. She's divorced. Two children. Lives fifteen minutes from me. She likes animals, skiing, and beaches.

Seems normal. I send her a message. There I did it. I'm not letting the fear of rejection stop me.

My phone dings with a new message from Stacy. That was fast.

"How soon can we meet?"

Should I bring Carrie in on this initial meeting with Stacy? I envision a large friendship group, not just one-off friends. I only have so much time, and if we all get along, we can keep going out together. Plus, having another woman there will make me less leery of possibly meeting a potential psycho. Always travel in pairs—I followed that philosophy through college, and it worked. I never got robbed, kidnapped, or killed.

I text Carrie, asking her if she would like to meet another potential new friend. She responds affirmatively. After a few back-and-forth messages, I find a time suitable for all three of us.

An alert for an email titled "IMPORTANT: Championship Game postponed" comes through. My shoulders relax. I had been dreading the game all week.

Of course, I want Maya to play the game and win, but it also means I'll have to see the Ma Spa Squad all together in one spot for a long period of time.

The email explains the messy state of the field from the recent storms. We got hit hard. I stare out the window at the threatening clouds. Tomorrow calls for more treacherous storms with lots of lightning. Because of other events going on at the park, they've postponed the game for another month. Just as well. I don't have to deal with the Ma Spa Squad now.

* * *

I wish Maya had asked me to volunteer for the book fair or the end-of-school party, not the second-grade music concert. I have absolutely zero music training. I scan the room and see Beatrice. *Great.* I didn't expect her to be here too.

"Hi, Mommy. I'm so glad you're here." Maya gives me a big hug. "Can Penelope come over after school today? We want to work on a science project together."

"Of course. That sounds like a wonderful idea." I make a mental note to confirm this with Elenore. My heart sings when I see Maya thriving at school and soccer. I kiss her forehead, and she rejoins her class.

The music teacher splits the second-grade classes into groups of ten and hands each of the volunteers the lyrics to the song the groups will be singing. Maya and Cecilia are placed in the same group. Beatrice and I are assigned to them. *Figures.*

I glance at the song. It's "Roar" by Katy Perry. I know the song well. I've sung it loudly and off-key in the shower a time or two. I scan the lyrics on the paper. *Are they appropriate for second graders?* The words hit me given the situation I find myself in with Beatrice. *Ironic.* Now I hear Alanis Morissette in my head.

We file down the hall to an open classroom to practice. Beatrice still hasn't acknowledged my presence. My mouth is dry, like a sandstorm swept through. It's getting more awkward by the minute. The music teacher texts me a link to the music file, and Beatrice arranges the kids in a line.

"I'm going to play the song," I squeak out, and clear my throat. "Let's listen, then we'll practice. Unless you have a better idea, Beatrice?"

She doesn't look at me. "That's fine."

I turn on the Bluetooth speaker and sync my cell phone to it.

A boy raises his hand. "Can I go to the bathroom?"

"Yes," I say.

A girl raises her hand. "Hi, I'm Skylar. I take singing lessons and I don't need the words. I know this song by heart."

Hmm . . . Skylar. This is the girl whose parents don't allow her to eat candy. I hold back my smile as I remember Maya's words: *A life without candy is no life at all.*

"That's nice, Skylar, but please hold the paper anyway."

Another boy raises his hand.

This is going to take forever. "One more question or comment, and then we will get started. Go ahead."

"Can I play the drums?"

"No, this is a singing concert only," Beatrice answers him.

Maya raises her hand.

"Maya, if you don't have to go to the bathroom, then please hold your question," I say. I can't play favorites.

"But, Mommy."

I shoot Maya a look, and she frowns at me.

Beatrice's daughter raises her hand. I ignore her. I'm not getting into this.

"Yes, Cecilia?" Beatrice says.

Ugh. Now I look like the jerk to my own child.

"I want to dance."

Maya sticks her tongue out at me.

"All of you can sway to the music," Beatrice answers.

Cecilia smirks.

I click to play the song before another hand is raised. The song pours out of the speaker, and the kids sway back and forth. Heat rises to my face as the words find their way under my skin. I sneak a glance at Beatrice. She stands with her arms crossed and her lips in a tight line. She's frozen, and it strikes me the kids should be singing "Let It Go."

I can't help but move with the rhythm as I tap my foot.

Once the song is over, I instruct the kids to sing with Katy Perry next time. Beatrice lets me take the lead. She's withdrawn. I assume her issues with Craig are taking a toll on her. Or maybe she just doesn't want to engage with me at all. It's unlike her. She's usually quite vocal. I think back to the confrontation in the school parking lot a few weeks ago.

I can't hear most of the kids over Katy Perry's vocals. The kids I can hear sound terrible. I refrain from covering my ears.

I can't sing and don't know how I'm going to teach them how in two short weeks before the concert. I'm about to switch the music off as Beatrice begins belting out the chorus. I turn to look at her with wide eyes. Beatrice can sing and she's singing to me. The words are echoing throughout the room: "'Cause I am a champion, and you're gonna hear me roar."

I want to shrink away. It's like everything she wants to say to me is in this song. The kids stop and listen. Beatrice flawlessly finishes, with cheers from the kids.

She does a quick curtsy.

"That's how it's done, kids," she says.

Beatrice smiles. I step back and allow Beatrice to take over the rest of the practice. By the end, I think the kids have a chance at singing decently. We walk them back to the gym for parent pickup.

"I didn't know you could sing," I say, pretending not to notice that the song was her way of saying to me, "Don't mess with me because I will tear you to shreds."

Beatrice shrugs.

I hold open the door to the gym. The kids file in.

"Cecilia, come on. It's time to go." Beatrice grabs Cecilia's hand and walks out of the gym, leaving me holding the door.

She turns around. "I knew I was right about you," she says. "You're nothing but a liar and a traitor."

I flinch. "What are you talking about?"

"Enjoy your new hashtag BFF."

I stare at the back of her head. *My hashtag BFF? Elenore? Or does she mean Carrie and the photo I posted?* She's clearly upset.

I thought hurting Beatrice would make me feel better. Surprisingly, I feel worse.

CHAPTER TWENTY-FOUR

Carrie and I agree to meet a half an hour earlier than Stacy, so we are in place when she arrives.

Carrie swirls the ice in her glass. "I'm dating someone," she says.

"Oh?"

"Yes, it's been a couple of months. I didn't say anything before because I didn't want to jinx it."

Avery is the same way. She says that she doesn't want to tell people too soon after meeting someone. Most of the time after telling her friends, it doesn't work out, and she feels dumb for thinking it will. She worries people will judge her. Like something is wrong with her that she can't make a relationship work. I often remind Avery that dating is a process, and she can't control douchebags.

"Did you meet on the Fireworks app?"

"No."

"Let me guess. You met him at the grocery store, and he asked you to squeeze his banana or something?"

I assume the grocery store is a legit place to meet, though I'm usually in a bad mood and having hot flashes there. I thank my lucky stars I don't have to be at my best while shopping. The pressure to always be in a good mood to attract a mate must be exhausting.

"That's funny, but no. I met him in my running club, but it wasn't until I booked an osteopath appointment with him that we started dating."

"Damsel in distress," I say. "Works every time."

I tell her how Max broke my toe, and I was once also a princess who needed rescuing. I roll my eyes now at the stereotypes and hope Maya's life will be different.

"Can he date his patients?"

"Sure. It's consensual."

Now I'm intrigued about this mystery man, and I can't help but pry. "So, tell me what he's like."

Carrie blushes. I can't believe I've embarrassed her. She's a lawyer. She must be used to being put on the spot.

"I never kiss and tell, but he is really amazing. I'll leave it at that."

I smile. "Okay, then tell me what dating has been like for you. I've been dying to know. Ya know, being married for fifteen years, I am so out of the scene."

"Before this relationship, dating hasn't been all that great. I can easily access background checks through work, so that's been very helpful in weeding out guys. You would be surprised at how many men have DUIs and drug arrest records. I've started to lower my standards a little and will let one DUI slide."

I sip my drink. "Wow. I had no idea. So, does this guy have a DUI?"

"Not that I can find. Assuming he's practicing under his real name."

I cringe. This all sounds terrible. I scan the bar and see a ton of men hanging around, thinking about creepy guys with arrest records, who may or may not be using their real names. One guy seems to be suspiciously staring our way. When he sees me staring back, he averts his eyes. I shake off the heebie-jeebies as a woman with a messy bun, wearing jeans, a sweater, and comfy boots, approaches us.

"Hi, Fallon?" she asks.

I reach my hand out to her. "You must be Stacy." I introduce Carrie and explain how Carrie and I recently met on the app.

"You got started without me." She points to my half-empty glass.

"Oh yeah, sorry. I had to get out of the house early."

"I understand."

Great, we're off to a good start. She is already sympathizing with me.

The suspicious guy is looking our way again. His appearance is like that of any normal guy, wearing a polo and jeans, except he's staring at Carrie over his phone. I ignore him and ask Stacy, "What do you do for a living?"

"The exciting business of commercial real estate."

I raise my eyebrows. That is exciting, but I detect her sarcasm.

She flags down the bartender. "I'll have what she's having, unless it's water."

Now I really like her. She will drink what I drink. She wrings her hands together as anxiety radiates off her.

"Rough day?" I ask her.

"I left work early to deal with an issue at my kid's school," Stacy says, then adds, "You're perceptive."

I want to tell her if that were true, I would have perceived my old group of friends would eventually exclude me. Would have saved me a bunch of heartache. I look to see if the creeper is still staring, but he's left the bar. *Good.*

"So," Stacy jumps right in. "Tell me why you joined the app."

I explain to her about the Ma Spa Squad. She listens intently, furrowing her brows and rolling her eyes at the appropriate times. I have to hand it to her—she's a good listener. I wave the bartender down.

"Wow, sounds like your friendships ended with a bang."

I nod. "Three shots of mind erasers, please."

"You poor thing. You need a shot. I can't believe they would turn on you, especially after you've known them for so many years, and you saved that one woman's child from the pool! Goodness gracious, how ungrateful."

She gets me. She really gets me. Carrie nods. She's been actively listening too, without interjecting. Carrie lifts a shot glass. "Shall we?" she says.

Stacy and I pick up our shots, and we all clink them together. I throw mine back and set the glass down.

"Okay, enough about me. Why are you looking for new friends? I'm intrigued," I say.

"As you know from my profile, I'm divorced."

I nod. I can't imagine what that's like *and* raising two kids.

"My husband cheated on me with my best friend."

I frown. Typical story. We've all heard it a million times.

"That's really low of him," Carrie interjects.

"I caught them."

I'm dying to know how, but I wait it out. Let her take her time to tell me. I don't know what to say in the meantime, so I just say, "I'm sorry." *What else can I say?*

"My husband had been acting secretive for a month, hiding his phone, going out at night, saying he had to go to the office. I knew something was up because he had a job where he could work remote. He wasn't very smart about the whole thing." She tips her drink up to her lips and takes a sip. "Sick of all the sneaking around, one day I tell him I'm going out with a friend. Sure enough, he hired a babysitter, and I followed him."

I like her. She isn't playing.

"To Down Low."

It takes me a few seconds to register where she is talking about, then it hits me.

"The gay bar?"

Max's sister used to hang out there all the time.

"Yep, that would be the one. I waited a few minutes in the parking lot, and that's when I saw Chad, my best friend, walking into the club. My heart dropped, but I was thinking, okay, maybe I'm wrong. Maybe my husband's planning a surprise for me and needs my best friend's opinion. After all, Chad knows me well and is really good with gifts."

"That's logical," Carrie says.

"I couldn't bring myself to go inside. What if they were planning a surprise for me and I was ruining it? But then I thought, why would they meet at a gay bar and not at a coffee shop or something? I sat there, trying to figure out my next move. I was in shock, praying that what could be true wasn't actually true. I didn't have to wait too long. An hour later, they walked out of the bar, holding hands. Then, right there against Chad's truck, Richard kissed him."

I throw my hand to my mouth. This is just as crazy as Elenore getting caught on stage with the principal. Both could be scenes straight out of a movie. "That must have been tough."

"Yeah, I met Chad in college. Never would have imagined he'd steal my husband."

I wave the bartender over and order three more mind-eraser shots.

"Anyway, all our friends were mutual, and instead of sticking by either of us, they all disappeared. I expected they would choose sides. I would have understood if they'd chosen to stay connected to Richard, because many of them played poker together, and I friended their wives, but the whole situation surprised them, and they left."

I feel a sudden kinship with this woman, and I want to hug her, but I maintain my distance so as not to come across too soon like a clingy weirdo.

"Wow. I'm at a loss for words," I say.

"So, that's why I'm looking for new friends. I considered moving, but I don't want to run away from my problems. I'm teaching my children how to be strong. I worry they're being bullied, but both are seeing a psychologist. Hopefully, it's helping."

Carrie tells her lake house story the same way she told me. She is a gifted storyteller and has Stacy on the edge of her seat. We do another shot.

After chatting for an hour, I genuinely like Stacy. We plan to meet up again next week. She asks me if she passed the screening process.

"Yes," I say, "with flying colors."

CHAPTER TWENTY-FIVE

Dr. Josie checks her notes.

"Do you think you're a likable person, Fallon?"

I've never thought about my likability. I answer her with a shrug.

"What does the voice in your head say about you?"

I roll my eyes up to my forehead, as if that will help me answer this deep question. *Where is she going with this?* I shift in my seat, thinking how to phrase the words that swirl in my head. If she's going to help me, I have to be honest with her. After a moment, I inhale, then choke out, "That I'm not worthy of anyone sticking around to be my friend."

Tears fall down my cheeks, and Dr. Josie extends a box of tissues to me.

"That's a harsh statement to say to yourself. Do you think this self-doubt stems from how you feel about your biological mom giving you up for adoption?"

I bite the dry skin off my lip. "I never correlated the two, but I guess it makes sense." She didn't want me. I'm sure, for the most part, other women in my life feel the same way about me too, especially now that I'm being ostracized.

"What would you say to someone else if she told you that she didn't feel worthy of friends?"

I blow my nose as tears continue to fall and converge at my chin. "I would say that's crazy talk and that she is definitely worthy." I wipe my tears. "Then I would hug her."

"Okay, then, what makes you unworthy?"

She waits for me to respond, but I can't form any words.

"Nothing," she says. "You are worthy, and it's time to start changing the narrative in your head from negative self-talk to positive self-talk. Can you do that?"

I blow out a breath. "I'm willing to try."

Dr. Josie hands me a small compact mirror she retrieved from her desk drawer. "Look in the mirror and repeat after me. 'I am enough. I am worthy of love. I am worthy of beautiful relationships.'"

I stare at my tear-streaked cheeks, brush my hair off my forehead and begin, "I am enough. I am worthy of love. I am worthy of beautiful relationships."

"Now, say it louder."

I repeat the words again with a raised voice. "I am enough. I am worthy of love. I am worthy of beautiful relationships."

"How do you feel?"

"Lighter."

"Good. I want you to continue to do this at home as much as possible. When you hear that negative voice harping in your head, squash it with positive affirmations."

I hand the mirror back to her and release my shoulders that had somehow ended up near my ears.

"Have you heard the saying that people come into your life for a reason, a season, or a lifetime?"

I remember reading that quote when I was sobbing on the couch, grieving over the friend loss.

"Yes, I've thought about that quote a lot recently."

"Do you agree with it?"

"I guess." I pick at my cuticles to distract myself from crying again.

"I have an idea. We can do an activity that may help you clarify your relationships."

Dr. Josie walks to her desk and gets a clipboard with a piece of paper and a pencil. She circles back around and hands them to me.

"I want you to divide this paper into four quadrants. At the top of the first quadrant, write 'Reason.' At the top of the second, write 'Season.' For the third, write 'Lifetime.' In the fourth, write, 'TBD.'"

Oddly, I feel like I'm back in third grade, hoping I don't break into a sweat. I hated school. I still have nightmares that I'm taking a test and can't fill in the little circles. I always wake up just as the teacher reaches for my empty Scantron test. I wipe my brow to swipe away the dread.

"Now close your eyes and think about some significant times in your life where someone you considered a friend may have helped you, but then moved on. Start with your earliest memories."

I close my eyes. My thoughts race around my head like they're being chased by aggressive dogs. After a minute, I open my eyes, and Dr. Josie tells me to write in the "Reason" box the names of the people I thought about.

I do as she says, then ask, "What's the fourth quadrant for?"

"That is to be determined. Those are for friends you may not yet know how to categorize."

I take the next few minutes to complete her assignment. I have four names in the reason section, three in season, and six in lifetime. The last time I did something like this was in middle school, when I was trying to decide which boy to ask to the Sadie Hawkins dance, except the categories were "yeah right," "no," and "never." Suffice it to say, I didn't go to the dance.

"Perfect. Please pick a person from the "Reason" section and tell me about them."

I take a deep breath and start with Casey. Dr. Josie had instructed me to think back to my earliest memories. It was the first day of kindergarten. I remember being scared and latching on to my mother's leg, much in the same way Maya does to me now. A girl with rosy cheeks and brown ringlets approached me and asked me if I wanted to be her friend. She introduced herself as Casey and held out her hand.

When I think back to that moment, butterflies swoop into my stomach. Casey had made my day. Her friendship lasted a week, until she found a new friend and they ran away from me at recess. I tried several times to play with them that second week of school, but they turned their backs on me and said I had cooties. Casey had served her purpose, though—she had gotten me through the first week of school.

Dr. Josie stops me before I can move on.

"How did it make you feel when Casey found a new friend?"

"I was fine. It was when they wouldn't play with me that I remember feeling sad. I spent a lot of time alone at recess after that."

"Did you tell anyone?"

"No. There was no point. I had to go to school."

"It sounds to me like this may be your first memory of friendship, and it is a sad one for you. What do you think might have been going on in Casey's life that could have led to the loss of your friendship?"

I hadn't thought about the fact that the demise of our brief friendship could have had anything to do with anything else but me. I can't believe we are talking about this, even though I brought it up from a place in my mind that should have trashed this memory a lifetime ago. It's been so long. I feel silly bringing it up now. I was five, and definitely not old enough to start ruining my life by harboring hurt feelings over poor treatment by other five-year-olds. This is the same age where you stick your head in between spindles of a railing and wail when you can't twist out of it. She had to realize this too.

"I'm really not sure. I was so young. I don't remember."

"Our childhood experiences mold us into who we are. They are important." She pauses, and I assume it's for emphasis as she waits for me to process her words. "Please tell me about one person in your "Season" quadrant."

I rehash Whitney Ross and the Great Hot Dog Hot Mess. I tell Dr. Josie I placed her in the season quadrant because we had been friends most of junior year until I got mustard on her prom dress.

Dr. Josie writes some things down and asks me to list the names in the third quadrant under "Lifetime."

"Avery, Mel, Vivian, Beatrice, Lyla, and Elenore."

"Your neighborhood friends. Why did you write them in this quadrant?"

"Well, like I've said before, because it's been seven years of friendship."

"Yes, and you became friends when your children were still in diapers. Your children are older now. Based on their recent treatment of you, do you think it's time to move them into another quadrant?"

Surprised by her question, I pinch the skin on my forehead. *They are lifetime friends.* I slowly release the hold on my brow. *Aren't they?* But since she raised the question, I'm not sure anymore. "I don't know."

"Who did you write in the fourth "TBD" quadrant?"

"My newest friends, Stacy and Carrie, who I met on the friendship app."

"What are your thoughts about moving some of your neighborhood friends into the "TBD" quadrant until you figure it out?"

I mull this idea over. I want them to be lifetime friends, but *am I forcing them into a box they don't fit in?*

"Okay," I say.

I cross out Vivian, Beatrice, and Lyla in quadrant three and lump them all together by writing "the Ma Spa Squad" in quadrant four.

"What was your intention of joining the friendship app?" Dr. Josie asks.

"To meet new friends."

"Why?"

I pause, thinking it over. "So, I'm not lonely." I swallow hard. "And to prove I have time for friends. That I *am* a good friend."

"Who are you proving this to?"

"The Ma Spa Squad."

"Okay, say you prove that you have time for friends. That you're a good friend. Now what?"

I sigh. She's like a drill sergeant firing questions at me. I'm tiring. I don't remember this approach. She's always been more methodical.

"The Ma Spa Squad is proved wrong," I say after a while, to slow her down a bit.

Dr. Josie raises her eyebrows, signaling me to keep going. "And?" she asks.

"Then it's not my fault we're no longer friends. It's theirs."

"Ah. Are you proving it to them or to yourself?"

"Both. I guess."

"Why is it important for you to prove anything to them?"

"Because I feel hurt and misunderstood."

She writes some notes on her yellow pad of paper.

"Have you thought about getting off social media for a while?" she asks.

I hope I don't go into a full-blown panic attack right here. This wouldn't be the worst place to have one, though. A therapist would know what to do. My face is burning, and I need a drink. I wish she had alcohol here. A whiskey shot would calm my nerves.

"Um. I hadn't considered it."

"Why not?"

"It keeps me connected."

"To whom?"

Good question. "Hmm . . . chocolate shops and groups, soccer stuff, family, school, a few friends, the news, shoe ads, acquaintances, people I know from college, the Ma Spa Squad, I guess."

"Could you keep in touch with family, friends, and organizations another way?"

"Text and email, I suppose . . ." *Like a cave woman.*

"How much time do you think you're spending on social media, checking on what your neighborhood mom friends are doing?"

"I don't know." *Way too much.* "I never timed it, but I'm sure it's a few times a day."

"How do you think that might be contributing to your emotional state?"

I pick at my cuticles. "It's probably not helping matters," I admit.

I guess I can live without knowing what people ate for breakfast, the food they serve their pets, random facts about their lives like how much weight they've lost; without reading their professions of deep love and gratitude for their spouse once a year on their anniversary, or about their beautiful vacations, new hairdos, etcetera. *But can I live without seeing what the Ma Spa Squad is up to?* It's become an obsession. Maybe I do need to step away, for my own mental health.

"I'll take a break from social media," I say, surprising myself.

"Good. You could start slowly by possibly taking off a day or two, and write about how you feel during this time."

I reach for my water bottle in my tote bag and take a long sip as she checks her notes again. I grip my water bottle tighter, already itching to grab my phone.

"How are things with Max?"

She must get the hint that I'm done talking about the friendships.

I clear my throat. "Fine." *Are things fine?* Based on that journal entry I found in the basement when I was looking for my grandma's china, my married life hasn't quite turned out like I hoped, and I can't help but notice everyone seems to be divorcing. Even Beatrice and her lobster, Craig.

Dr. Josie shuffles through my file and pulls out a paper. "According to my notes, the last time you and Max were here, two years ago, you promised you would go on a date once a month."

I stare at her as if she's mistaken me with another client who clearly had a solid plan for her marriage. I vaguely remember agreeing to that. Max and I have come a long way. We are having civilized adult conversations. We are no longer yelling at each other at the top of our lungs, and I've stopped screaming into pillows.

I blame some of our fights on my hormones, though. They were all messed up right after having Maya. Plus, I was operating on very little sleep. I resented Max for getting a good night's sleep so he could perform at his job the next day. I, on the other hand, was a walking zombie and still had to be on top of my game for Maya. The expectations of motherhood wore on me. I supposedly was more nurturing. I didn't feel like it with all the crabbiness that creeped in. But as Maya started sleeping through the night, things got better.

I had wanted four children, but God had other plans and had reminded me of them again recently. The all-knowing being was right. I couldn't do it again. I had failed at being strong. *Or was I strong because I knew my limits?* Either way— my marriage wouldn't have survived another child.

I scan my brain. *When was the last time we went on a date?* "Uh . . . no. The last time we'd been on a date was a couple of months ago for our anniversary."

She raises her eyebrows. "Are you interested in connecting more closely with Max?"

I could read between the lines. She was stressing the importance of my marriage as a priority over my female friendships. I had been content with the fact that Max and I were not living in a war zone anymore, and had failed to strengthen our relationship with time together. I take a deep breath.

"I am."

"Good," she says. "I remember your affinity for self-help books. Are you still reading them?"

"Yes," I say, although I had recently failed at my attempt at following the advice in *How to Win Friends and Influence People*.

Dr. Josie rises from her chair and walks to her bookshelf. She pulls a book off her shelf and flips through it. "This is one of my favorite books for couples. It's called *The Five Love Languages*. Have you read it?"

I've heard of it, but I read more personal development books rather than relationship books. Please don't tell me I have to learn five romance languages like Italian, French, Spanish, and two others to fix my marriage. My shoulders tense up again.

"No, I haven't."

"I thought about giving this to you back when you and Max were seeing me regularly, but then you mentioned reading was the last thing on your mind because you were exhausted from the sleepless nights with Maya." She hands me the book. "Here. It's yours. I think you'll find it eye opening."

And possibly tongue twisting. I pull out my phone and check the time, and notice I have several notifications of new Facebook posts.

Dr. Josie clears her throat. I look up at her. "How would you feel about turning off your social media alerts right now?"

I glance back down at my phone and refrain from clicking on the notifications even though I'm curious what they say. I suck in a sharp breath as a bead of sweat forms on my brow. Dr. Josie is right, though, like usual. I need a break for my sanity. In a few clicks, I take her advice one step further and delete Facebook from my phone. Not sure how long I would have taken to cut that cord without her prompting. I foresee hair-pulling withdrawals in my future.

* * *

When I get home, I pull my phone from my pocket to check Facebook, but the app isn't there. I'm on autopilot and addicted to social media. I jot this thought down in my notes app to pull up in my next session with Dr. Josie.

Hearing the mail truck in front of my house, I rush outside. Every day this week, I hurry out right after the mailman leaves. Peering into my mailbox, I pull out a bunch of junk mail. Another coupon for Bed, Bath & Beyond that I'll add to the overflowing drawer dedicated to them, some bills, but nothing yet from the adoption agency.

My heart sinks into my stomach as I think about what it will be like when the documents and letters finally arrive. So many thoughts circle in my head. *Will I be able to accept the past?* If there's an opportunity to meet my biological mother, *can we make up for lost time? What will she be like? Will we throw our arms around each other? Will she even be the type of person I'll want to hug?*

I swallow down the lump in my throat.

Will I be rejected again?

CHAPTER TWENTY-SIX

"Carrie's late," Stacy says, and looks at the time on her cell phone. The bartender places three mind-eraser shots on the bar.

Carrie rushes through the door, wearing a tracksuit and Nikes, which is starkly different from when we first met and she was dressed to the nines. She sees me staring at her and mouths the word "Sorry."

Hanging her bag on an empty stool next to me, she huffs and says, "It's been a hell of a day. I'm working on this new case, and I literally slept at the office last night."

"Oh, sounds like you have a juicy scoop," I say.

"I wish I could divulge information, but I'm bound by the whole client privilege thing." She pauses. "However, since someone already leaked it to the local paper that we are representing this client, I can tell you that much. It involves a school principal."

My eyes widen. "Who got caught with a mom on the theater stage?"

"Yes! That's the one."

What are the chances? "That's my daughter's school," I say.

"You've probably heard all about it then. It's a big deal for your school district," Carrie says.

"Small world," Stacy chimes in.

"Who are you representing?" I ask.

"The parents of the drama club students. Do you know any of them?"

Oh no! I sip my water, trying to disguise the shock on my face. I'm consorting with Elenore's enemy.

"I know of them," I say. "The woman who got caught is my friend, though." I drag my hand through my hair and avert my gaze from Carrie's.

"Really? Bad call on her part," Carrie says.

"She's probably going to lose everything, including her husband," Stacy says.

She's already lost him. I don't tell them they filed for divorce.

"I wonder if she's still screwing the principal," Stacy says.

I shift in my chair and roll my neck. Carrie will want to win this case. It's her job. I can feel the worry for Elenore etched on my face. *What if Elenore finds out I'm friends with Carrie?* I swipe the sweat from my brow. *Will Elenore think I'm a traitor?*

"Enough about this case," Carrie says, likely noticing my discomfort with this conversation. "Tell me something fabulous."

"I don't have anything fabulous, but I can tell you about my date last night. You're going to love this," Stacy says in her sarcastic tone. I lean in. It's been a long time since I've been privy to someone's dating life. This should be good.

I relax my shoulders, happy we've moved on to a much lighter subject.

"Yeah, so this guy, Bill, asks me to pick him up. Says his car's in the shop. Normally, I'm leery about this kind of thing, but I make sure I hide a baseball bat in my back seat, and I'm driving so I'll be in control."

"I would have done the same," I say. I'm glad I don't have to think about dating in this day and age. Some of these men are crazy.

"I pull up to his apartment complex. I'm scanning my phone when he knocks on my window, and I unlock the door. He gets in and immediately scoots down. I'm thinking that's odd. Is he hiding from someone?"

She takes a sip of her drink, and I'm wracking my brain, too, for this odd behavior.

"And he reeks of cigarette smoke. His dating profile said he was a nonsmoker."

Strike one.

"I would have asked him to get out," Carrie interjects. I have to agree with her on this one. I don't do smoking or lying.

"Oh, it gets better. The restaurant that he's chosen is a dive, but I try not to be too picky. He gets out of the car and rushes into the restaurant without waiting for me."

Strike two. I would have left.

"I should have gotten back in my car and driven away, I know. But I put on makeup for the occasion and had a shirt on that accentuated my boobs. I couldn't let all of that go to waste."

Carrie and I nod. That makes complete sense.

"When I get in, he's already at the bar, chatting with the bartender. Then he introduces me to the guys around the bar. I'm starting to panic. He must be a regular in this dingy place."

"That's creepy," Carrie says.

"The guys aren't quiet about anything, and they ask Bill if he can drive yet. Apparently, I had to pick him up not because his car is in the shop, but because he has three DUIs and his license has been revoked."

Strike three. *Buh-bye!*

Carrie shoots me a look that says, "See, I told you most guys have DUIs."

"I hope you left after that," I say.

"I wish I did, but I had ordered food and I was starving. When the check comes, he realizes he doesn't have his wallet."

"Oh my God! That's the oldest trick in the book!" I say.

"That wasn't even the worst part. He stands up to check his back pocket for his wallet, and it dawns on me why he scooted down in his seat and rushed into the bar. He couldn't be more than five feet two when his profile said six feet."

Now Carrie and I are laughing hysterically.

"I sure know how to pick 'em," Stacy says.

"Aw, it could happen to anyone," Carrie says.

"Anyway, enough about me. What's new with you, Fallon?" Stacy asks.

"I finished my business plan for my chocolate shop."

"I'll drink to that." Stacy picks up one of the shots. Carrie and I follow suit.

"That reminds me, I've been meaning to order a few boxes for clients. Can I email you an order?" Carrie asks.

"Yes. Yes, you can," I say with a wide smile.

"I want to order a box for my mom's birthday," Stacy says. "Throw in a box for me. The ones with alcohol."

For the first time in a long time, I feel supported. I forget about the Ma Spa Squad—even Elenore's case and Carrie's involvement in it, lest I give myself another panic attack—and I enjoy my new friends.

CHAPTER TWENTY-SEVEN

I turn up the volume on the car stereo, and Adam Levine sings "Sugar" to me. How appropriate as I am on my way to drop off chocolate truffles to Vivian's friend. Making a right turn, I brake for the cute old couple holding hands as they cross the street. Looks like they are perfectly speaking each other's love language. I tore through *The Five Love Languages*. It's nothing like I thought, and it is quite eye opening, like Dr. Josie said it would be. I've been doing this whole love thing all wrong. *Who knew people speak different love languages?* No wonder the divorce rate is through the roof.

I already know Max's love language is acts of service. I don't need to ask him. He likes when I make his favorite dinner or run an errand for him. My love language is quality time, yet we rarely spend any time together. *Is my marriage doomed like Beatrice's and Elenore's?* My marriage needs to be more than "fine." I must plan a date. Otherwise, before we know it, we could be headed straight to Splitsville like everyone else we know. And then I really would be all alone.

At the stop sign, I quickly text Max, saying we should go on a date tonight. His sister already said Maya could stay longer. Maya loves Maeve and Sarah and couldn't wait to visit today while I ran errands and delivered chocolate. I don't know when Max will see my text since he is at the driving range with a buddy, and he rarely looks at his phone.

I pull up to the address, realizing it's the same model house as mine. The subdivision has five to choose from. I liked this one with the porch with balusters. I had intended to relax on our front porch rocking chairs, but I never seem to make the time. The planters on either side of their front door are filled with gorgeous fuchsia begonias.

The door swings open as I approach, and a girl younger than Maya runs out screaming as a taller boy chases her with a squirt gun. A woman is screaming, "Don't get Cassie wet before the party!"

I step aside to let them by before they knock me or my chocolates down. I don't need a repeat of the bachelorette party Dirty Harry scene. My shoulders tense thinking about it.

"I'm sorry. It's a bit nuts here this morning," the woman says to me. "I'm Lisa. You must be delivering the chocolates." She eyes the box in my hand.

"Yes. Nice to meet you."

"Come in and I'll pay you. Right after I find my checkbook."

Noticing Lisa's bare feet, I enter the foyer and slide off my flats. Lisa smooths down her shirt that looks like it had been crumpled in a drawer. The two kids make their way back into the house and are now batting balloons at each other. They swat one at Lisa as she passes.

"Cassie and Micah, can you please stop before you pop the balloons? You can play with them during the party." Lisa sighs as I follow her.

The frenetic energy in the house is fraying my nerves. Hopefully, she finds her checkbook soon. I roll my neck and glance around. Either Lisa is an interior decorator or she hired one, because her home looks like it could grace the pages of *House Beautiful* magazine with colorful wall murals, oriental carpets, and elegant decor. It's a stark difference from my minimalistic style. The less I have in my house, the less I have to dust.

I set down the chocolates on the kitchen island, next to the cupcakes, as Lisa pulls her checkbook from her purse. "Found it," she says.

"Planning a party is always so stressful—at least for me anyway," I say over the loud, thumping music the kids have asked Google to play.

"Hey, Google, stop!" Lisa yells. With the silence, she says, "Now I can hear myself think." She runs her hand across her forehead. "I feel like a chicken with my head cut off. I haven't even showered yet, and guests will be arriving in less than an hour." Shaking her head, she hands me the check.

"Thank you. I hope your party goes well," I say, and smile. I let myself out, happy my chocolates are safely in Lisa's house, to be enjoyed and not strewn all over the floor.

A series of dings ring out from my cell. Before I drive away, I pull my phone from my tote, expecting to see a text from Max. But there are several from Elenore. *Did she find out about Carrie representing the drama club parents? Or worse, that I'm friends with Carrie?* My chest tightens.

As I look closer at my phone, I realize it's not that, but just as bad. Staring up at me are screenshots of the photo meant for Max's eyes only and the words, "My friends in Shitshire are jerks." I close my eyes. This can't be happening.

Forcing my eyes open, I read Elenore's texts. From what I can gather from her choppy rambling, with some words in all caps and several exclamations points, someone posted the screenshots to a community Facebook page. Lyla saw them and is spreading rumors I'm on the app to have an affair, which doesn't even make sense since it's a friendship app. Lyla also says that I said some nasty things about the women in Springshire. Elenore got all this information from her neighbor because Lyla isn't talking to her.

On the upside, the woman who posted the screenshots was meaning to give me props for being real. Little does she know it severely backfired. Once Lyla saw the post, she got on the phone immediately to broadcast it.

I quickly text Elenore back.

ME: *Mel created that profile as a joke, and it was accidentally published.*

This is exactly what I feared. My nose stings as I hold back tears. This is all getting to be too much to handle. My friend group ghosts me, then starts rumors about me. My work to win them back has been for naught. I'm about to lose it. I take one deep, calming breath like Dr. Josie advised me to do when I'm feeling anxious. *What am I going to do now? Tell the organizer of the Facebook group to remove the post?* I'm not sure damage control will work.

Stealing a phrase from Mel, I say, "Now I'm really up shit's creek."

CHAPTER TWENTY-EIGHT

I swallow down a mouthful of red wine as Sinatra sings "My Way" through the restaurant speakers. Quickly scanning my surroundings, I notice Antonio's hasn't changed in the ten years we've been coming here. Black-and-white photos of the family in Italy and America line the wall. This pizza parlor epitomizes the American dream, because everyone knows pizza is more popular in America than Italy.

My train of thought moves full steam ahead from the popularity of pizza to a self-help diet book that claims pizza causes weight gain. While reading the book, at the mere mention of pizza, I closed the book and ordered one. To my credit, I chose veggie toppings.

As I breathe in the scent of oregano and basil, my mouth salivates. Then I spy their award-winning cannoli being served to the next table, and my taste buds go bonkers.

Max is dressed in jeans and a soft red T-shirt that matches the signature red-and-white-checkered tablecloth. He's still the sexy man I met all those years ago, but there's an undeniable confidence in him now that makes him even sexier. With his black and gray-speckled hair, his warm cinnamon-hued eyes, and kind demeanor, he has an air of distinction about him. And he's not only a sought-after medical professional but a good husband and father. Water edges to my eyes as I think about how lucky I am to have him and how terribly heartbreaking it would be to lose him.

Before tears can escape, I rip off a piece of my garlic bread and pop it into my mouth, allowing it to melt, savoring the taste before swallowing. This helps calm my nerves, affected by my thoughts of my marriage not being as "fine" as I described it to Dr. Josie, and also by being preoccupied with Lyla's rumors about me. The thoughts swirl in my head like the pizza dough the chef is throwing and twirling in the air behind the counter.

"What's wrong?" Max asks. He can often read me like a book.

Instead of addressing the fact that we haven't been on a date in months, I tell him that Lyla is spreading rumors I'm on a friendship app to have an affair. The silence between us is palpable, and I avert my eyes to the couple sitting three feet from us, googly eyeing each other and playing footsie under the table. Those days are long gone for us.

I think back to falling in love with Max. I'm not much of a romantic, but sometimes I feel the love for him so deeply in my soul. It's in the quiet times—when I'm stirring chocolate. That's when my soul stirs too. Mostly my words drip with sarcasm, but if one listens closely to the pause, that's where my true feelings breathe. Always in the pause. And it was in the pause of our moments together where I fell in love with Max.

It wasn't one moment, but a series of silent moments. His lips to my brow. The hair he tucked behind my ear. The brush of his hand against my arm. His jacket around my shoulders. The smell of his cologne lingering on my T-shirt. His fingertips tangled in my hair. The rose left on my pillow. A heart drawn in the fogged mirror. The love letter placed between the pages of my favorite book. These were all the moments of pause. Every single one of them strung together like paper hearts caused my own heart to flutter deeper in love. Remembering all the pauses pushed me through the difficult times.

Swallowing down the last bite of my bread, I turn my attention back to Max. His shirt is on backwards, but I don't tell him because his smile is also upside down. I'm good at reading signs. For someone who seems so put together, he falls short on the details of dressing. I often see deodorant marks across the bottoms of his shirts and toothpaste on his collar. I don't mind it because it reminds me he's human.

"I'd like you to delete your profile," Max finally says to me.

I already met Carrie and Stacy through the friendship app, and I really don't need to meet others, but the fact that Max is telling me to take my profile down irks me. I get to decide when to take it down. Not him. He's not the boss of me. I've now reverted to ten-year-old me.

"My profile clearly states I'm looking for friends . . . female friends. It's a friend app."

"I know, but it seems a little, I don't know, desperate."

I lurch back in my seat. *Desperate?* That's not how I'd describe it. More like convenient. "It's my life." I run my fingers through my hair. "Wait, don't you trust me?"

Heat rises to my face as I realize we are supposed to be rekindling the romance in our marriage, and here we are staring each other down and not undressing each other with our eyes.

"It's not about trust, it's about being above reproach," he says as he takes a sip of his Lambrusco.

"Oh, so this is about keeping up appearances," I say, waving my hand in the air.

Max reaches for my hand, probably to stop me from making a scene rather than being endearing. "Wouldn't it be better if you got involved in some local organizations and met friends that way?"

Sitting back in the booth, I acknowledge it's a fine point, but I don't have the time to volunteer right now. It's easier to screen people online, but I don't tell him that.

The waiter places the pizza with fresh mushrooms, black olives, and green peppers in the center of our table. At least we always agree on the toppings. That's a win for us, but the garlic bread sits heavy in my stomach, and I've suddenly lost my appetite.

Max knows I'll take the profile down, and I know I will too, but he lets me have my moment of control. This is what we worked through in couples counseling. We butt heads for control. Instead of shouting now for the things we want, we have real adult conversations.

Excusing myself, I take my phone into the bathroom. This time I don't take a photo of my cleavage to send to him. Instead, I turn off alerts for the Fireworks Friends app. I'll delete it when I'm good and ready to.

CHAPTER TWENTY-NINE

Breathing in the fresh linen scent of Max's polo shirt, I fold into his arms. He's heading to the airport soon for a medical conference, and I don't want last night's tiff to be the turbulence that follows him onto the flight.

"I'm sorry about last night," he says. "I do trust you, and I want you to be happy."

"Thank you," I say.

Max squeezes me tighter. "I have to go, but I hope you have a good visit with Avery while I'm gone."

I could use a good friend right now. I'm excited Avery rescheduled her flight and feels up to traveling. I insisted she not come with her recent injury, but she wouldn't hear of it. She said she could use a break other than her leg. The least I could do was pick her up from the airport, but she declined, saying she would hire a car.

After Max leaves, I go through the house, picking up socks, shoes, books, and whatever else Maya's left lying around.

* * *

"You're here," I say through my car window, surprised to see Avery sitting on our porch rocking chair. "I'm sorry I'm late. It was crazy this morning."

"No worries. I'd come down to hug you, but . . ." Avery glances down at the cast on her leg.

"Oh, don't even think about it," I say as I park the car in the driveway.

I climb the three porch steps and bend down to hug her. "It's so great to see you!"

"You too!" Avery says as she pulls me tighter.

Releasing my hold on her, I sidestep to steer clear of her cast.

"Let's go in." I hold the door open for her as she hobbles into the house. "Here, I'll take your luggage upstairs."

"Thank you. I'm not used to being waited on."

"I know you would do it for me too. When do you get the cast off?"

"Not soon enough," she says. "Two weeks."

"Well, you're sure stronger than me. I don't think I would have gotten on a plane like that."

"It wasn't so bad. I was tired of sitting around the house. When I heard Max was going out of town, I thought you and I could use some time together."

"That's so sweet of you. I've missed you."

"I've missed you too. Besides, they sat me in the first row, with plenty of leg room, and there was eye candy."

"I hope you got eye candy's number."

"He was impressed with me getting on a plane with a cast. It was an easy conversation starter. We ended up exchanging cards for 'business purposes.'" She waggles her eyebrows.

"Oh, is that how it is these days?"

I prop some pillows up on the couch and hand her the remote control for the TV.

"I saved the latest *Dude and Dudettes* episode. I thought we could watch it together."

"Oh my God—this is going to be so much fun. Kind of like watching *The Real World* in college."

I drag her oversize luggage up the stairs and massage my back at the landing. I have no idea what she's packed in there, but I am certain she paid the overweight fee to the airlines. It's a good thing she sent the ten-pound hair package ahead of time.

As Avery catches up on emails on her cell, I make us some extra buttery popcorn. It's always been our go-to treat. It was one of the few snacks we could afford in bulk back in college. Now whenever we see each other, we can't go a day without eating it. I press "Play" where Avery has cued up the episode.

"So, what's new?" I say, stuffing my mouth with a handful of popcorn.

"Nothing too exciting. I swore off dating for a while."

"Oh, do tell."

"Well, I keep meeting Mr. Wrong. Kind of like Jerk Craig." She points to the TV.

"He is cute, though." It's as if the guy on the show hears me, because he looks straight into the camera, flashes his pearly whites, and winks.

"The cuter they are, the jerkier," she says.

"Hmm . . . could be a flawed dating app you're using."

"Or the pool of eligible bachelors is dwindling."

"My friend Carrie says dating has been difficult too, but she's recently found someone."

"That's encouraging. As we get older, it becomes harder. It's like which baggage are you willing to deal with?"

"God bless any guy who is willing to carry your baggage. What did you pack—your whole closet?"

Avery throws popcorn at me. "Oh look, you brought jokes."

"Always."

"I've really missed you," she says again, and places her arm around me. Warmth spreads through me. Being here with her feels like acceptance wrapped up in a bow. Avery's friendship has never wavered once over all these years. It's truly a gift.

We watch the show with lots of snorting, eye rolls, and snarky comments. Avery is my life jacket. She's the friend I'll always turn to when my life spirals out of control into the deepest waters of my soul.

* * *

I click off the TV. "Ride with me. I have to pick up Maya. She's going to be so excited to see you."

I avoid construction this time. I mapped out a different route to school.

"Are you still enjoying your job?" I ask as I turn the volume down on the car stereo.

"Yes. I am. It's crazy to think how our lives have turned out over the past twenty years."

Avery easily climbed the ladder in information security, which is mostly dominated by men. She has a great career, though demanding. She claims to be overworked but always says, "What else am I going to do with my time?"

"You're happy though. Aren't you?"

"Yes. It's not a *bad* life," she says, as if she is trying to convince herself.

My phone rings. It's Max. I answer it through the car's Bluetooth. After a quick exchange, he tells me his flight is delayed and he'll call me later.

Avery turns to me. "You hit the jackpot with Max."

"It hasn't always been good," I say. She's the only one I've ever admitted that to.

"I get it, Fallon. Relationships are tough work, but you seem to have weathered the storms quite well."

"I guess we have. If you had said that two years ago, though, I probably wouldn't have agreed with you." My "oh-so-perfect" marriage spiraled downward with the stress of trying to be the perfect mother and trying for another baby.

"You would have punched me."

"You're probably right." I laugh.

The first chords of "Achy Breaky Heart" play through the car speakers. I quickly change the channel.

"That song still gets under your skin?"

"Always."

Avery and I were assigned as roommates freshman year and continued to live together all through college. We attempted to join the same sorority sophomore year. She was more social than I was, and asked me to join with her. The sorority made us plan a country music swing dance party, and I was in charge of the music. Something went wrong with my mix tape, and it got stuck on replaying "Achy Breaky Heart" endlessly. Afterward, random frat boys would sing the song to me when I passed them on campus. I was so embarrassed and swore I would never willingly plan a party again, and I hadn't . . . until the Mexican Fiesta, and look how that had turned out.

CHAPTER THIRTY

I pull the ingredients for dinner out of the fridge.

"I have something for you, Maya Jambalaya," Avery says as she leans down to Maya.

"Yay!" Maya exclaims.

Avery digs in her purse and hands Maya a bag of her favorite gummy candy and a windup dancing robot.

"Thank you!" Maya throws her arms around Avery.

"Maya, you can have some of that candy after dinner," I say.

"No fair," Maya huffs. "How did you hurt your leg, Auntie Avery?"

"I'm clumsy. Fell down a few steps . . . it's no big deal, really."

"Maya, why don't you pick out a book to read to Avery."

"Okay, Mama."

I turn to Avery. "Fell down the stairs?"

She whispers, "I didn't want to scare Maya with the car story. Plus, it's embarrassing. I ended up with rotten banana peels in my hair and dog shi—" She looks over my shoulder to see if Maya is within earshot. "Poop smeared all over me. That was more traumatic than actually breaking my leg."

"Did you say *poop*?" Maya calls out from across the room. She would pick that word out from a mile away.

I stifle a laugh. "It sounds like a scene in a cartoon."

"See, even you think it's funny."

* * *

After tucking Maya into bed, Avery and I settle into the couch with our glasses of wine and some of my freshly made chocolates.

"This wine is fabulous," Avery says.

"Twenty years ago, this would have been cheap beer, and we'd be standing in a dank, sticky-floored basement shouting at each other over a thumping speaker while dumb frat boys humped our legs," I say.

"You're not kidding." She swirls the wine in her glass. "Do you ever think about those days?"

"Sometimes." College wasn't all that bad, given I met Max and Avery. Super social Avery met a ton of people. I wonder if it was all fun and games for her and if any of those friendships lasted. "Do you talk to anyone from college?"

She doesn't answer right away. She pops a chocolate in her mouth and groans. "These are amazing . . . I go back for homecoming."

I haven't attended one reunion or homecoming in the almost twenty years since graduation. "How many people do you know who still go to them?"

I think she's going to say five, but then she surprises me when she says twenty.

"Really? I didn't think homecoming was that popular."

"I don't know if it's about homecoming. It's more about catching up and bonding. We had a lot of great times at school. Don't you think?"

"Yeah, I guess." I have some good memories. "How come you never told me?"

"I didn't think it mattered to you. You've never seemed interested in going."

"I would have, had I known how important it was to you."

I hadn't warmed up to anyone in college except Avery and Max. I was going through a hard time back then. I probably wouldn't remember any of the people Avery knows anyway.

"But it has to be important to you," she says, and sips her drink. "Besides, I know you have a big group of neighbor friends who you hang out with, so I assumed you were focusing on bonding with them."

As I pour her more wine, I remind her about my terrible party and how I have fallen out of graces with the neighborhood women.

"Don't take this the wrong way, but you've changed since college," Avery says.

"Of course I have. I'm wiser."

"That you are. That's not what I mean. Back then, you would have ripped them a new one."

She knows the old me so well. The one I left behind when I became an adult. "You're right. I would have."

"So, why aren't you speaking up for yourself now? You didn't used to put up with drama like this."

I sip my wine and think about what she said. I know one of the times she's referring to is when I quit pledging for the sorority and gave them a piece of my mind. I told them that

I didn't need to buy friends or take their bullshit after they tried to make us do the polar bear plunge in our underwear. There was no way I was going in the frigid water, especially not in my bra and panties.

And the time the girls across the hall from us freshman year, who we hung out with, blasted their music for three hours straight in the middle of the night. I walked into their room, switched off their music, and told them if I heard one more of their crappy country songs, I was going to throw their boom box out the window. They never talked to me again, and I didn't care.

For the most part, I was laid back, but if I was pushed, I'd fight back. I know Avery thinks I've lost this fight in me. She's not wrong. I've mellowed out in suburbia.

"These are my neighbors. I can't go around telling them off like I used to."

"Listen, I'm not saying you should tell them off, but don't lose the person you are deep down in all of this. The person who stands up for herself." She points at my heart. Then puts her hand on my shoulder. "You should at least have a conversation with Beatrice and tell her exactly how you feel. Why did you really plan the party? To win your friends back?"

Initially, it was to win them back, but I know in my heart it was more than that.

"It was supposed to be about spending time with those I love—to make new memories together. To show them how much they mean to me. That I don't want to lose them." I lower my eyes to my hands.

"I thought so. You're a good friend, Fallon. You have a big heart. Being a good friend and having good friends are intricately connected, and you deserve good friends."

I look up and meet her eyes. "Just like you," I say.

"Let's not get too crazy. No one is like me," Avery says, throwing me a side-eye.

"You're right. You're simply the best," I say, and that is no lie.

*　　*　　*

We spend most of the weekend inside, playing games, putting together puzzles, and baking—cookies, brownies, and cake. Avery's sweet tooth drives us to make more than we could ever eat. I end up freezing most of it. Max will enjoy it when he gets back. In fact, he'll probably suggest Avery come visit more often just so he can have more dessert at his fingertips. Avery made two big batches of her mama's famous Jambalaya, and now I can't button my pants. Sometimes you don't have to try too hard to make memories.

*　　*　　*

"Do you have to leave?" Maya asks Avery when the town car arrives.

"I'm sorry, Maya Jambalaya. I promise I'll be back to visit soon. Once I get this cast off, we can go roller skating."

"Yay!" Maya exclaims, and I raise my eyebrows. Avery isn't one to shy away from sports that could hurt her.

I hug her. "So good to see you. Have a safe flight home."

"I will, and thank you for being such a gracious hostess."

"Anytime. I packed some cookies for you in your bag. Enjoy."

She waves to us from the car. The car turns out of sight, and Maya collapses into my arms, sobbing. I hold her tight.

It's always hard to say goodbye. Good thing I had anticipated this meltdown.

"So, I have a surprise for you," I say.

Maya pulls away from me, wipes her tears, and looks up at me with her huge, watery blue eyes.

"I invited Penelope over for a sleepover."

"Oh, Mommy. Thank you. Thank you. Thank you." She jumps up and down, and I may have just won Mother of the Year. And I could pat myself on the back, because tonight is Cecilia's birthday party, and I've managed to help Maya forget all about not being invited.

CHAPTER THIRTY-ONE

"I love what you've done with the place." Elenore walks around my living room. I invited her to stay for a glass of wine when she came to drop off Penelope, who immediately followed Maya to her playroom.

"Oh, thanks." I haven't done anything but clean up a little. I realize the last time she was here was outside for the Mexican Fiesta. I want to apologize for the flying cactus that punctured her leg, but I don't want to bring up the party if I don't have to.

"Please sit." I point to a kitchen stool. "Red or white?" I retrieve two wine glasses from the cabinet.

"Whatever you have is great. Any wine will take the edge off. I was up late reading through a bunch of legal papers."

I open the fridge and pull out a bottle of pinot grigio.

"How's it going?"

"Not well," she says, and tugs at her earlobe.

Is she talking about divorce proceedings or the suing moms? What a mess.

"Hasn't the drama club director come forward to say he was the one who saw you, not the kids?"

"That's the thing. He doesn't know. We shocked him, and he can't remember the sequence of events."

"I take it there were no cameras." A camera proving no kids witnessed her screwing the principal would be great evidence, but then again bad because she would be caught on video with her pants down. She couldn't win without further embarrassment.

She shakes her head. I give her a healthy pour before handing her the glass.

"Thank you."

"You're welcome," I say, filling my glass.

"I wish there was a way to prove that the kids didn't see me. No one is asking what the kids saw for fear of bringing up the traumatic experience again."

I breathe in the wine's aroma of peach and apricot before taking a sip.

"Maybe there is a way. I know the lawyer who's representing the kids' parents," I say casually as the oven beeps.

"You do?" Elenore sets her wine down.

"Uh-huh." Instead of meeting her eyes, I slip on oven mitts and open the oven door, glad for a reason to hide the guilt that's probably written all over my face. Heat spills out of the oven, and the strong scent of bacon fills the air. Elenore sits in silence as I place the cookie sheet with bacon-wrapped dates on the stovetop.

Turning my attention back to Elenore, she looks as if she sucked on a lemon, with pursed lips and narrowed eyes. Perhaps I should have offered her a lemon drop shot before dropping that bomb on her.

Before she can admonish me for fraternizing with the enemy, I say, "I met her on the friendship app. Anyway, I can talk to her and see if I can convince her that no children saw you on the stage." I move some bacon-wrapped dates to a plate.

Elenore leans forward. "You would do that for me?"

"Of course I would," I say, and place the plate in front of her.

She relaxes back into her chair with a heavy exhale. "That means a lot to me, Fallon. Everything is so overwhelming right now."

Between bites of the bacon dates, she tells me how Jeff will be representing himself in the divorce and how she's worried about him getting everything. Even with the evidence she's gathered of his cheating—phone and computer records—she doesn't think proving it will help her case. We live in a no-fault state. In the eyes of the court, it doesn't matter what happened to get them to this point. But Elenore wants to be prepared if Jeff starts a smear campaign against her. She's trying to be civil with him, but he's flipped a switch and become a monster. Elenore doesn't even recognize him anymore.

She's devoured the appetizer, so I pass her some chocolates. Her eyes light up, and I'm happy to offer her a little pick-me-up. She's going through so much, and I know how draining it's been on her.

"Chocolate is the remedy for everything," she says.

"That's what my Grandma Rose always said too." I pop a chocolate into my mouth, allowing it to melt on my tongue, savoring all its gooey goodness.

"Wise woman . . . gosh, I'm so sorry. I've been going on and on. How's the chocolate business?"

I tell her I'm working hard on my recipes. There's no need to toot my own horn on rehashing the award I won in New York, which I'm sure she saw on Mel's Facebook page. It's hard for me to share my wins while Elenore's life is in shambles.

"You've been busy. You know . . . the mom group, especially Beatrice, said you couldn't be bothered with anything that deterred you from your chocolate. I heard her make a few snide remarks at some of the kids' birthday parties where you gave your chocolates away for free. I was shocked."

I clench my fists.

"I was going to tell you, but then I found out Jeff was cheating and . . ."

Her words trail off, and I know she was going to mention the principal again but is tired of saying it.

She goes on. "Anyway, if you want my honest opinion, they're jealous. Jealous that you found something you enjoy and you're on the brink of success. I mean, look at these." She waves her hand over my chocolates.

"You think so?" I stare at her like she's a chalkboard with a complex math problem written on it.

Mel had surmised the same thing about the situation, and this had crossed my mind too. There's nothing to be jealous of. What I choose to do with my time shouldn't concern them, and it doesn't take away from how I feel about them. *Why should it make them change their minds about me and our friendship?*

"Most definitely. Some people can't handle other people's success."

Elenore's phone chimes, and she removes it from her purse to check it. She raises her eyebrows. "Seriously, this is getting out of hand. Did you know about this?"

She turns her phone to me. Photos of Cecilia and some other girls are plastered on Beatrice's Facebook page with the caption, "Happy Birthday to our darling Cecilia!"

I drag my fingers through my hair. "I did know about it. Maya wasn't invited."

"Penelope wasn't either. The nerve!"

They must have heard their names because Maya and Penelope come running into the kitchen, all smiles. "Mommy, can we have ice cream?"

"Sure can! With sprinkles?"

In unison, they scream, "Yes!"

Elenore mouths, "Thank you" to me, with misty eyes.

Several minutes later, as the girls enjoy their bowls of ice cream piled high with sprinkles, Elenore snaps some photos. Then she uploads them to her Facebook page with the caption "#BFFs."

Elenore's look of satisfaction fades into a frown as she stares at her phone. I wonder what Beatrice posted now.

"Fallon, did you deliver chocolates to Lisa Greggs?"

"Oh yeah. Vivian referred her to me."

She thrusts the phone at me.

Micah's birthday party went swimmingly, except for the chocolates that were delivered and placed in the hot sun by . . . oh I can't remember her name, but she's the one who started that chocolate side biz. It looks like my dog left a surprise on my table. What do you think?

In her photo, my chocolates look like diarrhea. *Gross. I didn't place them in her backyard, did I?* I wrack my brain, and I remember now.

"I put them in her kitchen, not outside." Heat rushes up my neck to my face. *Please don't have a panic attack. Not now.*

"This is horrible. At least she doesn't remember my name, but how many women are starting side chocolate businesses?"

"Read the first comment."

It was Fallon Monroe.

"Ugh. Leave it to Lyla to clarify."

Is anyone ever going to enjoy my chocolates without some sort of snafu? This is getting out of hand, and all signs point to me throwing in the towel on my dream.

"I'm sorry, Fallon. It is terrible to be accused of something you didn't do."

Elenore knows this firsthand. I bite my lip and give her phone back.

Elenore pushes back her stool. "I wish I could stay, but I have to meet with my lawyer. Are you going to be okay?"

I'm sure she doesn't want to leave Penelope here with a distraught woman, so I force a smile. "I'm fine."

"Okay, well, if you need anything, let me know. And thank you again for having Penelope over."

Elenore kisses Penelope, reminds her to show good manners, and takes three bacon wrapped dates and two chocolates in a napkin for the road.

I walk her to the door, and she gives me a hug.

"We should do this again. My place next time."

She gets two steps out my door and stops dead in her tracks. I follow her gaze. Her windshield is dripping with cracked eggs.

CHAPTER THIRTY-TWO

As I wait for Carrie and Stacy for our weekly ladies' night, I stand outside the bar and call Lisa Greggs. It's time for damage control.

She answers on the first ring, not giving me any time to back out. She's out of breath and irritated. *Is this woman ever not frazzled?*

"Lisa, it's Fallon Monroe. Is this a good time?"

"Fallon with the chocolates?" she asks, and huffs into the phone. A door slams in the background.

"Yes. I wanted to follow up to see if you liked the chocolates." Of course, I already know they ended up being a melted mess, but I play it cool.

"You put them in the hot sun, and no one got to taste them."

"I'm sorry that happened, but I placed them on your kitchen counter next to the cupcakes."

"Listen, I'm late for an appointment, and I don't have time for this."

The phone clicks. Silence. I look at my screen. I can't believe she just hung up on me. I head into the bar and order a stiff drink.

*   *   *

"You okay? You look like someone peed in your drink."

I look up from my glass at Carrie. Her eyes are brimming with sincerity. I don't tell her about my chocolate fail. Instead, I think of Elenore and my goal to talk to Carrie tonight about getting the charges dropped against her.

"Just lost in thought. I wanted to get your opinion on the situation with Elenore."

"Oh, okay. The woman my clients are suing, I assume?" Carrie slips onto the barstool next to me.

"That would be the one. Someone egged her car in front of my house," I say as Carrie orders a Tito's vodka and club soda with lime.

"Do you have a camera facing the street?" Carrie asks.

I shake my head. I wish I did now, but there isn't a need for one in our neighborhood unless we are tracking coyotes.

"Bummer." The unsympathetic vibes radiate off her.

"She thinks it was one of your clients."

She shrugs. "No proof."

Spoken like a true lawyer. I dismiss her comment because I need her on my side for what I'm about to say.

"Anyway, I want to tell you something so you don't waste a ton of time going down the wrong avenue."

Carrie sits up straight and raises her eyebrows. "Do tell."

I wait for the bartender to deliver her drink and leave, before saying, "Elenore's lawyer plans to request the kids be evaluated by a psychologist to prove they didn't see what everyone says they saw." I have no idea if this is true, but Elenore deserves a fair trial.

"Are they claiming the kids didn't see them . . . in flagrante?" Carrie swirls the straw in her drink.

"That's exactly what I'm saying."

"Interesting," she says with an expression that screams, *Doubt it.*"

"Sorry, I'm late." Stacy pulls up a stool next to us. "What did I miss? You look deep in conversation."

"Oh, nothing important," I say, and order another drink.

"I can't stay long," Carrie says. "I'm meeting Craig later."

"Craig?"

"The osteopath I told you about. I'm still seeing him."

"What's an osteopath, by the way?"

"You know, a chiropractor." She suddenly has a questioning look, takes out her phone, and taps at it. After a beat of research, she declares, "I guess they're not exactly the same. An osteopath has a medical degree." She looks up. "I thought 'osteopath' sounded better."

My mouth suddenly feels like it's full of cotton as I take in this new, possibly damaging information. *Her boyfriend Craig is a chiropractor . . .*

"What's his last name?" I reach for my drink. My hand shakes. Carrie never told me his name, and I never asked. It can't be Beatrice's Craig. *Can it?* We live in a small town that is feeling slightly smaller and more constricting by the minute. I pull at the collar of my shirt. Chiropractors are a dime a dozen, even in this small town. They're like dentists—one in every strip mall. I don't even know how they all stay in business. Surely there are lots of chiropractors named Craig.

She tilts her head. "Stone."

My stomach tightens like I've been sucker punched. I squeeze my eyes shut. Now Carrie has ties to Elenore *and* Beatrice. *Am I in the* Twilight Zone? Because somehow that makes better sense to me.

"Why? You know him?" Carrie asks.

"Yes. I know him. Our kids go to school together. I also know Beatrice."

"So, you know he's going through a divorce, then?" she asks.

Is she fishing for information?

"Yes." I remember when Vivian broke the news to me at the coffee shop and how much it saddened me.

It's a good thing I never mentioned Beatrice's name when recounting my friendship woes to Carrie, only referring to the much more vague "Bea." Around here, you never know who knows who. Now, I don't want her to know Beatrice was my best friend. I don't want her asking me about their relationship or anything about her. Even though Beatrice and I are on the outs, there is a part of me that doesn't want to hurt her further. I hope I don't come up in Carrie's conversations with Craig. Then another thought strikes:

Is Carrie the reason for Craig and Beatrice's divorce?

* * *

I toss and turn all night. Carrie's admission about dating Craig unnerves me, and the reality of Beatrice's divorce sinks in deeper. Craig and Beatrice were meant to be together. They met in college, like Max and me. I've heard the story a million times, Beatrice recounted it so often. I feel like I was there. I wish I had been. Their meeting was almost as good as Max running over my foot with his skateboard. It also had to do with feet. I liked feet-meeting stories. Well, shoe stories in particular.

Craig had gotten so sick at a party that he'd puked on her brand new, never before worn white Filas that she had saved for months to buy. I didn't comment on her wearing white shoes to a frat party, even though I questioned her judgment. As Craig was doubled over, she stomped on his foot for ruining her shoes. If he was there when she told the story, he'd interject, "Nothing like kicking a guy when he's down."

Over the next few weeks, Craig did everything he could to track down this mysterious woman. During that time, Beatrice scrubbed and scrubbed, but couldn't get the spots of lime green out of her Fila's. She said she cried for days. Once Craig found her and realized how upset she was, he bought her a new pair. The rest is history. I had fallen for Beatrice too. Any woman who would cry over a pair of shoes was my people.

Now he was screwing Carrie in her Christian Louboutins. I push the thought from my mind. I hope Carrie dumps him, but that seems unlikely. She gushed over Craig when she first told me about him. She admitted it's difficult to find men without multiple DUIs and how she'd had to lower her standards.

"Are you okay?" Max wraps his arms around me as I brush my teeth in the morning. "You were thrashing around last night like you were swimming your way out of a tidal wave."

Funny, that's exactly how I feel. When I came to bed last night, he was snoring lightly. I kissed him on the forehead, and he stirred a little.

"Uh-huh," I say with a mouth full of toothpaste. I don't want to get into this now. I need to think through what I want to do. I'm not sure if Max can offer any solid advice.

Men view situations like this differently. If I had to guess, he will probably tell me to butt out of it like he did about Elenore's fiasco with the principal. But I don't know how I can ignore this.

I think back to my social media page where I posted a photo of Carrie and me. *Is this what Beatrice was referring to at school music practice when she said to enjoy my new #BFF?*

I have to talk to Beatrice to tell her I had no idea Carrie and Craig were together. But I met Carrie *after* Beatrice started ghosting me, so I know Carrie is just another reason for Beatrice to despise me.

"You don't look all right," Max says as he stares at me in the mirror and runs his toothbrush under a stream of water.

I smooth orange-scented moisturizer over my face. The cream seeps into my pores, tingles on my cheeks, and relaxes my tense expression.

I sigh and realize I don't want to get into the whole thing. I decide to tell him about the other bothersome issue on my mind. "A customer complained about my chocolates on Facebook. When I tried to talk to her, she hung up on me."

Max sets his toothbrush down and turns to give me his full attention. "I'm sorry. What can I do?"

"There's nothing you can do. I'm a big old failure." I grab the hairbrush and drag it hard through my tangles. "I don't think I can keep doing this."

"Starting a business isn't easy." He pulls me into a hug. "You've come so far."

The floodgates open as tears pour out of me. The rejections keep piling up. My heart is heavy in my chest, and I realize this is what having a crushed dream feels like—an anchor tied to my legs, pulling my head under water.

CHAPTER THIRTY-THREE

"Maya, are you excited for your last day of school?"

I know I am. It means I don't have to wear my dark sunglasses and hat pulled low while rushing in and out of school drop-off and pickup. Maybe this summer I can grow a backbone.

"Yes, Mommy. It's sports day! It's going to be so fun."

"That is fun, Maya. And tonight is your concert. Are you ready?"

"Roar!" Maya mimics tiger claws with her hands. "You got my tiger makeup, right Mommy?"

"Sure did, sweetie."

After Max is at work and Maya is at school, I practice my speech in the mirror at least ten times before I have the nerve to ring Beatrice. I inhale deeply as I dial her number. My heart pounds. It rings once, and I hear, "This is Beatrice . . ." *Ugh.* I pull the phone away from my ear. She sent me straight to voicemail.

I put the phone back up to my ear and listen to the rest of her greeting. I debate hanging up, but I know how important this is. As it beeps, I clear my throat and put on my best friendly voice. "Hi Beatrice, it's me, Fallon. I'm calling because I want to say how sorry I am about you and Craig. I had no idea what you were going through. If I had known, I would have called you sooner. There are other things you should know. Maybe we can meet for lunch. Please call me."

After I hang up, I stare at my phone, willing it to ring back. I had hoped if I dangled a carrot in front of her, she might take the bait and meet with me. If she knows about Carrie, I want her to know I had no idea Carrie was dating Craig. One conversation could smooth everything over, if only she would just talk to me.

* * *

I check my phone one hundred times throughout the day. Beatrice doesn't even care what information I have for her. Fine. I'll see her at the second-grade concert tonight. She ended up bowing out of volunteering after the first day of practice. The kids are as ready as they are going to be, considering my lack of singing skills. I had gotten the music teacher to help me a few times.

In the school auditorium, I reserved two front-row seats for Max and me. The benefit of volunteering meant I could go in early.

Now, I stare at the stage. The same stage Elenore and Mr. Lox got busy on. I stifle a laugh. *Am I ever going to be able to look at the stage in the same light again?* Most likely not.

The seats fill in, and soon the auditorium is packed with parents and siblings. The front row on the other side of the aisle is occupied by Beatrice, Lyla, Vivian, and their families. Elenore waves to me from the back, and it makes me feel guilty for not thinking to save her a seat.

The assistant principal says a few words to get the concert underway. *When will he officially replace Mr. Lox?* There is no way Mr. Lox can work here anymore. It's a shame, too, because he's a great principal. He participated in every school event, including the dunk tank at the school fun fair. He won first place in the teacher and administrator pie-eating contest, which made me wonder if that's what attracted Elenore. *Ugh* . . . I have to stop with these thoughts. In all honesty, I'm going to miss Mr. Lox. I'm sure a lot of the parents feel the same way. If he could have just kept it in his pants on school property.

The kids in my group sway on stage, tiger makeup on their faces, and begin singing "Roar." They don't look or sound half bad. Max videos it while I hold back tears. Seeing Maya on stage almost always makes me cry. My little baby girl is growing up. The hour-long concert flies by. I file out of the row and almost run right into someone.

"Fallon!"

I look up. My eyes widen. *Oh no!*

"Carrie," I say. "What are you doing here?" I can't be seen with her, with Beatrice so close. *Is she here with Craig? Would Craig be that insensitive to bring her here?*

"Oh, I was invited by the moms of the kids from the lawsuit," she whispers.

I take a deep breath. *Good.* Craig didn't invite her.

"Gives me a chance to scope out the stage. You know, research."

I want to talk to her more for Elenore's sake. I want to give her a tour of the stage, so she can see that the kids could not have seen Mr. Lox and Elenore from here, but I need to get away from Carrie as fast as I can. If Beatrice sees me talking to her and she knows Craig is seeing her, I'll make an already bad situation worse. Max extends his hand to Carrie.

"I don't think we've met."

"Mommy! Mommy!" Maya tugs at my pants.

I bend down. "You did amazing! You are the cutest little tiger I know." Maya hugs me.

"Thank you, Mommy."

"You sounded like a croaking, dying frog," Cecilia says as she brushes past us.

"Excuse me?" I say to Cecilia as she turns and sticks her tongue out at Maya.

Carrie bends down to Maya and says she sounded wonderful.

"Cecilia, that isn't a very nice thing to say," I say.

Cecilia ignores me and walks toward Beatrice, who is glaring at me from across the room.

Maya's lip quivers, and water gathers at the edges of her eyes. I brace myself for Maya's tears, when Max swoops in and lifts Maya up, swinging her around. "You were brilliant, Maya Jambalaya," he says, stealing Avery's nickname for her.

Craig walks up, and Max sets Maya down. Craig asks Max about getting together for golf and places a hand on Carrie's back.

Shit, shit, shit.

I glance past Carrie and sure enough, Beatrice is staring right at us like she is witnessing a murder. And it will be mine if I don't get out of here fast.

I avert my gaze and unexpectedly meet Elenore's narrowed eyes. She must know who Carrie is from all the court proceedings. I hope she still knows I'm on her side and not Carrie's. I can't win in this situation.

"Mommy, I have to go pee," Maya says.

I grab Maya's hand and excuse us, taking her to the bathroom before all hell breaks loose.

"I'm sorry Cecilia said that to you," I say to Maya, squeezing her hand. I want Maya to know that we can talk about anything, especially mean bullies.

Maya takes a deep breath, rolls her neck, and says, "It's okay, Mommy. Her opinion doesn't matter anyway."

I'm surprised at her response, but also happy she didn't take Cecilia's words as gospel. Maya's much stronger than I give her credit for.

We emerge from the bathroom, and Elenore grinds to a halt, coming inches from slamming into me. I lurch back.

"There you are," she says. "I saw you talking to the lawyer lady. Did you convince her to have the charges dropped against me?" Her eyes give me a pleading look, and once again I feel deflated.

I wish I could say yes. That it all miraculously worked out, but everything in my life has been going south lately and this is one more added layer.

"I'm working on it," I finally say.

CHAPTER THIRTY-FOUR

I hug the oversized envelope to my chest, as if it is about to jump out of my arms. I know where it's from without looking at the return address. I release my grip, turn it over, and tear it open.

It took me years to contact the adoption agency. Only after bringing it up in therapy, did I realize I was ready. I'm not making that mistake again. I shove my finger in my mouth to quell the burning from the paper cut caused in my haste.

Inside, there is one official document along with two envelopes addressed to me, in care of the adoption agency, in pretty swirly handwriting.

Max watched me retrieve the envelope from the mailbox. When he realized my trancelike state, he took Maya out of the house. I know they will be back soon. So, I don't waste any time stuffing everything back into the oversized envelope and heading upstairs to our bedroom and shutting the door. Scooting across the bed, I prop up my pillow against the headboard. I make sure a box of tissues is still on my nightstand, and a glass of water sits there from last night.

I pull out the document from the agency with the "nonidentifying" information. "Your birth mother was sixteen and resided in the Midwest." She was only sixteen when she gave birth to me. Sixteen! *Whoa.* My hands tremble. That alone explains volumes. I read the physical description of my birth mother, searching for anything I can relate to.

Like me, she had blue eyes and blond hair. She weighed one hundred and fifteen pounds and was five feet six. I suck in a breath. We had similar builds at age sixteen. I close my eyes tight. This is where I came from. This is resonating. Tingles prickle me from my toes to the tips of my fingers. I open my eyes and scan my biological father's information. He had brown hair and brown eyes, was five feet eleven and one hundred and sixty pounds. I wonder if I have his nose, the shape of his eyes, or his jawline. *Whose ears do I have? Did we have similar interests? Am I more like my birth mother or my birth father?* This document isn't enough, but it's something.

After a moment, I set the document aside and move to the two envelopes and flip them over to determine when they were mailed. November 1982 and October 2002.

My hand trembles as I lift the glass from my nightstand and take a sip of my water, sloshing it on my shirt. I decide to open the letters in order. I'm afraid of what they might say.

November 15, 1982

Dear Sweet Pea,
I really don't know where to start. I am not sure when you are reading this, but I hope you are happy.

Sweet Pea is the name I called you when I was pregnant. You answered by kicking me. I think you liked the name. I also sang to you the song "Best of My Love" by The Emotions quite a bit.

When my parents found out I was pregnant, they were ashamed and sent me to my grandma's until after I had you. My grandma was there for me when my parents weren't.

I went back home to live with my parents after I had you, and I was told to pretend it never happened. But I want you to know that I will never forget you, even though I only gave you one kiss before you were taken from me by the nurse.

Your father was my high school boyfriend. I loved him and kind of still do. I haven't seen him or talked to him since we found out I was pregnant with you. Our parents wouldn't let us. I miss him and I'm not sure if we will ever be together.

The adoption agency said it would be good for me to give you a health history. I am healthy at seventeen. Your birth father is healthy for a seventeen-year-old too. Our families don't have any major illnesses. I hope this helps you.

Here is the hard part. I wanted to keep you, but because I'm so young and still a minor, my parents told me I should give you up. I didn't have anywhere to go except for my grandma's. Don't blame them, though. They think I'm too young to care for you. As they say, I'm basically a child myself. I thought they would come around as my belly got bigger, but I never saw them during my pregnancy.

I wanted a good home for you, where you would be loved and have everything you needed. I hope the adoption agency made the right choice for you.
I think about you all the time.

Sending love.

I cry my way through the first and second reading of the letter—big, ugly, snot-inducing tears. Then I read it ten more times. I spend an hour dissecting every sentence. Jumbled thoughts roll through my head like scattered marbles.

My pulse quickens at the thought of how young my birth mother was when she carried and delivered me. It must have been scary for her. At sixteen, I feared the pain of burning my forehead with the curling iron yet again—I couldn't imagine growing a tiny human and pushing it out of me.

It breaks my heart all over again, knowing she was forced to give me up and pretend it . . . *I* never happened, but she wanted me. I was wanted. My heart races as I let it sink in.

Now I wonder if she and my biological father ever rekindled their romance. My head says it's highly unlikely they continued their love story, while my heart hopes for their happy ending.

Can I find them? I have thought about my biological parents over the years. I never admitted it to anyone, not Max, not Avery, and definitely not my parents.

I reach into the oversized envelope for the second letter, stamped with the date October 1, 2002. As I pull out the letter, a loose slip of paper comes with it, and this one isn't written in the same pretty handwriting.

CHAPTER THIRTY-FIVE

It's Sunday morning. I'm sipping my coffee on the deck. Maya jumps and does flips on the trampoline. Max sits across from me, with his nose in a medical journal. My eyes are puffy, and my nose is swollen. I'm quick to tell Maya my appearance is a result of my allergies so as not to worry her. Max knows why I look like I got stung in the face by a swarm of bees, but he keeps my secret. I gave him the Cliff Notes version of my findings from the letters after Maya went to bed last night.

I flip open my date book. Now that Maya is out of school, I have to be a diligent planner. Tomorrow, she'll start an afternoon camp, which will give me time to work on the business. We'll spend most mornings at the neighborhood pool—one place Beatrice will not be because she has her own pool.

My phone dings. Speaking of the devil.

Beatrice: *I'm ready to listen.*

I think my eyes nearly pop out of my head at the unexpected text. I bet she's reaching out to me to find out more about Craig and Carrie after seeing them at the concert.

We need to meet on neutral ground. I suggest a late lunch Wednesday at a French bistro in the village. If it's a somewhat upscale café, she's less likely to make a scene. I'll have just enough time to get Maya off to camp and meet Beatrice.

"Everything okay?" Max stares at me.

"It's Beatrice."

He raises his eyebrows. "Oh?"

"Apparently, she's changed her mind about meeting."

"That's good news."

"Right," I say, not sure if it is. She may call me a bigger bitch this time.

Sensing my discomfort, Max doesn't inquire any further. He closes his journal and stands up.

"What do you say we go hiking today? It's a beautiful day. It's finally sunny. And we haven't done that in a while."

Or ever as a family. I tilt my head and squint. I don't remember the last time Max suggested we do anything as a family.

"Don't look so enthused," he says.

I know offering to hike is his way of comforting me after my discovery last night. Fresh air and nature will do me some good.

"I'm sorry. You surprised me."

Sundays meant Maya spent time on schoolwork and I cleaned. But she was out of school now. The cleaning, though, would never end. On Sunday afternoons, Maya and I cuddled and watched a movie until bedtime. Then I went to perfect my chocolates at the commercial kitchen. This time of year, Max takes care of the mowing and trimming outside, then usually buries himself in research. I am grateful he manages our lawn and bushes—I don't have any desire or a green thumb.

"I'll pack a picnic. Tell Maya," I say. Now I really do need to take my allergy medication.

From the kitchen, I hear Maya screaming in excitement at the news.

* * *

We pick an easy trail ten minutes from our house. Neither Max nor I know how long Maya will last without complaining. I'm banking on the spectacular views distracting her from aching legs. After only a few minutes up the rocky path, we stop to admire the hills and drink water.

"Which way do we live? Can we see our house from here?" Maya asks.

Max points. He has a better sense of direction than I do. I'm already turned around. Luckily, this is a well-traveled trail, and markers indicate where to go.

"That way. See those houses? We're in there."

Maya tents a hand over her eyes. "I think I see the pool."

"Here, let me take a photo of the two of you." I realize Max and Maya haven't been in a photo all year. I frown. "Be careful not to get too close to the edge."

Max holds his arms up in victory, and Maya copies him. It's a good photo. It looks like we are much higher up than we are. I'll frame it for Father's Day. We continue up the trail.

Maya jumps and screams, "Something ran over my foot!"

"Don't worry, honey. Just a harmless chipmunk."

Watching Maya to make sure she stays on the path, I stumble over a rock. Max throws out his arm and steadies me.

"Easy there. Are you okay?"

"I'm fine, thank you."

"Okay, we don't want a repeat of the last time we hiked."
I'm surprised he remembers. It's been twenty years. I can't
believe we've been together that long. It's not something I
gave much thought to. Our life together had become as natural as breathing. I had been with him for half of my life.

We stop at the top, and I remove my backpack, unzip it,
and pull out our lunches. I hand each of them a sandwich.
Maya is full of questions. "Who made this trail? What if we
got stuck up here? Are there bears or snakes?" She prattles on.
Max patiently answers all of them. I let them have this time
without me adding my comments. I'm with Maya more than
Max is, and these are precious moments for them.

The rolling green hills dotted with yellow, orange, and
purple wildflowers are gorgeous this time of year. The recent
rains have led to a beautiful blooming season. I'm glad I took
my allergy medication. A runny nose and itchy eyes would
have added to my somber mood. I finish the last bit of my
lunch, pull my legs to my chest, and listen to Maya and Max.
My mind travels back to the day Max and I went hiking
years ago.

Max planned a hike like this for us about thirty minutes
from school. He even made a picnic consisting of liver sausage and crackers. Not the most appetizing to look at, but
delicious. We were poor college students—liver sausage was
a luxury back then. He won some major points for effort. As
we hiked, we talked about our future and what we wanted
out of life.

Max told me his parents wanted him to come back after
college and help on the farm, but his heart wasn't in it. He
couldn't see himself milking cows for the rest of his life. He
worried he'd upset them. I didn't encourage him to follow

his own path. It was ultimately for him to decide. I couldn't see myself living on a farm. I was a city girl. I didn't tell him that. Instead, I told him I couldn't see myself returning home either. I wanted to live in a small town and raise a big family.

In the end, his parents forgave him and decided selling the farm would be the best for everyone. His sister, Maeve, didn't want to take it over either. His parents were happy to have their children living close by. My parents moved to Florida, so they weren't heartbroken I didn't move back. It had all worked out.

Then on our way down the trail on our romantic date, I tripped over a rock, landed headfirst in a thorn bush, and twisted my ankle. Bruised, bleeding, and embarrassed, I refused to make the situation worse by crying. Max carried me on his back for a quarter of a mile back to the parking lot.

He impressed me that day. I would give it a ten on a dating scale. In fact, I think that was the day I knew I'd marry him. That thought jogs my memory. It's also the day I wrote the journal entry about how great our life would be.

I think about the letters from my birth mother. I had an extra cup of coffee this morning to keep my eyes open after tossing and turning again all night. The final letter revealed she had breast cancer. Tears spring to my eyes, thinking about it now.

I tried to think back to what I was doing in October 2002. I was in college. I had the adoption agency information. The guilt shoots through me like bullet holes straight to my heart. Maybe I could have found her, but it's too late now. The slip of paper that fell out with the second letter was from the counselor, notifying me that my birth mother registered with the adoption agency and because of this they were able to include her name and contact information. My birth mother wanted me to know who she was. She wanted me to find her. Chills run up and down my arms, and I close my eyes tight, remembering the name on the document: Mary Brighton.

I immediately did an internet search. It took me a while, but I found what I'd hoped I wouldn't. Her obituary. Before she died, I could have contacted the agency in time. I know this is the thought that will haunt me for the rest of my life.

I look upward to the sky now and take a deep breath for Mary.

"What are you thinking about, starry eyes?" Max interrupts my thoughts. He must know where my head is today. I smile to push down the pain. But also for Maya and Max— to be in the moment now with them.

"Just how much I love you two."

Max throws his arm around me, and Maya crawls into my lap.

We take a family selfie.

On the way down the hill, Max tucks my arm into his and holds it close. I need his arm for support.

CHAPTER THIRTY-SIX

"I should have contacted the adoption agency when I found the letter," I say to Dr. Josie.

Why had I been so selfish? Why hadn't I contacted the agency in time? I could have found her and had at least a year with her. *What if I had found her and she'd fought harder to survive? What if the reason she died is because she had nothing to live for?* Maybe I could have saved her.

I'd let fear control me. Fear of rejection. Fear of knowing the truth. I protected my heart, but there was no reason to. I know that now. I should have been brave.

Dr. Josie gets up and pours me a cup of tea.

"It's guilt," she says as she hands me the mug.

I sip my tea. I know this, but how am I going to get through it? I don't know. That's why I'm here, sitting across from Dr. Josie as if she holds all the answers to my problems.

"This is not uncommon. When a person passes away, the survivors are often left wondering what they could have done differently. Do you think you could close your eyes and have a conversation with your birth mother as if she were still alive? What would you say to her to get it all out?"

I suck in a sharp breath. I'm not ready for that fake conversation. I stare past Dr. Josie at the beach scene on the wall. I want to be in the painting.

When Dr. Josie sees I'm not on board with that exercise, she continues, "Hindsight is twenty-twenty, and sometimes there are no answers."

I've poured my heart out to Max and to Avery. I listened to Max say he was sorry for what I was going through, trying to comfort me. I listened when Avery said I couldn't beat myself up—that anyone in my situation would have done the same thing. I didn't believe her. Not everyone would have waited more than twenty years to contact the adoption agency.

"I should have contacted the adoption agency," I say again. "Then I would have had the letters. And once I learned my birth mother was sick, I should have found her." My heart hammers in my chest, and drops of tears land on my cheeks.

Dr. Josie hands me a tissue. "That is good. Let it all out." She pauses. "You said you have the last letter from your birth mother. Would you like to read it to me?"

I inhale a sharp breath. I've read the letter what feels like a million times, and it doesn't get any easier. I pull it out of my tote bag and unfold it carefully, as if it will break under the pressure of my heart. I begin reading it to Dr. Josie.

Dearest Sweet Pea,

This is a tough letter for me to write, but you need to know for your own health that I have stage 4 breast cancer. I am losing the fight. There is a good chance you may receive this letter after I've passed on. For whatever reason you didn't contact me, I want you to know it's okay. I understand.

I pause. This is the sentence that cuts me to my core. She's absolving me of my guilt. I force myself to continue reading:

I never had another child because you were it for me. You made me a mother, and for that I am blessed beyond measure. My heart could only hold my love for you. I let half of it go with you, and no one could replace you.

I push the letter away so as not to stain it with my tears. I retrieve a tissue from the box, dry my eyes, and blow my nose as Dr. Josie patiently waits for me to continue.

I've included my favorite poem. Like the sweet peas in the poem, I always hoped you would fly high, and for you to do that, I had to let you go.
    I am truly sorry for the situation you were born into. I hope you know none of this is your fault.
    In my living years, there wasn't a day that went by that I didn't draw deep breaths for you. Always remember this.
All my love.

At this moment, I feel as close to my birth mother as I ever will, surrounded by her words and the declaration that she deeply loved me. I'm frozen.

I expected to be emotional, but what I'm feeling is indescribable. Love and loss combined, and it's almost unbearable.

"What a gift your birth mother left you," Dr. Josie says, and leans forward.

I close my eyes tight. It's quiet for a moment.

I fold the letter in half and place it in my purse.

"Do you think you will search for your birth father?" Dr. Josie asks.

The thought had crossed my mind, but I don't think I want to. Finding out my birth mother passed away is devastating enough. It sucked the life right out of me, along with any desire to continue searching for my birth father or any other relatives.

"No. I'm better off if the past stays buried with Mary," I say. This way I avoid further heartbreak. I drop my eyes to the floor.

"I can see why you would feel that way. It's a lot to take in," Dr. Josie says, and folds her hands across her lap. "I have an idea that may help you work through this. Do you keep a journal, Fallon?"

I shake my head. "I used to a long time ago. I came across it a few months ago."

"Did you read through it?"

"Just one entry. It made me sad."

"Why?"

"Because I wrote about what my life would be like." I pause. "And it isn't anything like I had imagined."

"Life rarely turns out the way we expect it to. While we're busy planning, life has other plans."

"I'm beginning to grasp that." I couldn't have foreseen that I was adopted, and after finding out, I'd vowed I would plan out the rest of my life so I didn't have any other devastating surprises.

"Would you be willing to start another journal to change the narrative? It may help you process all these emotions you have."

"I guess I could."

Dr. Josie reaches behind her chair and presents me with a journal. I reach for the brown leather-bound book and gasp. It's beautiful. The cover is laser engraved with a bird, its outspread wings ascending to the sky. The words "Rise from the Ashes" are etched in black below the bird.

"Thank you."

"You can get started immediately."

I run my hand over the journal, not knowing how I'll be able to start it. I'm so overwhelmed with grief.

Dr. Josie writes in her notepad and scans her page for a few minutes as I flip through the journal and read the quotes at the top of the pages. They're supposed to be uplifting, but my mood stays somber.

Dr. Josie sets down her pen, and I can feel her eyes on me now. I shut the journal and meet her gaze.

"Now, tell me. Did you read *The Five Love Languages*?"

"Yes," I say, and fold my hands together. Her eyes stay fixed on me as she waits for me to expound on the book. I say the first thing that comes to mind, "It's an interesting philosophy and makes sense." My thoughts aren't profound, but I'm not sure what else to say.

"What is your love language?"

"Quality time."

"Why do you think that?"

"It didn't take me long to identify it. I feel most loved when I am sharing an experience with others. That's why it's important for me to be included." I see the connection now with my fear of rejection and abandonment.

"What do you think Max's love language is?"

"Acts of service."

"Have you been speaking his love language?"

"Sure. I keep the house clean and under control. I make dinner. I do all the grocery shopping and laundry. I take his clothes to the dry cleaner . . ." I could go on, but I stop.

"What about quality time for you? Are you and Max spending time together?"

I tap my finger on my cup and bite the side of my lip, remembering our failed date.

"Not really."

"Okay, your assignment this week is to work on spending time together to bring more joy into your marriage."

Bring more joy. Her words reverberate inside my head as I mull them over. *Why didn't I think of that?* That's what's missing in our marriage. It's "fine," but where's the joy?

"Is there anything else you would like to talk about today?" she asks.

I've been debating whether I should bring up my dashed dreams of my chocolate business.

"You look like you have something else on your mind?"

"I've been having some setbacks with my chocolate business." I sigh. "I don't know if I should keep going with it. My last two big orders were flops, and I've had to deal with some nasty comments." My chest tightens as I think about all these rejections.

"Were you expecting that running a business is easy?" she asks as she sets her pen down and folds her hands in her lap.

I frown. "I never looked at it that way."

"In my own experience," she says, "there is a lot that goes into building a business, and I wouldn't ever claim that it's easy. In fact, I expected it to be difficult. That way when I was faced with an obstacle, I gave myself grace."

I stare at her like she just parted the Red Sea.

CHAPTER THIRTY-SEVEN

I'm emotionally spent and exhausted after my session with Dr. Josie. A quick nap sounds like a great idea. I head up to my bedroom, set my alarm so I don't miss picking up Maya from camp, and rest my head on my pillow.

"Should we add cinnamon?" I ask Grandma Rose, as she's melting the chocolate on the stove. I breathe in the rich cocoa and smile.

Grandma Rose stops stirring and looks at me. "You know I'm proud of you, right?"

"Why?" I tilt my head and stare into her ocean-blue eyes.

"For going after your dream. Life is too short not to create joy for yourself and others."

A noise jolts me out of my dream. Wetness covers my cheeks, and I realize I've been crying. It takes me a few seconds to figure out my phone is ringing, and I check my screen. When I answer, I detect excitement in Mel's voice, and I'm snapped back into reality.

"Are you sitting down?" Mel asks.

"Yes, why?" Technically I was still lying down.

"I pitched your business plan to some investors." Mel pauses for effect. "I included the sample of chocolates you sent me . . ." Another pause.

"And?" I inhale. She sure is dragging this out.

"They loved your chocolates and the business plan, especially your ideas for chocolate classes. They read through it thoroughly, checked into a few things, and . . ."

"What?"

"They've decided to lend you money!" I sit up quickly. *Did I just hear her right? This is huge.*

"Really? How much?"

"To be determined. They want to meet you first."

"Where? When?"

"We are coming to you. They want to see potential properties for your shop before they lend the money."

"You're coming back?"

"Yes, ma'am."

I squeal. I hadn't squealed in years, maybe ever for that matter.

"Do they have a date in mind?"

"First week in July."

I don't even check my calendar. There's nothing this important on it anyway. Well, except for my fortieth birthday.

"Yes!" I must have really wowed them with my business plan. Now I have to kick it into high gear to seal the deal. I have a few weeks to perfect some recipes and make more chocolates for the investors. I also have time to start scoping out potential properties. Sweat gathers under my armpits. *Is this really happening?* Someone needs to pinch me. I never expected for this to move so fast.

Mel goes on to explain more about her meeting with the investors and their enthusiasm.

"Okay, I'll book the hotel and flights and be in touch."

"Mel?"

"Yes?"

"How can I ever thank you?" This is the second time Mel has pulled through in a major way for my business. I don't know how I'm going to repay her.

"You know. Invest with me."

That sounds like a good idea. I'm surprised I hadn't thought of it. I will need somewhere to put my profits. "Of course I will."

"And buy me a drink when I get there."

"You're the best."

"I gotta run. Talk soon."

What are the chances that I would have a dream about my Grandma Rose right before Mel calls to say investors are interested? It's almost as if divine intervention is at play.

After I hang up with Mel, I call Avery.

"I got investors for a chocolate shop!" I say as soon as she answers. "I'm freaking over the mooooon!" I extend "moon" by several o's and throw my arm into the air.

"Whoa, Fallon. Congratulations!"

"I am so excited. I just needed to share my good news with you," I say as I bounce on my toes.

"Your chocolates are amazing. The world is ready for them."

"You think so?" I say, and stop bouncing.

"I know so."

I smile. This is why Avery is my bestie and I love her.

As soon as I get off the phone with her, I send an email to Stacy, asking if she can help me search for properties. Then I stuff my face with chocolates.

After picking up Maya from camp, she helps me make a few dozen truffles. It's time to celebrate.

When Max gets home from work, I share the good news with him. He opens a bottle of champagne, and I present my latest chocolates on my Grandma Rose's finest china platter.

"I'm proud of you, babe. Really proud."

I blush. I'm not sure I've ever heard Max utter those words to me.

"Me too, Mommy. You're going to be famous like Betty Crocker," Maya says, and pops a chocolate into her mouth.

"Well, I don't know about that. Mel says they do see me making a profit relatively quickly. Apparently, they think both an online e-commerce website paired with a brick-and-mortar store will be successful. They particularly loved the liqueur chocolates idea and hosting classes."

Max kisses me. "Of course they do. That reminds me," he says. "I have a request for a new flavor—bourbon-filled truffles."

"That's not a bad idea."

CHAPTER THIRTY-EIGHT

I rush into the restaurant, already five minutes late because of road construction. This isn't how I wanted this meeting to start. I slow my pace when I see Beatrice sitting with her back to me and her straight brown hair is swooped up into a floral fabric clip. As the hostess shows me to our table, I smooth down my skirt and take one calming breath.

"Hi, Beatrice," I say. My voice shakes, betraying any composure I've tried to muster.

"The waitress will be right with you," the hostess says, and leaves our table.

Beatrice lowers her gaze to her menu without greeting me. I sit and place my napkin on my lap. I eye her as she sets down her menu and picks up her lemon water, taking a quick sip. Her face is scrubbed clean of any sign of kindness. If looks could kill, I'd be dead twice.

I fill the silence. "I've never been here. Have you?"

She shakes her head and peruses the menu again, as if speaking to me would interrupt her important thoughts.

I shift my eyes to read the lunch specials, but I'm not sure I'll be able to eat with my nerves snuffing out my hunger.

"Construction was terrible," I say.

"Oh, did you take *Durand*?" she says curtly, and I remember that's the street I told her to take the day she screeched at me like a bonobo.

Now it's my turn to ignore her as I scan the menu.

After a few minutes, the waitress arrives to take our orders, slicing through the excruciating silence. When she leaves, I glance around, avoiding Beatrice's sudden glare.

She finally asks in a measured tone, "Why did you have the Mexican Fiesta?"

I'm caught off guard by her question. "Because you and I discussed having one."

"I don't recall that," she says, and taps her fingers on the table.

I wrack my brain for the conversation. I remember we were sipping margaritas by her pool. I said, "We should have a Mexican Fiesta," and she responded, "Oh yeah," while ogling Rocco, the pool boy, like usual. *Ugh.* It dawns on me. She wasn't even listening to me. She was probably fantasizing about Rocco spanking her with the pool skimmer.

I clear my throat and push the image from my mind. "Well, I thought you would be happy to attend the party and try Sergio's food. I know you had been wanting to go there."

She stares at me like I belched. *Was I wrong about that too?*

"It was my way of extending an olive branch to you. I did it all for you," I say. Saying this out loud makes me feel vulnerable, but if we're going to get anywhere, I need to lay it all out on the table.

Beatrice throws her head back, laughs, and says, "Yeah, right."

Her words sting like an electric charge zapping me, and I swallow hard, trying to figure out what to say next.

"I'm really sorry if I did something to upset you," I finally say.

"I saw the friends app screenshots. I'm appalled at the language you used to describe us," Beatrice says, and clenches one fist.

I'm afraid she's going to haul off and punch me, so I quickly say, "Mel wrote that as a joke."

Beatrice practically growls at me, "Now you see why I never liked Mel. She's always been mean."

Mel's been mean? *Mel never excluded me,* I want to say, but bite my tongue.

"Anyway, I know who Carrie is. I hired a private investigator, who followed Craig and saw them together. Then he followed Carrie right to you and your barstool."

I hunch over and rub my eyes, trying to place myself back at the bar with Carrie. I remember seeing that one guy staring at us oddly. He may have been the investigator. I'm a bit disturbed at the invasion of privacy but relieved he wasn't some creeper after all.

"I'm sorry. I didn't know about you and Craig," I say, and take a sip of my water as our salads arrive.

She bites her lip, and her eyes soften. I decide to stay in this direction. "I didn't know until my party, when you weren't wearing your ring."

Beatrice glances down at her hand, then picks up her fork and stabs an olive. I pour dressing on my salad. The silence is eating at me. This is as painful as a colonoscopy without anesthesia. I don't know how I'm going to make it through the rest of lunch.

She points her fork at me. "There's more." Her icy-blue eyes send a shiver up my spine.

Now we're getting somewhere. I narrow my eyes. "What?"

"The fact that you called me fat and that's why Craig doesn't sleep with me."

I lurch back like a bucket of water has just hit me in the face.

"What?" I set my fork down. "I have never once questioned your sex life for any reason."

"Oh, don't play innocent with me. I knew you said it when I saw you hanging out with his new skinny girlfriend— you probably introduced him to her. Does she meet your standards for him?"

"Beatrice, I never said such a thing. Who told you this?" I can't believe this is happening. *Are we in high school?*

"It doesn't matter."

"Whoever told you this is lying. Think about it. What does that person have to gain by telling you a lie like that?"

She doesn't answer.

"Was it Craig? Did he say this?"

"Lyla," she says.

"Lyla?" I clearly didn't hear her right.

"Lyla," she repeats.

I know I've never said anything like this. *Why is Lyla feeding Beatrice lies? And how can I prove she is lying?* It's her word against mine. Maybe she is jealous of Beatrice's relationship with me. *Is she the driving force behind all of this?*

"Why do you believe her?"

"Because who would make that up?"

"Um, Lyla, for some reason. What does Craig say about this?"

"Craig knows you and I aren't talking. I didn't tell him why. You think I'm going to tell him you called me fat and don't blame him for not sleeping with me?"

"I'm calling Lyla," I say, and pull out my phone. She grabs for it. I yank it from her grip and knock over my glass of water. It soaks my salad and spills over the edge of the table. I scoot my chair back so not to get my shoes wet and throw my napkin on the puddle. Holding my phone up, I click Lyla's number and put the phone on speaker. Beatrice is taking shallow breaths and balling each end of her napkin in her fists.

Lyla answers on the first ring. She probably thinks I have some great gossip to share. "Hello, Fallon?"

The women at the next table are gawking at us. I wave hi, and they quickly turn their heads.

I cut straight to it. "Lyla, did you tell Beatrice I called her fat and commented on her sex life?"

A woman from the other table audibly gasps.

Lyla clears her throat. "Yes."

"Why would you say such a thing?"

"Because that's what I heard you say."

The anger rises to my face.

"*What?*"

"At yoga. You were on the phone."

I wrack my brain. *What is she talking about?*

Beatrice folds her arm and sits back in her seat as if she's enjoying this shit show. All she needs is a bag of popcorn.

"So, let me get this straight. You supposedly overhear me on the phone with someone, saying things I would never say, and you tell Beatrice? You know Beatrice isn't talking to me, and you continue to pretend you don't know why?"

She doesn't answer. "And to top it off," I continue, "you're spreading rumors I'm on a dating app." If I could slap her through the phone, I would.

"Well, you are."

"It's a *friendship* app."

Beatrice rolls her eyes.

"Same difference," Lyla says.

"No, it's not. I joined to look for new friends because you all abandoned me."

I watch as Beatrice winces as if I'd pinched her. Maybe she is finally seeing things from my perspective.

"Whatever," Lyla says.

"I'm hanging up. And I'm glad you got glass in your ass," I hiss at her.

I click off the phone. Three tables of people are staring our way. I take out a twenty-dollar bill and throw it on the table.

"Keep the change."

Beatrice's lips are quivering, and she looks like she's about to say something, but I storm out of the café. And here I was worried Beatrice would be the one to make a scene.

I'm halfway down the block and almost to my car when it hits me. Lyla heard me talking on the phone to Avery about *Dude and Dudettes*. The lead guy—his name is Craig as well. We were discussing why he said he wasn't sleeping with one of the girls. He's a sleazeball.

"Wait!" Beatrice is huffing and puffing behind me.

I spin around to face her.

"I trusted Lyla. Maybe I shouldn't have."

"No, you shouldn't have." I keep moving to my car.

"Lyla is a gossip."

"You're just figuring this out now?" I ask.

"No, I knew that. Of course I knew that."

I have my hand on the car door handle now.

"I remember the conversation now. I was talking to my friend Avery on the phone, after yoga, about *Dude and Dudettes*. You may have heard of it? A guy on there . . . his name is Craig."

Beatrice is staring at me like I grew another head. "Oh," she finally says.

"Oh? That's all you have to say?"

"I was going through a rough time. Everything started to cloud my judgment. You hadn't been to a soccer game in a long time."

"My absence had nothing to do with you."

"I know. Like I said, I wasn't thinking straight. Craig left me. I was devastated. I latched on to anyone who was close."

I squint at her. Vivian told me it was Beatrice's idea to split with Craig, not that Craig left her. So many "he said, she saids" going on, it's driving me nuts.

"I thought we were better friends than this." My voice cracks.

"Why are you hanging out with Craig's new girlfriend?"

"I found her on the friendship app. As I said, I went on there to find new friends since you guys were ditching me. I had no idea she was dating Craig until recently. I swear."

"I can't believe you're friends with her," she says.

"Well, I can't believe you would ghost me after everything we've been through together." I scowl. "Why are you excluding me?" The reason must be more than my missing a few soccer games.

Beatrice's nostrils flare as she glares at me. I glare back and feel my own nostrils flare.

I give up on her answering me as I yank open my car door, scoot in, and leave her standing on the sidewalk. As I pull away, my hands shake on the steering wheel.

CHAPTER THIRTY-NINE

I sit in the bar and wait for Carrie and Stacy for our weekly get-together. I'm sweating, and not because it's the hottest day of the year. I'm going to be sick. Today is the day I am breaking up with them. Instead of cancelling and putting off the inevitable, it's only right that I officially sever our relationships. I don't want to ghost them like what's happened to me. It's important for me to be honest.

It's for the best to part ways with Carrie. I don't feel right continuing our friendship now that I know she is dating Craig. Beatrice is right—it's a betrayal of the lowest kind.

Unfortunately, Stacy is an innocent casualty, and I'm fully aware I'm sabotaging any chance of Stacy helping me find a property for my chocolate shop. I feel if I'm breaking up with Carrie, I need to with Stacy as well. They are my Thirsty Thursday girls. I can't separate them. Like a pair of earrings, shoes, or gloves. Like chocolate cake and ice cream. Okay, you could separate those, *but why would you?*

I have to make it quick and painless, like ripping off a Band-Aid. I get to the bar first and order three shots. Surprisingly, Carrie and Stacy arrive at the same time. This is a sign that tonight is a good night to break up.

We say our hellos. Before we get into a conversation, I take a deep breath and start my speech that I practiced in the mirror and in the car on the drive here.

"Carrie, Stacy, I want you to know that I've valued our time together."

Carrie takes a breath, as if she is going to say something, and I hold up my hand to signal for her to wait. "There are some complications in my life at the moment." I don't go into my reasoning. "And I'm sorry to say, but I need to break up our friendship." Now that I've said it out loud, I realize it sounds weird. But it needed to be said. Even though I am no longer close with Beatrice, I want to honor what we once had in the early days of motherhood. She got me through some really tough times, and I can't be witness to another woman taking her husband away.

Stacy's mouth drops open. "What?"

"You're not serious," Carrie says with a stiff jaw.

"Unfortunately, I am."

"Does this have something to do with Craig? Because he told me all about you and his soon-to-be ex-wife. Did you think I wouldn't find out?"

"Wait—hold up. What?" Stacy asks, confused.

Carrie turns to Stacy. "The guy I'm dating—his soon-to-be ex-wife, Beatrice, was Fallon's best friend and the reason Fallon was looking for new friends on the app. Beatrice is the reason we are all friends now. Or *were* friends, I should say."

Carrie points a finger at me. "So, Craig told me all about your falling out with Beatrice and how you're not really a good friend."

What? That's ridiculous. She might as well have just spit in my face.

"He's lying."

"Is he? Because breaking up with us now is evidence that you may not be the type of friend you think you are. I was willing to give you the benefit of the doubt. I went to bat for you with him, but now it looks like he was right all along."

My heart drops into my stomach. My mouth is dry. I finally squeak out, "I can't bear seeing Beatrice in pain over her split and the fact that Craig is with you."

Carrie stands up. "You and I were supposed to celebrate today. I got my clients to drop their lawsuit against your friend Elenore, which means I lost money, for you."

I throw my hand up to my mouth. I want to thank her, but she looks as if she's going to punch me.

"You're welcome," Carrie snaps at me. "This friendship should go down as the shortest friendship in the history of friendships."

She's right. A lot has happened in a short time.

"Stacy, call me. We can still be friends." Carrie knocks back a mind-eraser shot and stomps out.

Stacy stares at me, bewildered. "Is this really happening?"

Tears well up in my eyes. "Yes," I manage to say in a whisper.

"Okay. I can understand why being friends with Carrie might not be in your best interest because of your feelings for Beatrice, but I have nothing to do with any of this."

I know she's right, but I didn't think I had a choice.

"You don't have to do this," she says. "Listen, I'm not giving up on you."

Stacy wraps her arms around me. I stiffen, then slowly bring my arms up to return her hug.

"Thank you." I feel like I don't deserve her kindness. Apparently, I've been doing this friendship thing wrong. I release her hug and watch her walk out the door. I take the mind-eraser shot, hoping it actually helps me forget about Carrie. Then I delete the friendship app.

CHAPTER FORTY

The soccer field is muddy from last night's rain. All the girls' white uniforms are now a light shade of drab gray from the last time they played. The coach doesn't say anything about their ragged appearance. Next year they should choose a color other than white.

The bleachers are filled with smiling parents, and loud chatter and laughter surround me. Max and I sit a few rows behind the Ma Spa Squad. Not one of them turned to greet me. I assume Vivian's heard about the fallout at lunch from Lyla and has now joined forces with them.

For a moment, I close my eyes and relish the sun on my lashes. My mind drifts to the conversation with Max about moving out of Springshire. I had broached the subject a couple of days ago.

"I don't know. I haven't thought about moving since a few years ago," Max said to me. "Why?"

We had talked about moving into a bigger house closer to the downtown area and out of our subdivision when Max's practice doubled and his paycheck grew. I didn't want to move then because of my mom friends.

"Are you asking me this because of what's going on with you and Beatrice?"

I shrugged. I know it's probably not the best way to deal with the loss of friends. I think of Stacy. She commented she didn't want to run away from her problems after her husband cheated on her. *Could I be strong like her? Was it really a matter of being strong, or was it keeping one's sanity?*

Then Maya had interrupted us with an emergency: "I can't find my black marker!"

I didn't bring up moving again.

A tap on my shoulder interrupts my thoughts. I turn to see Lyla. "Can we talk a minute?"

My eyes widen. I didn't expect this.

She motions me off the bleachers. Whatever Lyla has to say, she must not want to say in front of anyone else. Curiosity gets the best of me, and I follow her.

"I owe you an apology. Beatrice told me that what I overheard was not about her."

I cross my arms over my chest. Maybe I was wrong, and she didn't intentionally try to ruin my relationship with Beatrice.

"You need to check your facts before you gossip. You are ruining reputations and relationships. You spread the wrong facts about the kids seeing Elenore on stage with the principal. You jumped to the conclusion that I was on a dating app. You thought I was talking about Beatrice when I wasn't. Do you realize the damage you've caused?"

"You're right. I'm sorry." Tears form at the corner of her eyes.

There were many times when Lyla had spread the right information, which I had been happy about for having a friend in the know. Like the time she warned us the cops were going to start sitting in our neighborhood to catch us rolling through stop signs. She had saved me from a hefty ticket. I'm sure of it. I can give her the benefit of the doubt now.

"I accept your apology," I say, and force myself to smile.

"Thank you. I truly am sorry," she says quietly, and drags her fingers through the ends of her hair.

The whistle blows, indicating the start of the game, and we both move back to our seats. Maeve, Sarah, and Max's parents scooch in beside Max. I greet them with a big smile. I'm grateful for their support of Maya.

It doesn't take long for the players on both teams to be caked in mud. It's everywhere. On their faces, in their hair. I'll have to hose off Maya before she enters the house.

Jeff is screaming at the ref again. If he gets kicked out this time, he'll most likely be suspended from the games next season. I assume he's taking out his frustration and humiliation at Elenore's cheating. I don't feel sorry for him, though. He cheated too. He just didn't get caught in public.

These divorces are getting out of hand. First Elenore, then Beatrice, *or was it Beatrice and then Elenore?* I hope no one else is next. It isn't fair. This isn't how it's supposed to be. We were all meant to grow old together and move to Florida into one of those golfing retirement communities where we sip margaritas by the pool and shout at each other because we can't hear. Then attend an all-you-can-eat fish dinner at the clubhouse at three thirty PM and embarrass our grandchildren with our flamingo hats. I realize all of this is a pipe dream anyway.

Max is on his feet now, screaming. Maya has the ball, weaving in and out of players like a little pro. She scores. I jump up and down.

"She's the best player," Max whispers to me. I know she is. If they were assigned a team captain at this age, Maya would be chosen.

The opposing team calls a time-out. Maya's team is winning—five to zero. The girls smear mud stripes like war paint under their eyes, and I snap a photo. I'll add it to the scrapbook I've been meaning to create since her birth. They stand in a circle, place their hands in the middle, and offer up a cheer before heading back on the field. I place my hand over my heart.

The husbands of the Ma Spa Squad sit in front of us and turn to talk to us a few times. Men don't hold grudges like women do. I glance at the moms in the front row. They're talking as usual. There are thirty seconds left in the game. The parents are high-fiving and cheering. The score is now seven to zero. Maya scored five of those points. She'll be named MVP. I'm sure of it.

There's a loud screech and a "Watch out!" Vivian throws up her arms to block a flying soccer ball. Mud splatters in all directions across the stands, and a lump of wet dirt lands on my forehead.

Parents of the other team snicker and laugh at us. The soccer ball may have been intentionally kicked into our stands by a player from the other team.

"Hey, the parents deserved that for their cheating kids. That girl with the pigtails touched the ball with her hands," a parent from the opposing team says loudly, and points at Penelope.

"Doesn't surprise me. One of those parents over there cheated with the principal. The apple doesn't fall far from the tree," another parent chimes in.

Jeff's face is beet red. He picks up a handful of mud and chucks it at their bleachers. Soon, mud is spraying above me and at me. I throw my hands over my head. Max is shielding me. Whistles are blowing. People yell obscenities. I hope Maya is covering her ears. I peer out at the soccer field. Both teams are kicking and throwing mud at each other. Max leads his parents, Maeve, and Sarah out of the stands, to safety. My first thought is to retrieve Maya, and as I move past the bleachers, something wet smacks me in the back of the head.

That's it. I can't take it anymore. I have all this pent-up anger and sadness eating at me. I'm in no mood. I pick up some mud and fling it. I mean to throw it at the opposing team's bleachers, but it slips out of my hand, and hits Lyla's cheek. I throw my hand up to my mouth. *Oh crap!* I didn't mean that, but it is a bit satisfying seeing gossip queen Lyla covered in mud. I lower my hand and feel the corner of my lip lifting into a smile and force it back down when I see Beatrice glaring at me.

I move toward Lyla to apologize, but her hand is raised high in the air with a perfectly formed mud ball. I watch in slow motion as she winds up and whips it at me. I try to get out of the way, but it hits me square in the chest so hard I fall back.

"Fallon, you think you're better than everyone else with your fancy chocolates and good-looking, rich husband!" Lyla yells at me. I've never seen her green eyes look so fierce, like a cat ready to pounce.

What? Lyla is jealous of me? Not more than an hour ago, she apologized to me, and now she's insulting me? The absurdity of it all. Mud is strewn across the front row. I grab a handful. I release it to throw back at Lyla, but my aim isn't that great, and it hits Beatrice's shoulder.

"Oh no, you don't!" Beatrice screeches at me.

"That's for excluding me from your girls' get-togethers," I say loudly.

Next thing I know, Elenore is beside me making mud balls. She hands me one. We hurl them at Beatrice and Lyla, who are not backing down.

"Well, this is for friending Carrie!" Beatrice lobs a mud ball at my head, and I duck.

Vivian looks on as if she's watching a train wreck, which is spot on.

"This is for calling me a bitch!" I send two mud balls at Beatrice.

Beatrice jumps back, and the mud falls at her feet.

"And this is for not inviting Maya to Cecilia's birthday party!" I fling more mud at her.

"Penelope wasn't invited either." Elenore kicks mud at Beatrice.

Beatrice is forming mud balls fast and handing them to Lyla. We keep catapulting them at each other.

"How did you like the eggs splattered on your windshield?" Lyla screams, and chucks more mud at Elenore.

"I should've known it was you! How juvenile." Elenore launches a huge chunk of dirt at her. "This is for the eggs and for the gossip. No kids saw me on that stage!"

The parents of the opposing team are still slinging mud our way. Parents on our side are retaliating. Mud is flying everywhere. One parent is using her umbrella to shield several people. The opposing parents can't make mud balls as fast. They begin retreating. I look down at my clothes. I am covered from head to toe.

Vivian moves in between us. "Stop the nonsense!" she screams. I step back. I've never heard Vivian raise her voice.

Craig joins her and holds his arms out like a referee.

"You said for better or for worse!" Beatrice screams at Craig and switches her aim from us to him. Craig crouches down with his arms over his head. Lyla joins forces with Beatrice against Craig. I'm glad to have the break. I breathe deeply. Vivian's husband, Andrew, drags Craig out of the line of fire.

The mudslinging stops altogether, but we're left looking like mud wrestlers. I wipe my face with the only clean corner of my shirt. I had given a lot of thought to trying to save my friendships with the Ma Spa Squad, but I could only do so much. At some point, I had to decide what was best for me.

I gather up my courage and turn to Beatrice. "I'm growing my chocolate business, and unfortunately that means my time is split. My new endeavor came at a time when you were going through a rough patch, and for that I am truly sorry. I've tried to make amends, but at some point, enough is enough." I kick the mud from my boots.

"You think that's the reason?" Beatrice spits back at me.

What the hell else could it be? I'm done playing these games. I take in Beatrice's strained expression and wait for her to go on. When she doesn't offer any explanation, I stomp away.

Right now, I need to find Max and Maya. I look to the field and see Cecilia push Maya. I watch in horror as Maya falls to the ground. My first instinct is to rush to Maya and help her up, but she's already scrambled to her feet and pushes Cecilia back in defense. I try to get there as fast as I can, but Coach Jack is closer and yelling for them to stop. Maya clenches her fists and turns away from Cecilia.

Max is right beside me now, and we get to Maya together.

"What happened? Why did Cecilia push you?" I say.

"I passed the ball to Penelope instead of Cecilia, and Cecilia got mad," Maya says, trembling. "She said I was arrogant like you, so I pushed her first." Tears form in her eyes. "I'm sorry, Mommy."

Max pulls us both close, and we fold into a group hug.

We celebrate winning the championship game, even though it was cut short by a mud fight, with a trip to Frosty's Ice Cream Parlor. where the three of us, covered in mud, devour the "Kitchen Sink"—six scoops of ice cream, three brownies, and whipped cream—and of course, three cherries on top.

CHAPTER FORTY-ONE

Stacy sent me five commercial property listings based on my criteria for the perfect chocolate shop. I am grateful she still searched after I tried to break up with her. I hadn't seen her since that night.

"You know, I didn't jibe with Carrie," she says to me as she unlocks the glass door to a space in a strip mall next to a fried chicken joint.

"Oh?" I guess I never thought about their friendship.

I can already tell this space won't work. Although the food smells delightful and my stomach growls in response, it's the type of smell that saturates everything. Chicken and chocolate aren't a good pair.

"Carrie's a little too cutthroat for me, which makes sense—she's a good lawyer. I didn't want to say anything during your whole—what did you guys call it? A breakup?"

"Yes."

"That's why I asked you to keep in touch. Carrie and I are not a package deal. And to me, you're a friend worth fighting for."

Her kind words surprise me, and my eyes mist over. "That means a lot," I say. She squeezes my arm as her phone beeps. She excuses herself to answer it.

I continue to walk around. There's not much to the wide-open space. I would have to do a ton of remodeling.

Stacy ends her call. "Carrie contacted me last Thursday to meet. I bowed out. I think she may have gotten the hint."

"You have to do what's right for you," I say. I miss hanging out with Carrie, but I know I made the right decision for me.

Stacy opens the door to leave. "Do you like this space?"

I take one last look around, trying to picture my shop here, regardless of the greasy chicken smell. *Where would I put my chocolates? The register?* Nothing comes to me. "No," I say.

"You're right. It's too commercial for a chocolate shop. You need something charming."

"Exactly."

* * *

The minute I see the large two-story Victorian with its signature gables and scalloped shingles, my heartbeat quickens. We approach the door to the burnt-sienna painted house, boasting a stunning, wide wraparound porch with ornamental spindles. Stacy explains to me that it was built by a wealthy textile merchant in the 1800s. Over the years, it housed affluent families until the residential street turned commercial with boutiques and specialty shops. Most recently, a stationery store occupied the space, with a wide selection of unique greeting cards, gift wrap, and rubber chickens. With more people turning to electronic cards and invitations and some kind of radical group against rubber chickens, the beloved paper store closed. Now it's up for lease. I'm in complete awe with heady exhilaration. *Could this be my chocolate shop?*

Driving past this house so many times, I admired the perfectly landscaped grounds, the brick pathway leading up to the porch, and the intricately carved and ornate wooden door. I envision children sitting on oversized rocking chairs on the porch, enjoying milk chocolate and caramel cashews in the shape of turtles. In the summer, I picture a musician singing and playing the guitar in the courtyard while patrons sit at tables, delighting in coffee and truffles.

We push open the door. I glide in as if I'm stepping into paradise. I smell lemon. Grandma Rose flashes in my mind. Wood stairs rise to the right. To the left, a stately room welcomes us. The room, once a parlor, is a perfect space for glass chocolate cases and a few small tables. A long hallway leads to a large kitchen used as a break room for the last shop. It can easily be turned into a commercial kitchen. As I take in all the incredible details, a happiness inside me is bursting at the possibility this could be my space.

The oak wood gleams in the sunlight shining through the bay windows. The rooms are cheery and bright, and there's a calm that passes over me as I take in every intricacy, from the elaborate gold trim to the light blue painted walls and the decorative panels and arches.

Could this really be mine?

The space where I, Fallon Monroe, can enter a new phase in my life, where possibilities turn into opportunities and my life will be what I've always dreamed it could be.

CHAPTER FORTY-TWO

Max crawls into bed next to me, and I set down *Slay Like a Mother*, my new engrossing self-help book.

He smells like mint and musk, and I scoot closer to him, laying my head on his chest.

"I think I found a place for my chocolate shop." I relay the Victorian's magnificent, charming features, with the caveat that it's not a done deal until the investors see it.

Max rubs my back in slow circles. "It sounds perfect. What did Stacy think?"

"She loved it too," I say. "Speaking of Stacy, I've been meaning to tell you I deleted the friendship app."

Max kisses the top of my head. "Thank you. I think you made the right decision."

I sigh. "Well, my friendships with Beatrice and Carrie are over."

"I'm sorry," he says. "Craig came to see me today at the clinic."

I pull back from him to look him in the eye with raised eyebrows.

"Not as my patient," he laughs.

That's what confused me. My mind is a bit muddled right now.

"He stopped in and asked if I could spare a few minutes," he says, and runs his hands through his hair. "I guess since Jeff is Beatrice's lawyer, she's taking Jeff's side in the whole Elenore and principal fiasco," he says.

"Yeah, I figured that," I say.

Max sighs. "Craig also apologized."

"For what?"

"Remember when we went golfing in March?"

I do. The guys made an impromptu decision to play on an unusually warm day. That was the last time all the women and kids got together outside of soccer. We met at the park. The kids played for hours while we got our vitamin D.

"I stayed after with Craig. We threw back a couple of beers at the clubhouse. He told me that he and Beatrice were having problems."

I lean forward. "Why didn't you tell me this before?" I don't understand why Max didn't think to mention this. Beatrice was my best friend, and this news is monumental. If I had known Beatrice and Craig were on their way to a divorce, I could have been there for her.

"I actually forgot about the conversation until he came to the clinic today. I thought they would work through it," he says.

Apparently, they couldn't. I sigh, feeling a weight of sadness. What's done is done now, and I decide it's no use getting mad at Max for not telling me sooner. "Did you give him any advice?"

"If you're asking if I told him we had our problems once too, no, I didn't tell him. I'm not sure I was much help. Before he told me, I showed him your anniversary gift. I know it was stupid of me to carry it around in my pocket, but I was paranoid you'd find it."

I couldn't believe Max had picked it out—a beautiful sapphire surrounded by diamonds, which is what I was subtly flashing in my social media post of us on our anniversary. I'm sure Beatrice saw it.

"I knew Craig bought Beatrice jewelry, and I wanted his opinion. That's when he said their anniversary was approaching and he went into their issues."

"I see."

"I guess I must have gone on about how happy you and I are. Um, of course, that was all before he went into his marital problems. I'm not that insensitive to brag about us while his marriage is on the rocks."

My heart swells. I had no idea how fondly Max spoke of us.

"Anyway, he went home that day after golf, and they got into a blowup. That's when shit hit the fan, and he asked for a divorce. The fight he and Beatrice had was about us."

What? I'm not understanding the connection. "Us?"

"Yes. He compared our relationship with theirs, saying how in tune we are with each other, and Beatrice blew a gasket. Craig apologized today because he used our relationship to get out of his, and he thinks he ruined your friendship with Beatrice."

I stare wide-eyed at Max. This all sounds so crazy. I replay what Max said. Max bragged about us to Craig. Craig compared us to him and Beatrice and asked for a divorce.

It takes a minute to fully sink in.

That's the reason.

I'm going to go out on a limb here and say they had issues that have absolutely nothing to do with me and Max. *Why hadn't Beatrice seen that?* She wants to blame me for her marriage failing. I'm furious. Furious that Beatrice discarded our friendship like a used piece of gum. Then I feel bad for her. *Maybe being with me enrages and embarrasses her because of what Craig said?*

"Truth is, Fallon, everyone thinks our relationship is good, and I don't air our dirty laundry, but I feel like I failed you." He takes a breath. "I couldn't give you the house full of kids you wanted." Now he blinks back tears.

My heart lurches into my stomach. *How did I not know he was struggling with this?* The words I should be saying to comfort him catch in my throat. I take his hand in mine.

I shake my head. "No, no. I'm sorry we never talked this through. We couldn't have prevented this."

"I'm just so sorry." He lowers his head.

I grab his hand and lift it to my lips.

"Should we revisit adopting?" he asks.

We had talked about adoption once before, but I had said no because of my own adoption experience and how my parents didn't tell me. I knew he was asking now because I had finally contacted the agency. He must think it's worth bringing up again in case I've changed my mind.

"No." I don't want to adopt after going through what I went through. The pain is still so raw.

"What will make you happy, then?"

I stare at him, taken aback. I don't answer because I can't find the words. He asks, "Then what can I do to lighten your load? When you were away in New York, I realized what you do for Maya on a daily basis, and I appreciate it. So . . . thank you."

My heart melts that Max acknowledges the time I put into raising Maya. I had gotten so used to being the main parent in Maya's life that I didn't even know where to ask for help anymore.

"I want more time, just us," I say.

"Really?"

"Why does that surprise you?"

"I didn't think you cared one way or another."

"What?"

"Fallon, we're like ships passing in the night."

"And you're okay with that?"

"No, but I didn't know how to fix it. I thought you resented me for being infertile. I failed you."

"I know our life didn't turn out the way I expected, and it's not perfect, but that doesn't mean that I love you any less or that our life isn't wonderful. Max, I love you more than the world. You and Maya *are* my world."

I couldn't imagine losing him too. I feel terrible that I didn't know Max was burdened with any of this. I'm determined to fix us. I'm going to put our relationship first. Over the past couple of months, I've seen relationships I thought would last forever take a terrible turn, with no chance of surviving. I refuse to let this happen to my marriage.

CHAPTER FORTY-THREE

Standing in the parlor of the Victorian house, I swallow down my nerves, find my voice, and relay to the investors—two women and one man—my vision for the space. The women gush over my ideas. The man walks around the room, deep in thought. I remove five boxes of my new recipes from my tote. I've gone gourmet on this batch. It's an assortment of four different customized truffles—Rose's Award-Winning Lemon Zest, Maya's Cookie Crumble, Max's Bourbon, and Mel's New York Cheesecake. I hand a gold ribbon–tied box to each investor and to Stacy and Mel.

"I encourage you to allow these truffles to melt slowly in your mouth as you take in this space."

Mel's smile reaches her eyes. She nods approvingly at me. She's the first to untie the ribbon and open her box. She gasps. "These look too delightful to eat." Then she whispers as the others continue to walk through the house and, I assume, open their chocolates secretly. "You're killing it."

I climb the stairs and drag Mel with me while Stacy gives the investors the grand tour. My heels click against the hardwood floors and echo throughout the upstairs foyer.

I haven't been up here before. I was most interested in the downstairs. The floors are being leased separately. I think about asking the owners to install a drop-down gate that divides the shop from the upstairs neighbors for after hours. Can't have the neighbors helping themselves to free chocolates. I mean, occasionally I'd offer them chocolates for being good neighbors—I will be a friendly business owner.

I marvel at the intricate detail of the carved woodwork and the abundance of cozy nooks. An ornate chandelier with drop crystals hangs in an elegant formal dining room with floral wallpaper and gilded wainscoting. High ceilings and deep archways add to the house's opulence. I gasp at the sprawling fireplace and fancy mantle. Whoever lives here is going to enjoy warm winter nights.

I run my hand over the gray granite kitchen countertops. The whole upstairs has been updated. My eyes continually widen as I investigate each room. Four bedrooms with ample closet space surprises me. Often, older homes have small closets because back then no one had one hundred pairs of shoes and counting, like I do.

"Are you thinking what I'm thinking?" Mel says.

"Hmm . . . I don't know. What are you thinking?"

"Fallon, you and your family could easily move in here."

I scrunch my nose.

"Think about it. A fresh start! It makes sense. You can roll out of bed, make your chocolates, open your shop . . . and get out of Shitshire. You could buy the building."

"The owners aren't selling."

"Not yet they aren't."

I raise my eyebrows.

"Everything can be negotiated . . . everything."

*   *   *

I had been looking forward to my date with Max all week. Ever since talking about making time for each other, we'd agreed to go on more dates. Tonight, we dropped Maya off at Max's parents for dinner, and then Maeve will take her to her house for a sleepover. Maya will be up way too late, but that's what aunties do.

"How are you feeling? More hot flashes?" Max lifts his water glass to his lips.

"No. I hadn't even noticed until you mentioned it."

"That's good. Maybe you're not as stressed anymore."

I hadn't thought about it that way. Maybe the friendship breakup was the best thing for my health.

As I butter my dinner roll, I think about the self-help book I've been reading. It's a good one. I wave the butter knife in the air like a sword, and Max stares at me like I'm crazy.

"What are you doing?"

"Slaying my self-doubt."

Max raises his eyebrows and grabs my hand to stop me. "Fallon, don't you see? You don't need these self-help books to fix you."

Oh, but I do! This is one every woman should read.

"I love you just the way you are. You are the love of my life."

I'm taken aback by his tenderness. Tears fall to my cheeks. "Max, I love you too. We need to keep making more time for each other."

Max lays his hand over mine. "I wholeheartedly agree. Why don't we start this new chapter with a toast?"

Max holds up his champagne flute. "To my smart and beautiful wife and to new beginnings."

"And to my supportive, hardworking, sexy husband."

We clink our glasses and take our celebratory sips. The waiter brings our entrees, and we dig in. I ask Max how he's doing with work. As we eat, we have a conversation like a normal married couple.

Max throws his napkin on his plate, and the waiter clears the table.

"So, give me all the details on the Victorian," Max says.

On the way to the restaurant, I couldn't contain my excitement and told Max the investors offered me five hundred thousand, which elicited an impromptu whistle out of him. The money will cover a lease for two years, upgrading the kitchen, marketing, supplies, and hiring a few people. I go on to tell him now how the Victorian is the investors' first pick out of the three properties we looked at today.

"With Stacy's help, I'm prepared to make an offer on leasing the space on Monday. However, there is one thing I'd like to talk to you about."

Max raises one eyebrow. "Oh?"

I take a sip of my champagne. "The upstairs is for lease too. It's residential."

Max tilts his head. "Go on."

"The owners will have to install a drop-down gate to separate the business from the tenants upstairs . . . unless we move in." As I say it out loud, butterflies flutter and overtake my stomach.

Max sips his champagne. "Have you looked at it?"

I describe the charm of it and its spaciousness.

"You're glowing," he says.

"Am I?"

"I'd like to see this Victorian that has you so mesmer-ized," Max says.

I smile knowingly. Max can't ever really say no to some-thing I have my heart set on. I reach for his hand. He's going to love it. I lean back in surprise as our waiter sets a piece of layered chocolate cake with a lit candle in front of me.

Max sings happy birthday to me in his best breathy singing voice, which is slightly better than mine, but not much. This morning Maya made me breakfast in bed, with Max's help—a smiley face made of sunny-side-up eggs for eyes, a strawberry nose, and a bacon mouth. Plus, coffee just the way I like it, with half and half and stevia. As a family of three, we snuggled in bed for ten minutes before Max headed to work. When I returned home from dropping Maya off at camp, I received the largest bouquet of flowers from my parents, and Avery sent me a heart-stopping per-sonalized Cameo video message from Mark McGrath of Sugar Ray, wishing me a happy birthday. *What!* I thought I'd died and gone to heaven. Then Elenore treated me to lunch at a cute café on the river, and Mel and Stacy took me for drinks after the investor meeting. I didn't order a mind-eraser shot this time. I had no intention of forgetting my birthday. I had been dreading forty, but it has been a fabulous day. Maybe turning forty is just what I needed to start a new chapter.

"Close your eyes and make a wish, my love."

I close my eyes, thinking about what I really want. After a long moment, I blow out the candle and smile.

When I open my eyes, Avery is standing next to the table. "I hope you wished for me," she says as my mouth drops open, and I let out a squeal. I jump out of my chair and hug her.

"What are you doing here?" I say in disbelief.

"Did you think I wouldn't come celebrate the Big Four-Oh with you?"

I'm still embracing her when over her shoulder I see Mel, Stacy, Elenore, Maya, Maeve, and Sarah walking toward us. "Surprise!" they say in unison.

Max rises from the table. "I think it's time to take this party to the private room I rented."

"All this for me?" I whisper.

"Yes, aren't we sneaky?" Mel says, and pats my arm.

I hug each one of my friends, then squeeze Max, with Maya sandwiched between us so tight that she screams, "I need air!"

In somewhat of a daze, I have one thought circling in my head: I am truly blessed.

CHAPTER FORTY-FOUR

"Someone caught it all on video," I say as I sit across from Dr. Josie and rehash the mud fight. She's biting her bottom lip to stop herself from laughing. I know she's trying to be professional, but I wouldn't blame her if she busted a gut right now. After all, she's human. I can't stop from laughing at my own retelling. I recount the story like I'm at improv night, using my arms to simulate throwing mud.

"That was quite the event," she finally says without cracking a smile. "I'll have to search online for the video." She pauses. "Are you talking to Beatrice again since you broke up with Carrie?"

"No. It's over between me and Beatrice, and me and Carrie."

"You do realize that the sacrifice you made to end your friendship with Carrie out of love for Beatrice is what a best friend would do, right?"

I swallow hard. I hadn't thought about it that way.

"You are starting to accept the way things are?" she asks.

I take in a deep breath. "Now that I've had some time to reflect, I didn't see what was going on with Beatrice, and I am to blame for that. I apologized, but it's too late. I take responsibility for my part in the friendship breakup."

"That's a very mature way to look at the breakup. How are you feeling about Beatrice now?"

I had given a lot of thought to our relationship. "I am grateful for the experience of our friendship. Rather than continuing to force the friendship at the cost of losing myself, it's okay to recognize the friendship has run its course and served its purpose, and to let it go." I pause. "When I think back to the term BFF, I realize the promise of forever isn't always guaranteed. It's more like forever for now," I say.

Walking away from a relationship that no longer works for either person is freeing. It's like a ten-pound weight has been lifted off my chest. Yes, there is sorrow, but I choose to focus on the good times we had, the tough times we shared and got through together, the growth we achieved, and the acceptance that some friendships aren't meant to last forever. I walk away with my head held high and a prayer in my heart for her happiness. Bearing ill will won't do anyone any good.

"Are you moving these friends to the season quadrant?"

"Yes."

Dr. Josie is right. They were in my life for a season. The season of my life that entailed first-time mother. The season where I would have lost my damn mind had I not had a group of mommy friends to commiserate with. We provided each other comfort, laughter, advice, and relief.

"I am happy to hear you are doing what is best for you and letting go. Are you still checking their social media accounts?"

I shake my head. "No, I've decided to stay off social media except for my business accounts. It's been much less stressful for me this way."

"You are handling this so well," Dr. Josie says, and smiles. She pauses for a moment and continues. "In that journal entry long ago, you wrote about the way you expected your life to be, and it hasn't turned out that way. Let's talk about this."

I clasp my hands together and lean forward. "I learned that life isn't perfect. It's messy, but that's what makes it beautiful."

Dr. Josie breaks into a clap. "Brava. You've grown so much through this experience."

I smile and bow slightly in my seat. "Thank you."

Dr. Josie turns her attention to my folder on her lap and flips through it. "Let's switch gears now and talk about your adoption."

I ball my hands into fists. "I'm still beating myself up over not contacting the adoption agency sooner."

"You were eighteen when you found out you were adopted, right?"

"Yes."

"Are you the same person you were at eighteen?"

"No." Of course not. I have responsibilities. I'm a mother and a wife. I've made adult decisions, sometimes half-assed, but the point was that I made them.

"You are looking back on your life with wise eyes. The eyes you did not have at eighteen. Do you hear what I'm saying?"

I narrow my eyes. Her words strike me hard over the head, like she's knocking sense into me.

"It's not the same choice you would have made today."

CHAPTER FORTY-FIVE

It's mid-January. I'm so overcome with giddiness that I hardly notice the blustering wind. Handling the huge pair of scissors, Maya helps me cut the red ribbon draped across the front porch of Monroe's Chocolates. I smile big for the camera. The mayor of our small town stands on my right, and Max and Maya stand on my left. *Is this really happening?*

The realization hits me. This is mine. I created this. The throng of people, my community, in front of me are here to support my business. A rush of warmth spreads throughout my chest and emanates from my heart. It's humbling and thrilling, and I've been on a happiness high for months.

I open the door and enter the shop. Stepping in feels like pure bliss—an elation so strong, I don't know when it will ever abate. My artfully arranged chocolate confections, wrapped in clear cellophane and tied with purple ribbon, line the dark stained shelves that perfectly match the oak wood floors. The ambiance reminds me of my favorite childhood candy shop minus the jumbo rainbow whirly lollipops that used to beckon me from the window.

Glancing at the bakery cases, I survey that every single piece of chocolate is perfectly positioned. Two dozen different types of truffles—milk, dark, or white chocolate, or some combination of the three—sit neatly in rows on the first two shelves. Presentation is everything. If the truffles look delightful, people will buy them. Once they taste my chocolate, I hope they'll become repeat customers.

The crystal droplet chandelier above me is gorgeous and casts sparkles against the freshly painted wall behind the counter. The dark brown paint starts at the ceiling and flows down the white wall, mimicking melting chocolate.

The first customers enter the shop. I stare out the front window at the line. My eyes follow it down the block until it disappears around the corner. I'm so honored at the turnout.

Stacy is helping me today at one of the two registers. She negotiated quite the deal on the whole building. Max and I are now proud owners. We sold our house in Springshire in two months and moved here. It took several months to renovate the chocolate shop, to set it up with a commercial kitchen and a room for chocolate classes, using the money the investors lent us. It's been a huge convenience for me, living upstairs like Mel envisioned.

I thank guests, one by one, for coming. The last time I welcomed people like this was on my wedding day. I'm just as joyous on this occasion. The difference is I planned this event all by myself. I'm getting better at this.

My parents and in-laws sit together at one of the five tables, enjoying chocolate, coffee, and conversation. My dad winks at me. I wink back. Max commandeers the other register, so I can flit around in my ballet flats, filling the cases with more chocolate from the kitchen and greeting customers. Max flashes me a smile and a thumbs-up. I watch Maya and Maeve place fliers in each customer's bag. They detail upcoming Mommy and Me chocolate classes.

I'm proud of Maya for adjusting to all these changes so well—a new house, neighborhood, school, and new friends. She likes taking the bus and feels special that it stops right in front of our home. The move has been good for all of us, including Max, who discovered a new hobby—woodworking. He's set up a workshop in our new shed in the backyard and made our first table for the chocolate shop, with the help of Maya. Quite impressive. And it warmed my heart that Max and Maya were spending quality time bonding.

It's surreal. I'm walking on clouds.

"This is an amazing turnout!"

Avery hugs me.

"You made it!"

She's added extensions to her hair, and her makeup is flawless and shimmery. Avery looks healthy and happy.

"Of course I did. I wouldn't miss this. Sorry I'm late. My flight was delayed."

"That's okay. You're here now and that's all that matters," I say. "You didn't stand in that line. Did you?"

"Girl, no. I knocked on your back door, and one of your employees let me in after I said you were my best friend. To her credit, she made me prove it by showing pictures of you and me on my phone."

"You didn't show her the one of me in my mismatched pajamas with messy Medusa hair you snapped of me the last time you visited?"

"Yep, that's the one."

I roll my eyes and she snorts.

"I'd like to introduce you to someone," she says cheerily.

I spy a tall, dark, and extremely handsome man standing next to her. He's movie star good-looking.

"Hi." I hold out my hand to him. "You must be Aaron."

He takes my hand in his. "Nice to meet you, Fallon. I've heard so much about you."

I smile. I had heard just as much about him in the past two months from Avery's more frequent calls and texts. He's the cute guy she met on the airplane when she visited me with her broken leg. I like to think I had something to do with their meeting. He sounded like a real catch the way Avery described him—funny, sweet, Ivy League educated, and CEO of a software company. I had no reservations. In all the years I've known Avery, she had never been this excited about anyone.

I grab Avery's hand. "Come with me. You too, Aaron."

I lead them to the glass cases and point to my newest product.

Avery reads the display sign, "Avery's Amazing Chocolate Popcorn."

"I'll take your biggest bag of that," she says, and throws her arm around my shoulder.

"Place your order with Stacy. Tell her to give you the BFF discount." I wink at her.

"I'm so proud of you for following your dreams and not letting anything stand in your way."

"Thank you," I say, and hug her. "That means a lot."

I glance around the space again. The best part of owning this shop is personalizing new flavors inspired by my family and friends. Good thing many of my relationships revolve around food. I even made chocolate in the shape of pigs for Max's mom, Milly. I think I'm growing on her.

I introduced the key lime cheesecake flavor in honor of my parents. They've already placed an order for five hundred chocolates for a party at their retirement community clubhouse in Florida in a couple of months.

My favorite, though, are the pink chocolate stilettos that are flying off the shelves. It wouldn't be my shop if I didn't incorporate both my love of chocolate and shoes. I smile as I remember making them. It was then, when I poured the chocolate into the mold, that I realized making chocolate for myself and for others is absolutely what I'm meant to do.

Someone squeezes my arm. It's Mel. I throw my arms around her.

"Hola, chica! I thought I'd never get a chance to talk to you," Mel says as she waves her hand around the crowded shop. There's hardly a place to stand without bumping into someone.

"Please pinch me." I can't believe all these people are here for me.

Mel obliges.

"Ouch. Okay, it's real." I rub my stinging arm.

"Of course it is. You aren't alone." She looks past me. "Is that Elenore?"

Elenore fills orders behind the counter. "Yes. She's my store manager. After the divorce, she needed a change of scenery and something to keep her busy. So I hired her, and she moved a few blocks from the shop. She's been a lifesaver for me, taking care of the business side of things while I focus on my recipes. I can't imagine managing all this without her."

"You're such a good friend."

I smile. After believing so long I wasn't a good friend to Beatrice or anyone, her words are like honeycomb, sweet to my soul, and a compliment I am now willing to accept.

"Speaking of friends, have you seen anyone from Shitshire lately?"

"Occasionally, I'll run into one of them at the local shopping mall, but if you're asking if I hang out with them, the answer is no." I adjust my sheer scarf over my shoulders.

"I've been thinking about all that, and I want you to know that you're probably not ever going to get an apology from Beatrice for excluding you. Some people just don't get it."

"It's okay. I've moved on," I say. "I joined the local Women's Club. The women are so nice. Bringing my chocolates to the meetings has really won them over."

I also tell her I started planning a fundraiser for teenage pregnancy, inspired by my adoption story. It's still in the initial stages, so I spare Mel all the details for now.

"That's wonderful news! Sounds like you're focusing on the things that truly matter."

Mel catches me up on her latest promotion at work and then says, "Remember, the guy we played a joke on in the bar? He was searching for someone who kind of looked like me?"

"Yes. Smith, right? He was an accountant from the Midwest."

"Yes! Good memory."

"I never forget a pair of shoes." I laugh.

"Well, I ran into him. He and Alejandra never made it past that first date."

"Oh?" I raise my eyebrows.

"Yeah, so we've been dating."

I lightly smack her arm. "You've been holding out on me!"

"I wanted to tell you in person."

"Oh, Mel! This is great news."

"It is. He's a keeper."

"I'm so happy for you."

"Excuse me, Fallon?" a woman interrupts us with a baby in a stroller and a little boy holding her hand. Mel tells me she'll catch up with me later.

The woman looks familiar. "I'm Tonya. I'm not sure if you remember me. I look a little different now. I met you in the Piggly Wiggly parking lot when I was nine months pregnant."

Now I recognize her. Her hair is brushed today, and she's wearing makeup.

"Yes! I remember you. How are you?"

"Much better now that Sophie is here." She reaches down and rubs her daughter's head.

My eyes drift down. "What a beautiful girl."

"Thank you. I recognized you on the Facebook announcement for the grand opening, and Benny and I wanted to be here."

"That is so sweet of you." I turn to her son. "Hi, Benny, you are being such a good boy for your mother." He looks up at me and smiles.

"I really appreciated that you helped me with my groceries. That was a rough day for me. Your act of kindness got me through the rest of the week, and I often remember your encouraging words. So, thank you." Tonya's misty hazel eyes meet mine.

"Those words got me through some tough times. I'm happy they helped you too," I say.

Benny runs to the chocolate jars of candy at his eye level. "Oh, gosh! I better get him before he puts his sticky hands into your chocolates."

I step aside and give her room to move through. "Thank you for coming, and always remember you're doing a great job, Mama."

She flashes me a smile before retrieving Benny. My heart is full and bursting in my chest.

A man with feathered hair and an unbuttoned white shirt, revealing his hairy chest, approaches me. He has a large boom box in his hand.

"Where would you like me to set up?"

My eyes almost bug out of my head as I realize it's Dirty Harry. This can't be happening. I have to get him out of here, and fast. Before I usher him out the door, Avery comes up behind him.

"Is something wrong?" she asks.

"Dirty Harry was just leaving," I say. The stripper raises his eyebrows in amusement.

Avery laughs. "Gotcha! I asked him to pretend."

I let out a slow breath in relief and shake my head. "You two almost gave me a panic attack."

Dirty Harry smiles. "I don't believe we've ever officially met. I'm Marco, not 'Dirty Harry,' and these are for you." He moves his hand from behind his back and presents me with a beautiful arrangement of lilies. "It's the least I could do."

I take the flowers and bury my nose in them, inhaling deeply.

"Thank you, Marco."

Marco glances around. "Now seriously, where do you want me to set up?"

Avery laughs and I shoot her a look.

CHAPTER FORTY-SIX

I remove the wilted flowers and replace them with a fresh bouquet of sweet peas. Bending down, I trace my fingers over the engraving on the simple headstone.

Mary Brighton

The times I've been to a cemetery are few and far between, so I'm not sure if I should sit or stand. I stay standing and staring for a long time. I talk to her in my head, but I'm not sure she hears me or if I'm making any sense.

I move my finger to the dates and trace them.

November 11, 1965–October 22, 2003

The dates register in my mind. I swallow hard at the realization she died at the age of thirty-seven. She was younger than me now when she passed. I hadn't even figured out what I wanted to do in my life until I was nearing forty.

I glance at the headstones surrounding hers, curious as to who her "neighbors" are, how they died, and who they left behind. Like Mary, their dreams died with them. Sadness lives in this place and latches on to me.

I made the two-hour drive here by myself. I told Max that he and Maya could join me another time. This I wanted to do on my own. I'm still in shock that Mary registered with the adoption registry before she passed away. This confirms she wanted to meet me.

My cheeks are raw and exposed. I pull my scarf up over my mouth and inhale the scent of the sweet pea fragrance I spritzed on it. I need to say what I really came here for. I don't know when I'll be back, and next time, Maya and Max could be with me.

I speak through the scarf as if it will help soften my words. "Mary, it's Fallon, um, . . . Sweet Pea," I say in case she has no idea who I am. There's no one around, so I feel comfortable talking to her aloud. I think she'll hear me now. "Happy Birthday."

I reach into my tote and take out a plastic framed photo of Maya, Max, and me, and lean it against the headstone.

She would have turned fifty-eight today. My heart aches at all the experiences she's going to miss—a relationship with me and being a grandma to Maya.

I sit on the hard, cold ground and sob for what feels like hours. Pulling my hat down to cover my ears, a shiver sweeps through me from a sudden gust of wind. Dead leaves lie scattered around the property, and I think about how eerily quiet it is now. Melancholy keeps a strong grip on my mood.

"Thank you for writing to me. I've read the letters repeatedly. I keep them in a box on my nightstand." I pause. "Having them near me when I sleep allows me to feel close to you."

I tell her about my chocolate and about Maya and Max. I keep talking. There's so much she doesn't know about me. I tell her about my recent mammogram results.

I think back to the news I received earlier this week. I underwent my first mammogram and took a blood test to determine if I have the gene for an increased risk of breast cancer. The results are cause for celebration. I am relieved about the gene testing. The few days it took to get results were excruciatingly painful. I worried more for Maya than for me if I tested positive.

What I really want to say sits quietly on the edge of my lips. I want to bury my head in my hands, but I know I need to be brave. I stand now to give myself confidence. The words finally come in one fast sentence that leaves me breathless.

"I'm sorry I waited so long to contact the adoption agency, and now it's too late. Please forgive me."

There's chaos in my mind, but words from her letter swoop in like quiet in the storm. *For whatever reason you didn't contact me, I want you to know it's okay. I understand.* A calmness overtakes my whole being as acceptance replaces my feelings of rejection. Even when I felt it the least, I had been loved all along.

* * *

I run my hand over my journal. I love the way it feels and the smell of the leather. I promised Dr. Josie I would write down my thoughts, but I wanted the first page to be monumental. Something I could read back on and recall with happiness. It couldn't be ho-hum. So much had happened. I hadn't even had time to go see Dr. Josie. I hope I won't have to go back. I miss our talks, but I don't have anything pressing to see her about. My panic attacks and hot flashes are gone. Life is good. Actually, it's better than good.

I click my pen and open my journal to the first page. I take a deep breath and put the pen to the paper.

On my fortieth birthday, I blew out the candle and wished for understanding and growth. Mainly because they were the first two words that popped into my head. I went with it. I sounded grown up to ask for something other than a new pair of shoes.

With all the events that I've experienced, I can look back now and say—I survived and thrived. I've officially turned my pain into power, and I repeat to myself every day, "I am enough. I am worthy of love. I am worthy of beautiful relationships."

In the end, I've surrounded myself with the best of both worlds—my new business and friends who support me no matter what. I've let go and found joy in the unexpected and that has made all the difference.

Life doesn't have to turn out exactly as I pictured it all those years ago. It's not perfect, but that's okay. It's perfectly imperfect.

ACKNOWLEDGMENTS

There are so many people to thank for supporting me on my author journey. It takes universal laws or at least a small country to bring a book baby into the world, and I'm eternally grateful.

To my agent, Lindsay Guzzardo, for taking a chance on me, and working with me to make my book sparkle. You have extraordinary editing and agenting skills, and I'm forever indebted.

To my editor, Faith Black Ross, for loving my book, your brilliant edits and guidance, and enjoying chocolate as much as I do.

To the team at Alcove Press, for your support in bringing my book to market, which is no small feat: Madeline, Dulce, Melissa, Rebecca, and Molly.

To my first beta reader and editor, Kimberly Hunt. I am so happy we met on Critique Match. Your enthusiasm for my book kept me going and your edits helped me take it to the next level.

To my critique partners, Skylar Shoar and Erica Mae, thank you for your feedback in the margins, especially where you commented LOL. Your laughter made all the difference.

To my author coach and friend, Camille Pagan, for your wisdom, encouragement, and fabulous advice.

To Lainey Cameron, thank you for knowing exactly how to send feedback in two emails: (1) the good and (2) the bad. I'd like to add a third email to your process: (3) the ugly (crap you should delete).

To my mom, my first reader of *all* my writing and for being my biggest fan. You've lifted me up not only as a child but as an adult—does your back hurt yet? I hope I've made you proud.

To my brother, Eric, for holing up in a hotel room to read my book. Your comments made me snort with laughter!

To my ride-or-die bestie, Jenny, thank you for reading every single iteration of this book and all my manuscripts that landed under a huge pile of clothes on my desk. I couldn't have dreamt up a better friend—my sister from another mister.

To Lauren, for being an early reader with impressive proofing skills, for cheering me on along the way with bubbly, and being one of my first mommy friends in the trenches.

To Katie, for taking this journey with me, waiting impatiently with me, and passing the time with wining. Red is better.

To Susan, for setting aside a million books on your TBR list to read mine. I cannot even put into words how much this touched my heart. You're my Booksta Bestie.

To Jean, our dog walks and gifted wine kept me moving forward. Thank you for reading this book and the ones before it.

To Jamie, thank you for our many outings in different cities over the years. Your energy always uplifts me.

To my dear author friend Selimah Nemoy, for answering my many questions about adoption from your alternate universe to mine! You have the "Best of My Love."

To Ira, for your countless hours behind the scenes wielding your magic wand of expert technical skills on my website.

To my beta readers, author Rebecca Prenevost and soccer aficionado Marty, thank you for your valuable thoughts. If Fallon were real, I'm sure she'd thank you by making chocolate.

To my subject matter experts: Amber Trueblood for bringing Dr. Josie to life, and Nina and Jackie from The Cradle for walking me through the adoption process. You helped make Fallon's story authentic.

To my intern, Madison, it's so fitting how your taste in shoes matches Fallon's. Thank you for all your work.

To my talented writer friends whom I met decades ago, Janine, Allison, Eileen, and Jonathan (in heaven now)—I may have rolled my eyes at your tiny, pink-pen edits, but it's the little things that make the biggest impressions.

To the authors who've guided me along the way: Lisa Roe, Sara Goodman Confino, Barbara Newman, Rochelle Weinstein, Liz Talley, Glendy Vanderah, and Camille Pagan's 2022 Career Author Mastermind Group.

To the Author's Guild, for the many resources you provide, including contract review services.

To Kristyn @delightfullybooked, thank you for your stellar author services. It's a delight to be booked with you.

To the Women's Fiction Writers Association, for your numerous member benefits, including your wonderful workshops and critique partner program.

To the Bookstagram community, you've kept me sane throughout this whole process. Thank you for your continued support.

Special thanks to my friends and family, who provided moral support and assembled an amazing cheering section: Dad, Faith, Kathleen, JP, Karen, John, Sue, Phil, Tom, Tracy, Debbie, and Donna.

To Pat, who predicted this book many moons ago and to my cousin, Geri, for reconnecting us and all your support.

To my readers, I'm overwhelmed with gratitude. Time is precious, and I am grateful you spent it with Fallon Monroe.

To my daughter, Skylar, thank you for inspiring parts of this book. I often wonder, between you and me, who is teaching whom. I hope you know you can be anything you want to be and that you never lose sight of your dreams.

To my incredible husband, for providing endless support and encouragement—believing in me when I started to lose hope. You were right—it happened!

I offer this book back to God and my Muse, from where it originated.